Tijuana Weekend

A Mick Murphy Mexican Mystery

By Michael Haskins

LIBRARY OF CONGRESS

CATALOGING-IN-PUBLICATION DATA

Haskins, Michael.
Tijuana Weekend: a Mick Murphy mystery
Michael Haskins. - 1st ed.
ISBN- 13(alk. paper)978-1456595142
ISBN- 10(alk. paper)1456595148

1. Journalists-Fiction. 2. Key West (Fla.)-Fiction. 3. United States-Relations-Mexico-Fiction. 4. Mexico-United States-Relations-Fiction. 5. Political fiction. I. Title.

Copyright @ 2011 by Michael Haskins.

Published in 2011

www.michaelhaskins.net

Introduction

This is the second Mick Murphy novel and I wrote it in Mexico in 1994. Like most of us, Murphy came from somewhere else before he showed up in Key West, Florida, and I began the short stories and mystery series.

I reread *Tijuana Weekend* recently and thought it held up pretty well – better than I have – and with only minor editing what you see is what you get. I added the date and time to each chapter because I want the reader to remember the story takes place in the past. Some of the political facts of Central America at that time date the story and to update it to present time would have changed what I wanted to say.

Unfortunately, not that much has changed in Central America since I wrote this. The murder of the Jesuits by the military in El Salvador is true and these many years later, the organizers of the murders go unpunished. In May 2011 General Rene Emilio Ponce died. He was considered the mastermind behind the killings and was never prosecuted. However, the new president of El Salvador was once a guerrilla fighting the government, so there has been progress and there maybe justice in the future, as has happened in countries like Chile, Brazil and Argentina.

I spent more than twenty summers in Tijuana, attending the bullfight, and used those experiences in the story. My twin daughters, Seanan and Chela, almost grew up in Tijuana when spending their summers with me. For many years it was their second home on the West Coast. It was an education for the three of us.

During the time I was there, I made friends and met many good people. Today, Tijuana is caught up in the Mexican drug cartel wars and it saddens me because the residents of the city deserve better.

Tijuana Weekend is dedicated to my Mexican friends, those living and those who have passed. A special thanks for years of friendship to Alfonso Ruiz Padilla, a long-time friend who helped me chase Selma Hayek around *el río*. Don't know what we would have done if we found her. He helped me understand the people by introducing me to them and showed me life in the city. I learned so much more than if he had only told me or if I had stayed on the sidelines. Show, don't tell, I learned in writing 101 and it's true with life experiences, too.

I have to give a special thanks to fellow writer Wayne Gales for his help with the cover. I couldn't have done it without him.

May 4, 1995
11:50 a.m.

Chapter ONE

When I first came to Tijuana, Mexico, more than 20 years ago, it was a sleepy border town, minutes from San Diego, California, where liquor was cheap and women plentiful. Dirt streets, dusty with summer breezes or impassable from winter rains, were everywhere. A few main streets were paved, but not to American standards.

You entered most places free, but a bribe usually passed onto someone in a uniform when you tried to leave, a lot drunker than when you arrived and a little less horny, if you'd been lucky.

A few *gringo* dollars could keep you out of a Mexican jail, or so you were fooled into believing. The bribe was part of the excitement of Tijuana. Changes had forced their way into the border town in the past twenty years, some good, some not so good.

It was Thursday, close to noon, and I sat in the small, almost empty sidewalk cafe in front of *Hotel Caesar,* sipping my first beer of the day. As I watched from my seat, sheltered in shade, ancient busses and cars of every make and model year passed on the busy sun swept street - a paved street as good as any in Los Angeles. This was an old section of town, filled with tourist shops in quaint buildings, a few trendy structures nestled in between, their large glass windows catching and reflecting the hot Mexican sun.

The last day of April. The streets were crowded with all kinds of people moving rapidly by, talking to one another, bumping, smiling, and growling. There were no Anglo faces, no English spoken. It was too early for the American servicemen to be wandering the crowded sidewalks and weekend tourists wouldn't show up until Saturday to begin their shopping spree.

Maybe because it was Mexico, the sun seemed hot for the time of year. That was okay.

Sunday would be the first bullfight of the season and that made it a special weekend for me and some friends who would meet me, beginning Friday afternoon. Heat was as much a requirement for a bullfight as were the *matador* and *toro.*

I'd purchased everyone's ticket for Sunday and deposited money on all reserved hotel rooms. The afternoon and evening were mine, to do with as I pleased.

Cafe América would be my next stop. Dick Dowly, the owner and enigma, an American who never crossed the border.

Whenever I knew I'd be visiting Tijuana I'd call and bring some item he wanted, videotape, music CD or book. Not much, but always something. Something easily purchased a few miles away in San Diego. We swap fish stories about life and I'm not sure which of us is the biggest charlatan.

Chuy, *Caesar's* outdoor waiter brought me a fresh beer. He was used to my spending long afternoons in the shade of the patio bar. His was a good job because it dealt in dollars. He always smiled his thick nose wrinkling as he did. His brown eyes squinting from the sun, searching the tables, making sure everyone had what they wanted, his English as good as the customer required. When he thought someone might want him, he wove his thin frame through the crowded patio, squeezing between tables placed much to close together, smiling while he listened to the requests.

"Juaquin?" I asked him, accepting the beer.

"*La farmacia,*" he said and moved onto another table.

Juaquin was the handy man of the hotel. He shined shoes, kept street urchins and unwanted street salesmen away from the customers and made deliveries for the pharmacy.

He was about five six, which made him tall since he looked Indian. His skin a reddish brown, aged like leather, a full head of hair, just now showing white strands. He's been sixty-five for the past 10 years, or so he tells everyone. Deep black eyes watch you as you speak to him. If he thinks you understand Spanish, even just a little, he tries to converse in his language. If he sees you failing to understand, he'll speak in English.

I missed him. He's consistently full of gossip, political as well as social and has always kept me up to date on what has happened since my last visit.

Mexico has a lot of poverty. Tijuana has more than its share, since it's a stopping off point for illegal entry into the United States. You see all forms of poverty here.

I observed the busy street, foot traffic darting from one side to another, dodging between cars, busses and trucks. As I sat back and sipped my beer, I noticed a man leaning against one of the pillars that held up the second floor of *Caesar's*.

His appearance made me think of the poverty. He was tall; his clothes dirty and slept in. A battered old hat pulled down on his head, long grimy hair hung from under it. His beard was matted and his face looked like an ancient death mask.

He stared at me, hard, and a small smile formed where his mouth was hidden in the beard. He looked nervously around. Was he used to Juaquin chasing him away? There was a look on his soiled face that told me he knew he had nothing to lose by asking for money. He attempted to stand straight and began a slow pace toward me.

I could smell him from two tables away. I reached into my pocket and hoped he'd take a dollar and leave quickly. He stopped a table away and scanned the street behind him. The thought of Juaquin catching him must have been frightening. He looked past me at the other tables. Three had people at them, couples who spoke in whispers too low for me to hear.

He stood there, a smile on his face, smelling like gym socks. I forced a smile and held out the dollar bill. He leaned against a table, tired.

"Mick," he mumbled slowly, forcing the words. "You owe me more than a dollar." He sat at the next table.

He knew me. How the hell did he know me? I studied him and recognized something that wouldn't come to me. Chuy came out, saw the bum sitting there, and looked at me.

"*Dos mas*," I said and held up my beer bottle.

The beggar looked anxiously around again. He'd paid little attention to Chuy, but something out on the street concerned him.

Chuy brought me the two beers and looked at the derelict again. I picked up the beers, smiled and walked to the next table. He took the beer from me and drank quickly from it. He smelled worse than old gym socks and looked tired, hungry, thirsty, and very scared.

"You okay?" I said, not wanting to be caught in a game with a wanderer who, somehow, recognized me. I couldn't call to mind what it was about him I recognized. Up close, he could've been Latin or a sun burned American.

"We've had better days, Mick." He drank right after saying my name. "You here looking for me?" His English came slowly, as if he were relearning it.

"I can't place you," I finally admitted. "But I'm not here looking for anyone"

"Do you believe in miracles, Mick?" He finished his beer and took mine.

"Sometimes," I said. I let him drink my beer.

"Well Mick," he drank slower now. "If you're not looking for me, then you're my miracle." He raised his open hand, thumbs facing his nose and made the sign of the cross. "Bless you," he cried.

"*Padre Seámus.*" I yelled.

"You're not lying, Mick, are you? You're not looking for me?" He wiped tears from his eyes, his hands filthy.

"*Jesús.*" I moaned, looking at the battered figure I'd known long ago.

"Mary and Joseph." He finished the blessing for me and smiled.

"Seámus," I murmured, "what's happened?"

He looked impatiently around, scanning the crowded sidewalk and busy street.

"Ah, Mick," he mumbled, finishing my beer, "it's a long story. One you'd love," he said with a small smile as he stumbled through the English words. "Still a newspaperman?" He played with the empty bottle.

"Yes . . . but you?" I fumbled for words.

"Can we go inside?" he asked quietly, still searching the sidewalk and street.

I looked at him, I smelled him and wondered how long we'd be allowed inside *Caesar's* bar. In my mind I put Roman collar on him, but couldn't bring back the vision of *Padre Seámus*, the Jesuit. Seámus McGillicuddy, as Black Boston Irish as me and a Jesuit to boot. My up bringing wouldn't allow me to say no to a priest.

"Of course," I answered, fearing he felt my hesitation. We both stood, he turned to glance around again and then followed me toward the door.

Seámus McGillicuddy, a few years older than me. We met while I was at Harvard; he was studying something, already a Jesuit. Our Irish-ness brought us together. In those days, he must have been five ten or so, and now he looked so stooped you couldn't tell how tall he really was. He kept his hair cut close back then, but even so, you could tell it was thick and wavy. Clean-shaven, he was easy to blush, which made his blue-green eyes stand out even more. When he wore his collar, he broke hearts.

A year or two after leaving Boston, he went to Central America to teach. It wasn't long before he was at odds with the wealthy landowners, concerned for the living conditions of the Indians. With the help of a Boston church, he began a co-op farm program, using donations to buy an old truck to take crops to an open market. The military, at the request of the landowners, put a brutal end to the co-op, the truck, and open market.

Soon he was *the rebel priest*, working and living with guerrillas deep in the mountains of Central America. I went there and did a story on him in the late 70s. I saw him again in El Salvador and Nicaragua. On each encounter, I did an updated story. Now he stumbled through the table-cluttered patio and followed me into the dark bar. I waited for him at the entrance, watched him look back again at the street and saw fear in his tired blood shot eyes as he looked at me.

Thursday, at noon, *Caesar's* bar was not busy, almost empty. It would be filled by two. I pointed to a booth, far from the bar and he followed me there. As I raised my hand to signal for two beers, he pushed it down.

"Is there a back way out, Mick?" he whispered.

"Through the restaurant and out the kitchen," I said. Was he paranoid? Then I remembered the time two Cuban born CIA agents seized him at the Guatemalan border, stuffed him in the trunk of their car and drove him north to the Texas border. Dumped him there, where American authorities took him to the nearest Catholic Church. He'd been in the trunk for days, no food, no water, no nothing. Maybe he was paranoid, but it didn't mean someone wasn't after him.

May 4, 1995
12:25 p.m.

chapter TWO

We walked through the kitchen slowly, the help giving Seámus stares, leaving him alone because we were together. I smiled politely at the few I knew and wondered if Seámus cared about the looks we received. I doubted it.

I stopped as we exited the rear of *Caesar's* and waited for him to catch up. He stared at the dozen or so parked cars. A noon sun reflected off their windshields, lighting the boxed in parking area with a sparkling brilliance, as heat waves rippled off their hot frames. Sighing, he turned his scrutiny to the vacant alley and the street it ran into.

Seámus was an old friend, no matter what he looked like, or smelled like. Whatever his problems, real or not, I felt a responsibility to him.

He looked ill. Physically, for sure and, after all these years, probably mentally. I could clean him up, get him across the border to help and be back in plenty of time to see Dick Dowly tonight.

"Padre Seámus, let's go to my hotel," I said, pulling his concentration back to me.

"How?" he said, staring at me.

I returned his stare, trying to see those old blue eyes, but couldn't get past the dirt and bloodshot gaze. I realized, to my surprise, he didn't trust me.

"We'll take a taxi."

"What hotel?" His voice was low and the words came slow.

"*Hotel Inca*. It's on the *Rio*," I said, not knowing if he knew these areas of Tijuana. "Padre Seámus, you can trust me."

"Who wouldn't trust their miracle, Mick?" he said, staring around the parking area one more time. "We have to go on the street?"

"There'll be a taxi by the side of the hotel, I'll get it." I began to walk toward the alley.

"No," he yelled hoarsely. "Away from the hotel, Mick. I'll explain," he said and walked down the alley with me.

As we walked away from the hotel, the sidewalks became narrow and crowded. Many of the small shops displayed merchandise on out door tables, forcing pedestrians into the congested street.

Seámus was slow, stumbling a couple of times before I caught him. Small Indian women with babies wrapped in colorful *huipiles* that hugged their chests, yelled at him as we passed, in a dialect I could not understand. He paid no attention.

We walked two blocks from the hotel, into an area only a brave tourist would venture, before he allowed me to call a taxi.

"The market area is near this hotel?" he asked, before I hailed the taxi.

"Yes," I said and saw him scan the street. For what? I wondered.

"Take the taxi there, not the hotel," he ordered and then added, "please."

"Can you tell me what's wrong?" I said as we waited for a light to change.

"Yes I can," he said. "At the hotel."

We got into the taxi and the driver zigzagged us through the busy streets and, in a round about way, got us to the *mercado*. The hotel was a half dozen blocks away, it was noon and hot. I doubted Seámus could walk the distance.

"There is a taxi over there." He pointed toward the far side of the large parking lot and began to walk.

I followed, more concerned now than ever. Changing taxis to lose someone following you is right out of spy novels by Gayle Lynds, but that's what we did. In Central America he was a fugitive, here in Mexico, so close to the United States, he should have felt safe.

The taxi dropped us off at the rear of the hotel and we took the stairs to my third floor room.

"Clean up," I said to him, trying to make my tone as friendly as possible. "I'll find some clean clothes for you," and pointed toward the large bathroom, hoping he understood I meant for him to shower.

"These aren't worth saving," he mumbled to himself, as he looked in the mirror. After he closed the bathroom door, I heard him going through the drawers, searching for something.

I called down to the hotel's kitchen and ordered two chicken soups, a plate full of soft tacos and four beers. As I hung up, I heard my beard trimmer humming from the bathroom. While searching for clothes I hoped would fit, I heard the shower running. I found him everything but shoes, unless he had small feet like mine.

I waited, glad to hear the shower running for such a long time and I tipped the waiter after he set the food down on the small table, let him out, and opened a beer.

Sipping the beer I stared down at the front parking lot, where the hotel office overlooked the busy street. No strange men lurked about outside. There were two taxis, a dozen or so parked and empty cars. No one even walked the street, not from where I could see.

"Waiting for someone?" Seámus said suspiciously, a hotel towel wrapped around his waist.

He was skin and bones and his gaunt appearance startled me.

With his shaved head and beard cropped to a day's growth, he was the portrait of a Nazi death camp survivor.

Draped in the towel he seemed taller than when he was in his ratty clothes. Fright entered my mind for the first time. Not frightened of him, but for him. Even in Central America, living with the guerrillas in the mountains, Padre Seámus had never looked so haggard.

"I was curious to see if we'd been followed," I finally said, deciding to play his game for the time being. "No one out there." I walked to the food.

"Smells great," he said and sat down. His bony hands shook as he used the soup spoon. It embarrassed him. He smiled at me and I could almost see blue eyes. To help brace himself he gulped beer and then returned to the soup.

I sat across from him and ate my soup. He smelled and resembled clean, the dirty matted beard gone, his scalp buzzed, but still looked sickly. His bony chest was covered with small scars and held fresh black and blue welts.

"There's clothes for you," I said, looking toward the bed.

"I've lost weight," he replied matter-of-factly. "Think they will fit?"

"One way or another," I smiled.

Seámus returned my smile and for the first time I saw an image of the man, the priest I knew.

"When I saw you sitting there in the shadows," he began without my asking, "I couldn't believe it. Red beard and shaggy hair. Could only be you, Mad Mick Murphy," he cheered into the stillroom, remembering our Harvard days and the source of my nickname. "You were one of two things, Mick. A miracle or my killer." He stopped and ate a soft taco, adding salsa.

"And I thought I was just another crazy Irishman. A miracle, you say?" I teased, drank some beer, and waited.

He looked at me, a sad expression on his face. He drank some beer, his expression unchanged. "You've blundered into something, Mick that is very dangerous. I could use your help." He paused for a moment and decided quietly to go on with his story. "Actually, we could use you. I don't know how many of us are left, but originally there were twelve. I doubt there are that many still alive." He inspected me with his gaze while he spoke. His soup was gone, so he munched on the soft tacos and drank from a second bottle of beer. "If they don't kill you, you'd have one prize winning feature. You still writing?" He wouldn't take his eyes off me.

He knew I still wrote and he remembered from our past interviews how I always hoped for a Pulitzer. The paranoia seemed to have gone the way of the dirty hair and grimy body. As he spoke, there was confidence in his tone and the way he held himself. Soap, hot water and a little food had made a big change in Padre Seámus.

"Of course," I said, taking the last beer. He sipped from his half-filled bottle. "What is it that's going to win me the Pulitzer?"

"November 16th, 1989 . . . San Salvador. Mean anything?"

I thought to myself, knowing it meant something. He had me too confused to think straight. Was he paranoid or plain crazy? Or was he into something that might cost him his life?

"Salvadoran troops murdered six Jesuits, their house keeper and her fifteen year old daughter at the University. There was a rebel offensive happening," he led me along like a high school history teacher.

"The same people involved in murdering Cardinal Romero during Mass in 1980." He knew he had my attention. "We have copies of documents from the Arena Party, to the military, in regard to the Jesuits. A low ranking officer has pictures of people from your embassy at the University before the murders. With them are Salvadoran military officials. These same Salvadorans are seen with the Jesuits bodies in the background in other photos. Bodies of my friends. My protectors." The words exploded from him as he wiped tears from his angry eyes.

"Can I try on the clothes?" He stood and walked to the bed, composing himself, getting back his self-control. Leaving the painful memory for a moment.

I remained at the table, running what he had revealed around in my pessimistic, journalist's mind. He dropped the towel, his naked body flimsy and bruised.

I thought of questions for him, while he dressed in the loose fitting clothes. He didn't look great, but he looked better than a few hours ago.

He wouldn't stay, even though I tried to argue with him. Once he was gone, I knew I would be of little help to him and his paranoia.

From my pocket I pulled ten, $20 bills and handed them to him. I walked to the closet and took down one of my wide brim hats. "Take the money and wear the hat," I told him. Standing there, I felt how frail he really was.

" "Some change," he smiled and turned to me. "Well?" He lay back on the bed and pulled the hat over his eyes.

"What about the officers convicted for the murders?"

"One of them, a *Benavides*, is in the pictures. He and *Mendoza* were sacrificial lambs. They'll be quietly released from prison and the true murderers will go unpunished." He lay still.

"Where did you get all this information?" I sat at the table and finished my beer.

"When I became involved the underground already had it. The war's over," his voice couldn't hide his anger, "and the murderers are walking the streets. Visiting Washington, lecturing in California.

"I was told the officer who took the pictures, did so without permission. When he realized what he had, he became frightened. He gathered the written memos and notes as insurance. When he understood it wasn't going to keep him alive he went underground and our people got him. That's when I got involved. I have met him and believe him. I don't know if he is still alive." Now he sounded exhausted.

"What's your purpose?" I said, my beer gone. "What is it that's worth your life?"

"Purpose?" he bellowed from the bed. "Friends have been murdered. Innocent people . . ." His anger tapered off.

"I'm sorry, Seámus," I said quietly, "but these are questions I have to ask."

His expression showed how confused he was, how tired this journey had made him. "Each of us . . . "

"The twelve of you?"

"Yes." He began again, more quietly. "Each of us has three original negatives, along with thirty-six, five-by-seven prints, a proof sheet, and copies of ten memos.

"Our only hope is to get this information, as much of it as possible, to your congress." He said *your* again, forgetting he too was an American. "Maybe they will do something? A senator or congressman." He spoke to himself, half hoping, and half praying.

"Are the Americans in the photos diplomats?"

"No," he said with a sour laugh. "Our sources say they're CIA, working out of the embassy with cover. That is why we can't deal with your embassy in any country." He was almost asleep.

"You can prove this?"

"We have the names they're using, or were using while there. We know what their positions were in the embassy. Enough information so Congress should be able to locate them."

"An obvious question, Seámus."

"Yes." His voice was weak. He stretched his thin frame and yawned. "I must go," he said without getting up.

"Why haven't you crossed into California?"

"You wouldn't have asked that question in Boston," he yawned. "Or El Salvador or Nicaragua." He pulled on a fresh pair of my tube socks. They were not big enough, but did the job. "Small feet," he said.

"In Mexico I ask that question," I answered trying to put some humor in my words.

"The border is closed," he answered harshly, got up, found his old torn tennis shoes and sat again, putting them on.

"I came in this morning," I said, trying to ignore his tone.

"Did you notice the back up going out?" He was angry.

"There's always a back up," I said.

"Don't humor me, Mick," he yelled. "I am not lying. I have been here a week and the border is closed."

"I can't cross?" I challenged him.

"Sure. If you have a couple of hours to kill. Have you gone liberal and soft on me, Mick?"

I wanted to believe him. I wanted the story. An expose on Central American death squads was something I had always wanted to do. The more the corrupt elements of government were involved, the more I wanted the story.

"Seámus, explain, in simple English, what you're saying," I said, taking a Mexican cigar from the bureau. He refused one. I lighted mine and sat back down.

"There is a secret government, within the governments in Central America. You know that," he said.

I nodded in agreement.

"That government has a secret police . . . death squads. They work clandestinely, quietly sometimes. Not so quietly, other times. Secret police forces are at the Mexican border to stop the others and me. They aren't Mexican police, they're not *Federales*."

"Mercenaries?" As unrealistic as his story sounded, I knew some of it had probabilities.

"If you prefer that term. From Texas to California borders, they're here. No illegals are crossing, I guarantee you. Any coyote that tries, dies and the deaths don't show up in the paper.

You have friends here, ask them. Every car crossing is checked. That's the tie up, not the American custom agents. The Mexican police have backed off, turned and looked the other way."

"I know the chief of police here. He's honest."

"I am sure he is. But remember, I am a fugitive and I am being sought. There is a list of my associates, pictures too. We are being sought. We are not heroes here, Mick. We are not heroes anywhere," his voice weakened.

"We are trying to correct the death of innocent people, friends," his voice ebbed, "and the dead, friends or not, don't have the clout the living privileged do. You used to understand that. Can you now?"

I smoked while he talked. The anger waned and turned to challenge. I knew he believed what he was saying. He had lived within that world for many years and brought that awareness with him. That he could be right concerned me.

"You have the proof?" I blew smoke toward the ceiling.

He almost hid his laugh. "Not on me. But I have it. You want to see it?"

"If I'm going to win the Pulitzer for this story, I have to see it. I have to see everything, Seámus."

"Christ had his Seámus," he smiled, "I have Mick Murphy," he said, referring to the Apostle Seámus.

"Christ had his cross to bear and I have you," I tossed back at him, remembering how he always quoted the bible in arguments back at Harvard. "I believe you, but I can't do a feature without hard evidence. It won't sell."

"I understand," he sighed.

"Still don't trust me?"

"At this point, Mick, I have to trust you." He stood and looked out the window. "These men will know we met. They will get to you." He didn't look at me. "Tell them the truth, what you've done for me. That you think I'm *loco*," he turned and smiled, reminding me of the old Seámus. "You know the patio bar at *Tia's*?"

"Yes," I said, holding my cigar.

"If everything is okay, you be there in a couple hours and I will have evidence for you. If there is a problem and you are not there, I will go on my own. If you are forced to be there, or think you are being watched, drink coke and someone will get to you later. Otherwise, drink beer." He stood by the door, looking much different from before.

"I'll be there," I told him, trying not to think of Gayle Lynds' characters. "And Seámus, I am not Judas."

"I certainly hope not." He didn't look like he'd make it. "Burn the clothes, Mick. They are full of lice." He opened the door and gave me one more sad smile, nodded and left.

I thought it was the last I'd ever see of him or hear of his fable.

May 4, 1995
2:05 p.m.

chapter THREE

After Seámus left, I carefully placed his old clothes in a hotel laundry bag and tossed it in the trash bin down stairs. There were no hairs in the sink, so Padre Seámus somehow managed to flush his cropped beard and buzzed head hair down the toilet. I was grateful.

At the hotel bar, I talked with the owner, Luis, about the three *matadors* who would fight that weekend. We both considered two to be good, but I knew nothing of the third.

"First year coming north," Luis said. He was tall and light skinned. Most of his black hair had gone with middle age. His brown eyes darted about as we talked, keeping track of the few afternoon customers. Every year at this time, we began an argument about the *matadors* that continued through the summer. We agreed on some, like today, but not all.

"Last year was his first year as a *matador*. An excellent *novillero*." He spoke as if he had followed this *matador* as an amateur. "He fought in the south and along the shore. Once in Mexico." Mexicans refer to Mexico City as Mexico, as New Yorker's refer to New York City. "So, so reviews," he said, raising his hand and making half circle motions with it. "We will talk this evening," he said, excusing himself. He went and sat at a table with two other men.

Thoughts of Seámus and the things he said played around in my head. I pondered story possibilities and felt ashamed of myself for being so selfish, considering what I thought was his paranoid condition. But, kept popping into my thoughts. But, if he wasn't totally paranoid and what he said held some truth, even half true, what a story.

How hard could it be to cross the border? I'd done it for years and the only annoying prospect was the U.S. Customs delay. That delay was one reason I didn't cross until Monday mornings. If there were a private police force there looking for him and the others, I could talk with the chief of police and handle that. We could walk right into the American consulate. Maybe not. He could be right about them returning him.

I surprised myself by putting together scenarios of how to get Padre Seámus out of Tijuana with his information. I became excited with the idea of exposing the Salvadoran death squads. Their leader, *Roberto D'Aubuisson*, was long dead and the civil war over, but the true story still had to be told. Political and military decisions in that small country were being decided and the expose could change some minds.

There was an hour left before I had to be at *Tia's* to meet Seámus. I finished my beer and went to the front for a taxi. The lobby was empty, except for the employees who smiled and wished me good afternoon. I looked around as I got into the taxi and didn't see anyone sinister. Maybe it was their *siesta* time too.

Good, I thought to myself, stupidly, after I told the driver where to take me, because it was too early for rum and coke.

Tia's is the locals name for *Tijuana Tillie's* sidewalk cafe. It was located next to the *Jai Alai* stadium on *Avenida Revolucion* and usually filled with tourists in the afternoon. The large open patio looked out onto the busy street and served Mexican fast food and liquor.

On Thursday afternoon, there were only a scattering of American servicemen, boys really, seated, eating tacos and drinking.

Horse drawn taxis waited out front, on the *avenida*, for some romantic fool. The taxi drivers dosed and the horses looked bored. I sat by the railing, close to the sidewalk, from where I could see up and down the busy street. I ordered a beer, just the bottle, no glass and waited. The beer was ice cold, the bottle damp and I sipped. I didn't want to have to order another one.

Seámus stood in the shadows of a restaurant parking lot, half a block up the street. When I noticed him, it was ten past three. He stood there, not moving. I raised the beer bottle in his direction, toasted him silently and drank. He exited the parking lot, looking carefully around, and walked toward 7th Street.

He looked into shop windows and then up and down *Avenida Revolucion*. I caught him staring at the tables around me, all empty and then at the few with the servicemen.

Even from this distance, he looked a lot different than he had earlier. He looked like a tourist. Busy Tijuana residents passed by, ignoring him. Street urchins tried to sell him trinkets and Chiclets. When the light changed at the corner, he crossed over.

The weariness was still in his walk. He passed the horses and dosing drivers, passed by me and walked toward the *Jai Alai* entrance. He stopped, stared at the servicemen, and then entered the sidewalk bar from the far end. A waiter said something to him, he shook his head no and pointed toward me. The waiter left and Seámus came, sat down, and forced a tired smile.

"You're okay," I said and realized how wrong I was. He looked exhausted. "Want something to drink?"

"No," he mumbled, scanning the patio. My old hat helped cover his eyes. Something was wrong.

"What's wrong?" I said, nervously. After all my planning, was he going to turn out to be crazy? All a made up story of some burned out, paranoid, priest?

"I made contact," he said to assure me. "First I found a room." He looked at me and then turned his eyes down. "I need to sleep."

"I can tell," I said, trying to hide my anxiousness.

"Two friends did not make it to Texas," he sighed.

"What's that mean?"

"They did not make contact at the border." He looked at me, a grim expression on his tired face. "Two days late means they are dead." He didn't take his eyes away this time. "If they are lucky."

"I'm sorry." I was at a loss for words and my belief was close to being lost.

"Thank you. I cannot get the articles until later. I need you to believe me, Mick," he pleaded. "I might not make it, but what I have, you must get across. I know you think I am insane or whatever and I do not blame you. Humor me, if that is what it takes."

"I believe you, Seámus," I lied and took a drink of beer. "I'm also concerned." "

"Someone will contact you this evening and bring the proof you want." He scanned the street knowing if they showed up, he couldn't run. "You will be where? Not your hotel," he said after a moments thought.

"From here I'm going to *Café Américan*, later I'll be at *Alfonso's*. You can find them?" The thought that this was all a hoax, irritated me. I finished my beer.

"Someone will find you," he said.

"Why not you?" I said and a little frustration came into my tone.

"You still do not believe me," he sighed.

I looked at him and tried to see the Seámus of old, but found it hard to remember what or who that was. In front of me was a tired, beaten man. Long ago expelled by Rome, if not his brethren within the Jesuit community.

This was an important weekend for me, friends from the States and Mexico were to meet here, and it should turn into one hell of a party. Not one you'd want to take a priest to, with, or without Rome's blessings.

"Padre Seámus," I began, looked at him, and searched for something I could remember, without success. "I want to. I really do. I want you to have the documents and I want to get you and them, safely across the border to Rockport and home. That's God's truth."

"You know, Mick, it sounds like you have faith about the size of a mustard seed," he said clearly, almost with a smile.

I smiled back, remembering our duels in Boston and thought that maybe I was seeing a little of the old Seámus. ". . . if you have the faith the size of a mustard seed, you shall say to the mountain, move from here to there, and it shall move; and nothing shall be impossible to you."

"You still remember," he grinned. "Some things stay with you." He was stating a fact, not asking a question.

"I remember, Seámus, Sister Patricia Alicette saw to that. What's more important, do you still believe? A priest is a priest is a priest?"

"Remember once you told me you never left the Church?" He spoke clearly, but sill kept his voice low. He checked the street again, waiting for my answer.

"The Church left me," I smiled. "I'm still waiting for it to come back for me. Maybe when another Pope John comes around?" I was asking him for an answer.

"Maybe it will pick me up then too?" he smiled his tired smile.

"Between us, Mick, maybe we can pull this off? I have run out of options and am quickly losing friends.

"Copies of everything I have are being made for you. But you must understand to make copies of these things is dangerous. People are risking their lives and I do not want anyone of them to be wasting their time . . . *for nothing*," he said as firmly as he could.

"Believe me, trust me and you will get your proof. If you have a doubt, any kind, say so and you are out. You will not be bothered by me again." He waited for my answer.

"How do we keep in touch?" I hoped my question assured him.

"We will keep in touch with you." He hesitated and then said, "They will get to you, Mick. Believe me, they will."

"The secret government's police?"

"Yes," he mumbled. "Be careful with them. Do not lie to them, just be careful what you say."

"That's why I can't contact you?"

"You will have no secrets from these men," he said again. "What you know, you will tell them." He sat up, yawned, and ran his fingers through his stubby beard. "Feel naked," he joked. "Do not watch which way I go," he said and stood. "For you, Mick, when you are contacted, the person will give you something green. You do not accept it, I will know it is not safe. Okay?"

I looked up at him, standing there, holding the wrought iron chair for strength. I knew there were blue eyes behind his squint.

"Okay," I answered, wondering what I was agreeing to.

"Something green," he mumbled with a soft laugh as he walked behind me, out of my vision.

May 4, 1995
2:55 p.m.

chapter FOUR

I ordered another beer. No matter what I really believed – and I wasn't sure what that was – I had committed myself to Padre Seámus and his problems. To see what I had gotten myself into, I decided to check with Dick Dowly at his *Café Américan. Avenida Revolucion* was busy with traffic, it was always busy, congested with cars and busses and trucks. The sidewalks were jammed with people and peddlers. I decided to walk and hoped I could sort out my options before I talked with Dick.

None of the dozing taxi drivers or their horses paid attention to me as I passed. The avenue was lined with small, colorful shops that sold everything from leather to jewelry, blankets to clothing and a multitude of native crafts, all aimed at the tourists and the American dollar.

Along the way, second story restaurants and bars with patios overlooked the avenue, the patrons, mostly American servicemen, peered over, whistling at the pretty Mexican women who passed.

I often wondered, when seeing this, what they and their neighbors would say if Mexican men did the same thing to American women, while visiting their hometown bars. I was sure I knew. I didn't need anything so I hurried by, knowing that in the next day or two I would return with my friends and assist them with their shopping.

On *Calle Benito Juarez,* I turned and walked toward the Cathedral. Here I passed vendors selling boiled corn, tacos, tamales and, mixed in, hawkers peddling religious items. Elderly Mexican women, bent with years, dressed in black and holding children by the hand came and went from the church. The very old and the very young. There were few men. Maybe, like the Irish, the men only showed up at Easter. There were no second story bars or restaurants, simply small businesses. The streets and sidewalks were crowded and there was little chance of hearing English spoken.

As I continued on, the buildings got older, the sidewalk more aged and less cared for. The sun was low and the traffic dusted the area with fine soot. Though mostly in shadows, the air seemed humid, the heat held in by the buildings and traffic. Dick's place was a few doors before *Avenida F.*

I entered, from the street, using the bar entrance. Inside was dim and cool. The room was large, a miniature stage set far back, arranged for a small group. Usually the group played jazz on weekends.

Dick liked jazz and booked groups from San Diego. The dark, hard wood bar was long and high, with tall hand carved stools placed in front. The back wall was aged brick and had primitive wooden shelves for the liquor and glasses. Defused light from over head flowed down. Tables for four lined the stucco wall that divided the bar from the restaurant, arches built in for those who passed between the two areas.

Six men sat together at the bar, drinking. Half way down, two tables were pushed together and five men played or watched others play dominos. The slapping of the dice cup was loud and the excited cries of men rumbled off the walls.

"Mick Murphy," My name was howled from a door by the stage. Dick stood there, back lit by light from his office. He closed the door. Everyone looked toward me and then resumed what they were doing.

He was five ten, my height, with a head full of brown hair that had streaks of gray in it. I guessed him to be in his mid fifties, but never asked. If it weren't for a small gut, something he had from spending so many days and nights in a saloon, he would've been slim. His round face was made handsome, or so women friends had told me, by his pug nose and green-gray eyes.

"Christ. It's that time again?" He kept his voice loud. We shook hands and then hugged, *abrazo* the Mexicans called it. He'd been here a long time.

"First Sunday in May," I assured him, stepping back. "You're looking fat as ever, "I lied. The walk hadn't helped me sort through my options.

"Lost five pounds," he lied, sucking in his stomach and smacking it with his hands. "Drink?" We walked to an empty section of the bar and sat down.

"First one on the house?" It was an old joke. "Isn't it always?"

The young Mexican bartender hurried to his boss.

"A shot of Irish and a tall beer," I said as seriously as I could. "A boiler maker," I grinned and Dick nodded to the bartender. "Only kidding," I said, but not until he pulled a bottle of Jameson's from it's hiding place.

"*Tecate,*" I said, slapping Dick on the back.

The bartender smiled. To drink it properly, you take a can of *Tecate*, ring the opening with lime and salt, and drink it, one large gulp at a time. It doesn't work with other beers, but it's refreshing with *Tecate*.

We both prepared our beer and drank. The saltshaker and plate of cut limes stayed on the bar.

"The party beginnin' Thursday this year?" he asked, gulping from the beer can.

"No," I answered and followed with my own gulp. "Paying for the hotel rooms and buying the tickets. Got yours," I said, finishing my beer. "Left it in my hotel."

"Don't do that on Sunday," he said and tapped his empty can on the bar. The bartender hurried to us with two new, cold cans of beer. "How many joinin' you this year?"

We prepared our beers and drank.

"Too many as usual. Not the asshole from last year," I assured him.

Last year a girl I knew from the Caribe West in Rockport came with her current boy friend. He turned out to be a jealous drunk and almost ruined the weekend. She stayed, Dick got him across the border the second afternoon. It was that or we were going to have to draw straws to see who received the honor of killing him.

"Good. Good," he smiled and drank. "We get a chance to talk before the craziness begins? I look forward to that."

"There is something I would like to talk to you about," I said matter-of-factly.

He pulled the beer can away, just as he was about to drink and put it on the bar. He had a questioning look that could've gone into a smile or frown. He frowned. "Sounds like you got a problem?" He drank from his beer.

"Not a problem, really. I just heard something and I'd like to see what you know about it." I finished my beer, tapped it on the bar, and watched as the bartender delivered two more. I hesitantly turned back to Dick.

"I thought your rule was this was a non-working weekend?" We prepared our beers.

"Weekend begins tomorrow,' I said, unable to put any humor into it.

"Go ahead and ask." We both sucked on squeezed limes at the same time.

"I heard the border's closed. Even to the coyotes. Maybe one or two of 'em have died trying to cross. You hear anything?" As hard as I tried to keep my tone low key I couldn't. Too many years of asking questions, especially to those who don't want to answer.

"Somethin' up?" he said as he turned to look at the six men sitting further down the bar.

"You tell me," I said. Was he checking customers or was he nervous, like Seámus?

"Let's sit at a table," he said and stood.

We walked back toward the entrance. Where the bar turned toward the brick wall, there was a small alcove with two tables. Dick sat down, I joined him.

"Why do you want to know this?" he said seriously.

"Is it true?" I ignored his question.

From where we sat, we could see both the restaurant and bar's entrances. We could also see the six men at the bar and the heads of the domino players.

"I heard," he began slowly, reluctantly, 'that about a week ago special police arrived, lookin' for a fugitive, a terrorist from Central America. They're lookin' for him and about six or so of his supporters. They've been able to do what American Immigrations hasn't, effectively close the border. In some places, I've been told, they've repaired the fence. Now, what are you up to?"

"What about dead coyotes?" I insisted.

"There haven't been any funerals."

"Dick," I said, staring him down.

"There's a couple missin'," he mumbled, staring back at me. "Nobody knows for sure. Okay? Now, why?"

It was my turn to nervously look around. No one had come in or gone out since I arrived, but I looked anyway. The few patrons couldn't have cared less about us and they were all too far away to hear anything we might say. Even the bartender ignored us and our beers were empty. There must have been an understanding between Dick and his employees about this location.

"Remember the pieces I've done on the Irish priest, Seámus McGillicuddy?" I said, keeping my voice low.

"Padre Seámus," he said remembering and then his expression changed. "Sweet Jesús," he moaned. "The terrorist is the priest?" he guessed. "Mick, tell me no. You aren't here for him?"

"I'm here for what I'm here for every first weekend in May," I assured him. Then I told him about meeting Seámus and what he had told me.

"What are you gonna do?" he said after a moment of quiet.

"Go to the bullfights," I said. "Dick, I don't even know if what he's telling me is the truth."

"You don't think what he's telling you is possible?" he said, surprised.

"We both know what he's saying is probably fact. What I'm getting at is does he have the documents?"

"You think the Mexican government would allow these goons to close the illegal exits and tie up the regular crossings for a paranoid priest? Hell," he almost yelled. "The American DEA doesn't get that kind of cooperation."

"Can you check into it?" I drained the last drop of beer.

"Jesús, almighty," he mumbled. "Ask me to cut my own throat, why don't you?" he went on as he walked to the bar and then came back with two cans of beer. We prepared the lime and salt in silence. "I'll ask around, but I got a feelin' you aren't gonna like what I come up with."

"That's all I ask. I don't have to like what you come up."

"Bullshit. How you gonna get him out?" He drank beer and grinned at me. "So, that's not all you're gonna ask. Is it?"

May 4, 1995
4 p.m.

chapter FIVE

I stopped at *Caesar's* for *caldo*, Mexican chicken soup, with lots of chopped up peppers and onions. I squeezed fresh lime into it, sipped my beer, and ate the hot soup. Dick would go about whatever it is he goes about doing, and we would meet for breakfast at the hotel in the morning. His offer of help was greatly appreciated.

First, he would look into the special police, Seámus' death squads, while I waited around to be contacted. By someone offering me something green, I reminded myself.

Juaquin walked in from the outside patio, waved and came over. He wore a baseball cap, advertising an American business – everyone gave him hats – polished cowboy boots, faded jeans, and an old western shirt. He didn't dress like a man his age was supposed to, whatever that was.

"Tomorrow all the *gringos* come?" he said, sitting, his large black Indian eyes excited.

"Yes," I smiled. He didn't drink, so I didn't offer to buy him anything.

"You need me to buy the *boletos*," he smiled.

"Bought this morning," I said.

His expression saddened. "Why you don't come here first?"

"I did." For years, he had always gone with me to buy the tickets, assuring me that he would not allow me to be cheated. The only places I'd been cheated at in Tijuana were bars I shouldn't have been in, in the first place. "I was early," I said to reassure him. "I have everyone's ticket, including yours."

"*Gracias,*" he smiled. "If you had waited, maybe I could have gotten better seats."

"Front row," I said. "You've been busy." I finished my soup.

"*No trabajo sabado, domingo,* have to work now."

"Anyone looking for me?"

"*No hoy,*" he smiled. He knew once the weekend began the patio café out front was the meeting place for all my lost bullfight stragglers.

"Many police," he pointed toward outside. "Not good to be *borrachin* this weekend. You say to your friends."

"I will thank you." I wondered if he was talking about the beefed up security at the border or just the local cops gearing up for the *Cinco de mayo* weekend. "I didn't see many police."

"Not in uniforms," he said and stood. "I have to go outside to work. You go to *Alfonso's*?"

"Later. You be there?"

"Too much drinking," he grinned. "I see you tomorrow morning? Okay?"

"*Mañana en la mañana*," I said. "If you hear why so many police are in street clothes, you let me know. Okay?"

"You don't want to ask Vargas?" he questioned with a stare.

He was talking about Chief of Police Rául Vargas. He knew I would see Vargas that evening and during the weekend.

"Just curious," I smiled, but his questioning look didn't change. He was very perceptive and I saw his confusion with my question.

"*No problema*," he nodded and left.

I finished my soup and beer. It was a little before seven, which meant it would be dark and cool outside. Where had the afternoon gone?

Juaquin sat by himself watching over the scattering of patrons. His shoeshine stand closed for the evening. I sat with him. He watched the street hawkers offer their goods to the customers, jewelry mostly, but some blankets and gum. Those that sold American cigarettes found the only customers. The hawkers watched him as they moved between tables, knowing he would force them out of the patio if they were too persistent.

"You baby sit for *los gringos?*" I asked.

He smiled at me, his stained teeth a reminder of when he smoked, the smile friendly and knowing. "*Por qué no?*" he said.

Years ago, while staying at *Caesar's,* I got very drunk and woke up the next day with only a few *pesos*, and no wallet. Hung over and panicked, I came down to the patio for a beer – hair of the dog, or maybe bull, if you will.

The only thing I appreciated at that moment was that my room was on American Express. I could eat and drink here and sign the tab.

Juaquin and I were not as close at that time, but always spoke. He sat with me and joked about the past evening. He drank and smoked in those days. After my third beer, he shined shoes and left me to myself. During that time, he shined maybe five pairs of shoes, earning about twenty dollars, American, and a few cents in tips. When he returned and sat, he handed me a small paper bag. He was all smiles and his eyes were lit up. He ordered a beer and I opened the bag. Inside was my wallet, with close to three hundred dollars cash and another couple hundred in travelers' checks. He could see my confusion and then my elation.

"You left on the bar," he said, and pointed toward the inside hotel bar.

"Gracias," I said. I certainly felt dumb. As I started to count the money, I felt guilty for doing so, so I peeled two $20s off and gave them to him. He didn't want to accept them. I insisted and told him it was for babysitting me. Finally, he accepted. I took him to the bullfights and we were friends. Since then he has always acted as my and my guests' protector.

I gave him $100 in $20s, which he put into his pocket without counting.

"Many people?

"You know most everyone," I said.

"The *loco?*"

"No," I said. "They come tomorrow about noon."

"Todo?"

"No." I laughed. "Some tomorrow, some on Saturday. They all know to see you when they arrive."

"A working vacation for me," he said shrewdly. "I baby sit," he said, the excitement still in his eyes.

"Thank you." I slapped his shoulder in a friendly way as I stood. "I will see you tomorrow."

"And I will see about the police without uniforms," he said, the curious look still in his eyes.

At the corner, I got in a taxi and asked to be taken to *Alfonso's*. So far, no one had offered me anything, green or otherwise.

May 4, 1995
6:10 p.m.

chapter SIX

    Alfonso's Restaurante y Bar was located within walking distance of the bullring. Years ago, after a bullfight, I stumbled in, lost, thirsty and hungry. I had found a home. During the years, many interesting friendships had developed there and most everyone had forgiven me for helping so many *gringos* discover the place.

    Inside was smaller than *Café Américan.* The bar was brighter and the restaurant busier. The front entrance opened to a vestibule that gave you two archways to choose from. The bar, to the right and the other to the dinning room. Many local politicians ate and drank here.

When the governor came from Mexicali, the capital, of *Baja California Norte,* he and his aids always stopped by. I've been told that every president of Mexico in the last 10 years has had a drink at the bar.

In Mexico, the president serves one six-year term, so in all it means two presidents have stopped by. Alfonso and Natale, partners in the business, proudly say that since they've been opened every president has stopped by. And that's the truth.

Alfonso was at the bar, on the phone, when I walked in. He looked taller than his five, seven because of his full frame. Not fat, but well conditioned. His hair was black, no gray, brown alert eyes sat deep in their sockets, and his light skin was clean-shaven. A bright white smile wrinkled his thin straight nose as I nodded. He pointed to an empty stool. I sat and the young bartender brought me a cold beer and said hello. Luis, from the hotel, stood by a table in the corner, watching men play dominos.

Natale came in from the dinning room. He was the same height as Alfonso, but stockier. His face was fuller and except for his mustache, he was clean-shaven. After seeing me, he peeked back into the dinning room and said something I couldn't hear. Then he came over and we shook hands.

"Your *aficionados* are already eating," he smiled, his eyes hidden behind tinted glasses. "I told them to wait." He looked at his wristwatch. It was close to eight.

"I'm late," I said and drank some beer.

"I save for you a big plate of *camaron con ajo,*" he smiled and pointed toward the dinning room.

"Fantastic," I grinned, glad he remembered how I loved shrimp with lots of garlic and that's the way he prepared it in the kitchen for me.

When Alfonso got off the phone the three of us headed toward the dinning room. Luis stopped us to show the newspaper articles he had brought along regarding the new matador.

We would join him later in the bar.

The dinning room was full. Each table had a crisp, clean, white tablecloth, real crystal glasses, one for water, and one for wine and freshly cut flowers were centered in a crystal vase. Waiters, dressed in black and white, hurried from the kitchen to the various tables bringing orders or clearing away empty dishes.

At our normal table, in the back, from where you could see everyone and everything that happened, sat Manuel Ruiz, the *empresario* of the bullfights, promoter in English. He was short, balding, with patches of white-white hair over his ears, a round happy face that told everyone he enjoyed himself and life in general during the past 50-odd years.

Next to him sat Chuy Padilla, a local businessman who traveled north of the border quite often. He was almost six foot, topped off with bushy white hair, gray eyes, a hardy appetite and a thirst that knew no end.

It was rumored that, at one time or another, he had helped out and/or bribed every politician in *Baja*, showing no prejudice to party affiliation. When I tried to find out what business he was in, he'd told me he had retired and was no longer in business. I think if he were an American, he'd be considered a lobbyist.

The third man at the table set for six, was Rául Vargas, chief of police, *Tijuana, Baja California Norte, Mexico*. I don't think I had ever seen him in uniform and hoped to keep it that way. Like everyone else, he was dressed casually. He was average height, kept himself fit and his dark, curly haircut short. Under his loose fitting shirt, I could see the bulge of his service revolver.

He appeared to have a permanent tan and spoke English like a native, which he almost was. He was born in East Los Angeles and went to school there until the sixth grade. His family returned to Ensenada, Mexico, where he finished his education. He went to a Mexican University and attended the FBI school. I knew he had close contacts with the DEA across the border. When I asked him about the FBI and DEA he smiled and asked, "Why would I do that?" I didn't have an answer for him.

Tired, blood shot brown eyes looked up at me as Rául greeted the three of us. I wondered if the problems at the border had kept him awake for the past week. Something had.

Alfonso and Natale had begun to eat before I arrived. We all sat and my food was brought to me. Natale had it waiting in the kitchen. There was a lot of small talk as we ate, about the new *matador* and the two, Lomelin and Silveti, that we all knew. You either loved Antonio Lomelin or hated him, I loved him. David Silveti was a toss up. Lomelin was a showman who worked in so close that sometimes he and the bull were like one. On a good day, he would receive two ears and a tail. On a bad day, he would receive a standing ovation from the crowd.

Two young couples sat alone at different tables, ignoring the world. The six of us finished eating and were well into an evening of drinking, arguing, and all around enjoying ourselves.

It was almost 11 p.m. and the waiters were ready to close up. Alfonso and Natale were up and down, seeing to the customers, the kitchen, and the bar. It seemed like the past ten or so first weekends in May, as we talked about the bullfights throughout Mexico, the political situations in Europe and Central America.

I excused myself and went to the bar's men's room. The bar was half filled – or I should say half empty, since I am a pessimist – with most everyone up at the far end, by the entrance, watching a rerun of a soccer match on the TV.

Raúl stood at the end of the bar, waiting for me as I left the men's room, ignoring the soccer match. He motioned for me to sit next to him. There were two beers waiting. He smiled a tired smile and sipped from his glass.

"You have many friends," he began, sounding as if he were reciting, "some good to know, some not so good. You travel, you make friends. Europe," he laughed softly, "England, I don't think so, but Ireland yes. Central America, yes and maybe even in Colombia?" His eyes questioned me. "Someday you must tell me the truth about you and the Colombians."

"Someday," I promised him with a grin, waiting for him to say what it was he had to say.

"The terrorist you met today, Mick, is not a good person to know," he said firmly, like a policeman. "You plan to help him?" He stared at me and sipped from his glass. "Or have you already?"

"I've met a lot of people today, Raúl," I said in a low voice.

"Don't be a *yanqui,* Mick," he said, holding back the anger. "I have spent all afternoon defending you, damn it. Do you know where the terrorist is?"

"No." That's all I said. He stared at me.

"Did you come here to meet him?" He looked away, toward the soccer match.

"No. I didn't know he was here and I have no idea where he's at now."

"You would think that as chief of police, I would be in control of Tijuana," he spoke into the emptiness of where we were seated, "wouldn't you?" He waited and I said nothing.

I wasn't supposed to.

"I get a call about ten days ago, from Mexico. From the attorney general himself. He tells me about the search for a terrorist from Central America. An American national, but wanted for acts of terrorism throughout Central America. It seems the man wants to reenter the United States and he has a fugitive from El Salvador with him. You following me?" he asked, looking back at me.

"I'm listening."

"I'm to cooperate by pulling my men back from the border and letting . . ." he paused. "I don't know what to call them."

"Secret Police?" I suggested. "Death squads?"

"You are being overly melodramatic, don't you think?"

"Dick Dowly mentioned the border closing," I said. "What do you know of this man?"

"I know I am to cooperate with the secret police," he forced a tired grin. "I object, but like all men in positions of mine, I am over ruled. Maybe one day I want to be mayor or governor and I will need the men in Mexico for support. Understand?" He didn't wait for me to answer.

"I bite my tongue and pull my men from the border. Nine days ago, these men arrive and set up a command post at my police station. I complain to Mexico when they hire some of my officers to work for them. Mexico tells me it's okay as long as the men are off duty.

"I'm pissed, Mick, but can't do much about it." He took a long swallow of beer. "Today I find out you are an old friend of this terrorist . . . I can't call him a priest. That's all I know about him, all I need to know. Find that strange?"

"I can't call him a terrorist."

"I didn't think you would. Anyway, you're an old friend of his, you're here, and he's here. You lean, should we say, to the left and these men lean to the right. They think you're here to help the terrorist. I tell them you have come to Tijuana for years, before I was chief, to attend the first bullfight of the season. I mention people here who like you, are your friends. Lucky for you, it's an impressive list. But these men, they think you would've planned the meeting this way . . . to cover yourself. They were very convincing, Mick." He finished his beer and signaled for another.

The bartender pulled himself away from the soccer match and brought us two beers. Mine was only half-full, but I took the new one.

"You can tell me what took place or you can tell them," he murmured. "My advice is to tell me."

I told him the truth up until Seámus left the hotel.

"What's your opinion?" he said after I stopped talking.

"I haven't had time to consider it," I said. "But of Seámus, I think he's paranoid . . . or thought so until now. I think he's more a danger to himself than to the secret police," I lied.

"Do you think you'll see him again?" He was being a policeman.

"I don't plan to, Rául."

"I don't like any of this, Mick, but it comes with the job. I've done all I can to keep you out of this and don't know if it's been enough. I'll relay what you've told me and I'll tell them I believe you. Will I be safe in telling them that?" He watched me with policemen's eyes.

"I've told you the truth," I answered and drank some beer to help moisten my parched throat.

"Okay," he said dryly. "We keep it between us?" He looked toward the dinning room.

"Whatever you say. I'm here for the bullfights, nothing else," I answered. "Thank you for standing up for me," I mumbled between swallows.

"That's about all I can do, Mick. Every man has a price and mine is my future. After I talk to them, it's out of my hands. I gotta run," he said and stood up. "I'll do what I can, but you might want to consider missing the bullfights," he said and walked out through the front entrance.

I watched him leave, feeling fear and confusion snake into me, and then went back to the men's room. I felt dizzy and sick to my stomach. What Seámus had said was true, or so it seemed. If that was the case, maybe he did have the papers and photos he said he had. The thought frightened me, then excited me, but my stomach turned and I vomited, hoping no one heard.

A flower girl was in the shadows as I came from the men's room. She smiled. She was pretty in her jeans and multi-colored blouse. Her long black hair, thick and wavy, was pulled back into a ponytail, tied with a bright ribbon, a few strands falling over her forehead. Her Indian features added to her beauty, her skin clear and smooth. Fervent black eyes stared out at me, a thin smile showed white teeth.

"*Flores, señor?*" she said, stepping out of the shadows, pushing the loose stands of hair back in place with her free hand. She looked toward the dining room, then back at the bar and me. She nervously pushed the loose strands of thick hair back from her forehead as she stood there and with the slight movement of her head the strands fell back.

I drank from my glass at the bar, trying to rid my mouth of the sour taste it had. I stopped because she was pretty. Usually the flower girls were younger and not so well dressed. She was older. Maybe it was all the beer, but I wanted to talk with her, buy her flowers and talk. I pointed to a stool by the bar and she shook her head no.

"*Flores, señor?*" she said again, nervously playing with her hair. She held out a small packet of carnations, wrapped in newspaper. "*Por favor?*"

I reached into my pocket for money and as I did, I noticed in the middle of the colorful carnations, a green one. I looked again, smiled nervously, and said, "*Habla inglés?*"

"Little," she said softly, pushing the flowers toward me. "You buy," she said, not a question. "Pretty colors," she continued softly.

I gave her five dollars, she looked at it, not sure what to do.

"*Gracias,*" she finally mumbled.

"*Como se llama?*" I asked her name.

She looked nervously around and then at me. It seemed she was forcing herself to speak. "Sonia," she finally said, forcing a small smile. Her large black eyes could not hide her nervousness.

"Its okay, Sonia," I said. I held the flowers and could feel the heaviness in the stem area. "You know my name?"

"Mick," she said with a simper, not sure if she was supposed to or not.

"Yes," I grinned. "Do you know Seámus?"

The soccer match ended to the cheers of the men watching it. The noise frightened Sonia, I could see it in her eyes. I touched her hand and smiled at her. She smiled back, nervously. I was about to say something to her when the loud screeching of breaks came from out front and then the slamming of doors, followed by rapid bursts of automatic gunfire. The loud retorts stopped as quickly as they began.

Sonia froze, her face panicked. I held her by the arm, she dropped the dozen, or so packets of carnations and roses she held. For a moment, there was silence. The men watching the TV rushed to the windows and looked out. I heard my friends in the dinning room open the front door. The reflection of flashing red lights bounced into the bar. Sonia held onto me tightly.

"*Ay dios, mio.*" she cried.

May 4, 1995
8:15 p.m.

chapter SEVEN

Sonia held onto me for a few more moments. I could feel her trembling. Then she pushed away and wiped at the tears on her cheeks. Her expression was grim as she looked toward the door that allowed the flashing police lights to pierce the bar.

"Somebody to meet you?" I said, keeping my voice low. We were alone and seemed to have been forgotten, the way I wanted to keep it for as long as possible.

"*Quizas,*" she whispered, her voice tottering.

I took her answer to mean what we heard had to do with the person or persons who were to meet her. "You're safe," I said to assure her.

She looked at me like I was from another planet.

"My fear is for the person there," she nodded toward the front, "not myself," she lectured me in an ice-cold challenge.

I believed her.

She moved further away, bent and picked up the flowers she'd dropped. I still held onto the packet with the green carnation. A commotion was taking place at the vestibule, the door closed, there was some yelling, and it reopened, letting the flashing police lights penetrate the room again. Two men entered the bar carrying M-16s. They were Latin, maybe a mix of Indian, almost my height, dressed casually and seemed angry. Police or military? I didn't think it mattered. They stared in our direction. I turned to place my carnations on a table and saw two more armed men standing behind us at the restaurant archway. Sonia placed her arm full of flowers over my carnations, the look on her face very ardent. She stared at the men behind us, duplicates of the two by the entrance and moved closer to me.

"Are you the American?" One of the men at the entrance yelled in Spanish.

"*Yo soy norteamericano,*" I said, hoping he hadn't mistaken me for Seámus.

There were only six of us in the bar, the four-armed men, Sonia, and me. I hadn't noticed the others leave, or maybe they were seated in the restaurant.

These men held their automatic weapons at the ready, something that frightened me since we were standing in a restaurant I considered a second home.

I didn't know for sure what was hidden in the stem of my carnations, but I knew if it was discovered, I was in trouble. My stomach turned and I held back the retching as it tried to work its way into my throat.

"Sit down," the man ordered in Spanish, using the M-16 to point at an empty table. "Please," he finished in English.

I sat and Sonia pushed in next to me. The men behind us laughed. I had no idea what they saw that was funny. They walked past us, to the men in front. They spoke quietly and the four of them laughed. Sonia and I looked at each other, both distrustful of their humor.

"You wait there, Murphy," one said in English. I couldn't tell which one spoke, but he had a thick accent. "You wait," he ordered again.

"I'll wait," I answered in English and the four of them walked to the vestibule.

We'd heard sirens after the first gunshots, then the sirens stopped. We were able to hear small pieces of commotion from out on the street each time the door opened and closed. Sometimes it stayed open for a short while. There was no order to the commotion or the sounds we heard.

"What's in the flowers?" I looked toward the pile of roses and carnation on the next table.

"Papers," she whispered.

"No photos?" Seámus had promised photos.

"Paper copies of photos," she said, unable to hide her confusion with my questions.

That confusion, in her voice, led me to believe she thought I was more involved than I was. That wasn't good, especially if these were the people looking for Seámus and they were as good at extracting information as he had said.

I glanced around quickly, making sure no one had come in from the restaurant to watch us. We seemed to be alone. I pushed Sonia out of her seat and we moved to the next table. We both looked around, unable to hide our nervousness.

From beneath the pile of wrapped flowers, I pulled the packet with the green carnation and quickly unwrapped it.

I didn't take time to read or look at the copies that were there, I folded them and slipped the sheets between the booth's cushions. I scattered the flowers in with the pile of wrapped flowers. We returned to the other table and smiled tensely at each other.

"You think the papers are safe there?" Her dark eyes searched for something from me.

"For the moment," I said, trying to keep a blank expression, hoping it would pass for being in control.

"When the moment passes?"

"One moment at a time," I said curtly, adapting the alcoholics' motto to our situation.

"Yes," she said after a pause. I wasn't sure if it was ridicule or agreement.

The door closed up front and the flashing police light stopped its annoying reflection. I heard someone walk through the restaurant, behind us, and talk to whoever was still seated there. Sonia and I both tensed.

"Damn you Murphy," bellowed from the vestibule.

I recognized the voice instantly. Norm. He walked into the room with the bartender in tow.

"Drinks for my friends, *amigo*," he said and let the bartender go. I expected to see him carrying an M-16, but he wasn't.

"*Si señor.*" The jittery boy ran behind the bar. He placed three bottles of beer on the bar, looked nervously at me and then at Norm.

Norm must have been in his early 50s, he was muscular, kept his six-foot frame in shape at his own health club-gym by the Los Angeles International Airport. His round face seemed ageless, his crooked nose a monument to his profession.

He was a boxing trainer, pro and amateur, or so he posed. I first ran into him in Panama, where he saved my life. I was researching an article on drug smuggling and seeing a girl whose brother was a Colombian drug czar. He sent a couple of his men to bring me to Colombia, a place I wasn't interested in being. One thing led to another, there was a shoot out, and Norm got my happy ass on an airplane and back to the States. I figured he was DEA, now I think he's CIA. Freelance, maybe, but CIA. He denies it.

"Relax, son," Norm told the bartender as he picked up the three beers and brought them to our table.

His tan sport coat was tailored to give him extra room in the back, where he carried his 9mm automatic. All his jackets were tailored like that. He wore starched jeans, a faded yellow cotton shirt, and western boots. He smiled at us, his eyes a cold blue-gray, giving Sonia an extra second's attention.

"Always exotic, Mick," he said giving us the beers.

Sonia left hers on the table. I took a long swallow of mine.

"Sonia, this is a friend," I said after my drink. "Norm, this is Sonia"

They smiled at each other, Norm's blue-gray eyes not telling anything. Sonia's black eyes frightened, anxiously trying to see past this moment, as she pushed loose strands of hair from her forehead.

"You're early," I said, not knowing what else to say.

Norm and Wayne were supposed to join me for the weekend. Somehow, I knew, he was involved in the hunt for Seámus.

A coincidence? How could either of us have known about Seámus being in Tijuana this weekend? I fought the thought of how Norm knew about things. A sharp pain tore at my stomach as I wondered how involved he was. Was he using me, by offering to join in the long bullfight weekend, or did he think I was using him? Did he think I was involved? I wasn't feeling any better. I took hold of Sonia's hand a gave it a small squeeze, hoping she understood I was telling her it was okay.

"I have business to take care," he said with indifference. "The weekend begins tomorrow"

"Boxing?" I said, not able to hide the smirk on my face. "Or something to do with the shooting outside?"

"Cute, Mick," he answered and drank some beer. "Would you excuse us, for a moment?" he said to Sonia. Before she could answer, he had his large hand on my shoulder, leading me to the bar. We sat down, each holding a beer bottle.

Wayne walked in from the restaurant, as if on cue. He was about six, two. From Brazil, originally, his skin the color of weak coffee, his eyes brown and intense. He wore a brown sport coat, tailored to hide his side arm, a blue oxford shit, faded jeans, and tennis shoes. The bartender brought him a coke. Wayne smiled, a large friendly grin, but didn't say anything.

"Do you know what you're involved in?" Norm asked and then gave the young bartender a look that sent him to where Wayne sat. "These are not nice people," he said firmly.

"I didn't know Padre Seámus was here," I said as honestly as possible.

"Tell me about it," he asked, but it was an order.

He seemed edgy and that concerned me. For the third time in only a few hours, I told the story of how I met Seámus that afternoon at *Hotel Caesar's* and what we did. I covered everything until he left my hotel room.

Norm listened. He watched me closely and twice glanced at Sonia. When I finished he drained his beer and signaled the jittery bartender for two more. He brought the beers and quickly returned to Wayne.

"I got these?" he said, pulling two bullfight tickets from his shirt pocket.

I was surprised since I'd told him I'd buy the tickets. "I have two for you," I said. "They're at my hotel."

"These are them," he taunted.

"How . . . ?"

"How do you think?" he irately cut me off. "I'm sitting at the gym this afternoon and get a call. Is my friend Murphy in Tijuana, Mexico? I tell 'em, yes. Then I'm told your ass is gonna be mowed into compost. Damn it, Mick. Vargas is the only thing between you and an interrogation room and it ain't a nice room.

"While we're flying here, I'm briefed on what's happening and given copies of your articles on the priest. I'll tell you, Mick, their idea that you set it up his escape to fall on this weekend rings true to me and I'm on your side. Remember, I've seen some of the shit you've pulled. You figure to sneak the priest through with us as a group?" He drank some beer.

"I didn't know he was here," I said again, trying not to be angry. I swallowed beer, not tasting it.

"What I told you is the truth, not matter what you think. My question is, why are you with a Central American death squad?"

He placed the two tickets on the bar, thought about it and picked them up. "I took these from your room," he mumbled, looking more at the tickets than me. "I'm with you and I am trying to keep it that way," he said. "She staying with you?" he nodded toward Sonia.

"I'm not sure, after this," I sipped some beer.

"You won't be alone," he warned me. "Understand?"

"They'll follow me?"

"Yeah," Norm grumbled. "And listen too."

"They've bugged the room?" Things were beginning to move a little too fast.

"The bedroom, the bathroom, your car," he sneered. "They have someone at the switch board, to see everyone who comes and goes. See who asks for you. Are you getting the picture?" He put the tickets in his shirt pocket.

"Yeah," I said slowly, not knowing how frightened I sounded.

"They almost had the priest and you saved his holy ass." Norm explained with clenched teeth. "I got here just about the time they discovered where you were staying. They went through your room, your car and found the priest's old clothes in the trash outside. The fact that you admitted to Vargas about giving him a change of clothes, shows you're being honest." He almost winced when he said honest. "They don't know you as well as I do.

"Who's the exotic little creature?" he said, not taking his eyes from me.

"I hit on her a couple of times this evening and she was coming around. We were talking when all this happened." I tried a chauvinist smile.

"If you care," he said matter-of-factly, "keep her with you, she'll be safer that way. I wouldn't let her go on her own." His stare was cold and his meaning chilled me.

"I care," I said nervously. "What are you really doing here?" I finally found the nerve to ask.

"Trying to keep you alive," he said, showing some humor, even if it was from the dark side. "Maybe I can scare some sense into you?"

He went over to Sonia, spoke to her, and helped her up. I thought he would bring her to me instead she walked to Wayne.

"*Agua mineral,*" Norm ordered from the bartender, as he stood next to me.

I looked toward Sonia and Wayne. When the bartender gave Norm the bottle of seltzer water, a look of terror emanated from Sonia. I looked around, thinking someone had come in, but we were still alone. Wayne put his hand on her shoulder and spoke to her. I could see her shake her head violently. They were arguing. I looked to Norm for an explanation.

With a vice like grip, he moved me from the bar stool to a chair by the table covered with flowers. He sat me down forcibly. With his large thumb over the opened bottle, he shook it fiercely.

"I'm not sure how to get through to you, Mick," he spoke slowly, shaking the bottle as he circled me.

"See, you're a romantic. You believe in lost causes, the underdog. You chase wind mills," he yelled, jarring me.

"I like you. I even owe you and I don't owe many people. All your heroes are dead, Mick. You ever think of that? Dead," he clenched his teeth again, but the words came out harsh and loud.

"All romantics, like you . . . and Padre Seámus." He lowered his voice when he mentioned Seámus.

"You can't save the god-damn world because it don't wanna be saved. No matter what anyone does, there'll always be the exploited . . . the poor.

"You wanna buy a truck to help some Indian farmers in Guatemala go to the market, buy it, and know what happens? Those farmers make a little money and they become the exploiters. It's a big cycle and you can't do a damn thing about it." As he spoke, he stopped, stared at me, and then circled again, shaking the bottle.

"These people after the priest, don't have respect for human life, not yours, not mine, not hers." He stopped moving and pointed toward Sonia.

She looked frightened. Wayne kept his large arm around her, holding her in her seat. I'd never seen Norm look the way he did as he spoke. There was anger in his voice and cruelty in his expression.

With a swiftness I couldn't have expected, Norm moved behind me, clasped his large hand across my mouth and pulled the chair and me backwards. He stopped me at about forty-five degrees. I tried to pull his hand away with both my hands, but couldn't. Then I became frightened. I was helpless, I couldn't escape from the chair or his grip.

"They'd have you tied to this chair," he said coarsely, his words coming quickly and with malice. He shook the bottle in front of me.

"Then, while they had your mouth held shut, they'd let the spray from this bottle shoot up your nose. You'd choke, gag, and maybe puke."

He let the spray from the bottle hit me in the face. I closed my eyes and felt myself gag. I couldn't get free. My arms flew wildly around, trying to hit him, to make him release me.

"If you didn't choke to death on your own vomit," he said, his words icy, "they might pull you back more," he leaned the chair back so I looked at his piqued face and the old ceiling, "and then pour what was left in the bottle right into your nose." His expression was as callous as his words. He poured the water from the bottle onto the floor, letting me see it as it flowed past.

He put the chair back up right and let go of my mouth. His strong hand kept me from standing. My legs shook too much for me to stand, but I didn't want him to see that. He probably knew it, though. The bottle fell to the floor and he kicked it away. I wanted to yell, but feared how powerless I'd sound if I attempted to speak.

"That's what they'd do, before they really care if you answer them or not," he taunted me. "I forgot to tell you, you're naked when they tie you to the chair."

Images ran through my mind that frightened me. "If you want to scare me . . . " It sounded as if my words came from somewhere else. He cut me off and I was thankful.

"Scare you, Mick? You'd better be scared," he said.

"Next they might bend you over a table," he kicked the table with the flowers, its sudden movement made me jump. Packets of flowers fell to the floor. "You know what a cattle prong is, right?"

"Yeah," I mumbled, staring at him. The anger in me was as frightening as the fear.

"There wouldn't be a condom on it."

"Jesús," I moaned. "What the hell are you doing?"

"I'm trying to save your useless Irish life, you dumb shit," he whispered and walked to the bar. He sipped some beer. "I'm almost out of time," he sighed and finished his beer.

"What's that mean?" I asked and stood, surprised my legs held me. Slowly, I walked to the bar. Sonia stared horrified. She had to be thinking, if these were my friends, what were my enemies like?

"Just listen to me," he said. "I told them you work for me."

"Doing what?" I said before he had finished.

"Damn it," he yelled. "They know you've written about the leftist movements in Central America. I told them you went in, the journalism a cover and came back with information for me. I don't want your cover blown and as long as they believe it, you might make it. Her too," he said, meaning Sonia.

"I never . . ."

"But they don't know that, Mick. And I got bad news for you," he said, with a cold grim expression.

"And what was that, good news?" I looked toward the chair he had me in earlier.

"A lesson," he said. "No, more an example of what might be."

"What's the bad news?" I was regaining my strength. I reached for my beer and took a sip. Wayne was no longer holding Sonia back, but she wasn't rushing to me either.

"Neil Cluny, Jr.," he said, staring at me, waiting for some form of recognition. He didn't receive any.

"Who?" Sounded like a Limy name.

"Neville Cluny Sr. was a MI-6 agent. Did a lot of work on the Irish problem. His son, junior, followed in his foot steps, but he got a little too sadistic, even for the British."

"I've lost you," I said, confused.

"Junior is running this operation," he sneered. "He's working for the Central Americans. Tijuana to Tecate is his area. He's the one that closed the border."

"Shit."

" Wait, it gets better. He's read your Irish stuff. I think he'd like to kill you." There was a lack of humor in his demeanor.

May 4, 1995
9:30 p.m.

chapter EIGHT

I don't know which was worse, my fear or my anger. Fear for myself and anger toward the cause of my fear. I was angry with Norm too. His little demonstration had scared me, but I wasn't afraid of him.

Sonia sat next to Wayne, resigned to her predicament. I couldn't tell from looking at her, which I did a lot of, but she had to be puzzled. I had a feeling she'd been angry long before that evening, but confusion must have been scarce in her life. I wanted to tell her how uninvolved I was in all this, but knew she wouldn't believe me. I doubted, at that point, if anyone would believe me. She didn't touch the drink that was in front of her, she sat there, no longer arguing with Wayne and occasionally glanced toward the flowers. Those flowers that went to the floor when Norm kicked the table stayed there.

"You play this my way," Norm said, his voice taut, "you might get to spend the evening with the young lady." He hadn't missed my glances at Sonia.

"I'm a spy," I said without enthusiasm but with a lot of sarcasm.

"I'll be the spy, smart ass," his tone lighter, "you be my researcher. Okay?" A thin smile formed on his stern face.

Before I answered, the front door opened, harsh noises jolted the still bar from outside and then the door closed again. There were no flashing police lights.

"Time's up, Mick," Norm warned me in a whisper.

Wayne said something to Sonia and she quietly acknowledged whatever it was. Fear was quickly over taking my anger. Fear of what I know, is bad enough, but fears of the unknown, has often proved more frightening than the end result. However, thanks to Norm, I knew what the actual result could be.

A well-dressed Latin man entered the bar, looked around and then signaled to someone else. He stepped back to let a man enter. Norm nodded his head slightly, crossed over to a table and sat down. I knew the man was Cluny.

He was short, about five, five or five, six and weighed close to 170 pounds, which he carried poorly. His mousy colored hair was thinning and he tried to make up for it by growing an uneven mustache that only highlighted a weak, cruel mouth.

He was dressed off the rack of a safari store, a tan bush jacket, and pants to match. His safari shirt did little to hide his large stomach.

As he walked, I saw an old military holster on his right side, the top flap unsnapped, ready for a left-handed draw. He walked without expression and didn't acknowledge Norm. His face was flabby with beady brown eyes hidden deep in their sockets. His thick nose and cheeks were covered with small broken capillaries from too much drinking. His flabby neck gave him multiple double chins to go with the weak one below his meager mouth.

He stared around the room, finally nodded to Norm, ignored Wayne, but I caught a short pause when he saw Sonia. His stare settled on me, briefly and his runty mouth had a depraved sneer on it. No one said anything for what seemed an extremely long time. Cluny reached into one of the bush jacket's large pockets and pulled out a Polaroid photo.

"Know 'im?" he said as he handed the picture to me.

It was a head and shoulders shot of an old man laying in the street. His bushy hair was mostly gray, with a few strands of black remaining. He needed a shave and a haircut, but his glassy-eyed expression told me he was past caring. I handed it back.

"No," I said, trying not to be harsh, but not wanting to sound coerced. "Who was he?" I mustered the courage to ask and sipped from my beer, sighing to myself.

"An associate of your terrorist friend," he said without emotion and put the picture back in his pocket. "We caught 'im outside. Thought maybe 'e was to meet you. Take you to the terrorist?"

"You thought wrong," I said, trying to mimic his emotionless tone. "There's no reason for the priest to contact me." I stared at him and he stared back.

He forced an evil smile, his pulpy face turning to wrinkles as he did. With a harsh movement of his arm, he signaled for the young, nervous bartender to come where we were. Wayne said something and the young man rushed to us. Cluny pointed at a bottle and was given it with a small tumbler. I watched him pour a good shot of *Oso Negro*, Mexican vodka, into a glass and swallow it down.

The bartender slowly backed his way to Wayne and Sonia. Cluny poured another shot, but didn't drink it.

"You're the only friend 'e 'as left," Cluny said. Moving away from the bar, he held the glass of vodka. "Now that the old man is dead," he mumbled and nodded toward the street.

"How would he have known to look for me here?" I asked, my stomach beginning to knot. He was toying with me, working up to what he really wanted to say or do. The or do, was what tore me up inside.

"You may 'ave told 'im," he said without any emotion.

"I didn't."

"All we 'ave is your word on that," he grinned again and sipped from his glass. "I keep trying to remind myself that you are an employee of our friend there," he pointed the glass toward Norm, "and 'is agency. I find it 'ard to believe." He sipped more vodka and walked back to fill the glass.

"That's why it works," I said, feeling myself tense as he neared. I looked away, toward Norm, hoping it made me seem confident, but I needed to read Norm's expression. He looked relaxed and gave a short, thin smile as our eyes met. What the hell did that mean?

"What you want me to believe is, the articles you 'ave written on Central and South America are not representative of your true beliefs? Is that right?" He said, sitting next to me. I could smell the thickness of his sour breath.

"If I got into the sanctuary of the guerrillas, say in El Salvador, spent time with them, moved about with them and then went and wrote a pro American or *pro Arena* article, do you think they'd ever let me back? There or in any other leftist strong hold?"

Words came out of my mouth that I never thought would. Fear for my life caused me to deny my beliefs. And doing so because of a foul smelling asshole like Cluny only made me feel worse. But I did and knew I would keep it up for however long it would take to separate us.

Another vile smile, while he drained the vodka from his glass. "That is not an answer," he yelled, banging the glass onto the bar. "Damn you."

Two armed men entered from the vestibule, but stopped when Cluny raised his arm. They waited there, their M-16s pointing toward the floor, their fingers on the trigger.

"Answer me," he said, his voice dropped, but his anger was pronounced.

"I wrote what I did to create my cover. I have continued to write that way and because of it, I've been invited into areas our friend," I pointed my empty beer bottle toward Norm, "and members of his agency cannot go. I have no political beliefs." I continued to hold onto the beer bottle as if it were a weapon. Maybe it was.

"And your pieces on the IRA?" he said, his face flushed from anger.

"They part of your cover?" He poured more vodka and swallowed it. He stood, his bitter breath smothering me.

The bar was quiet, too quiet. I first looked toward the two M-16 toting Indians and then at Norm. He offered no clue as to what I should say. Wayne seemed to have moved closer to Sonia.

"If you 'ave no political beliefs," he didn't wait for me to answer, "I should assume that includes Ireland?" His voice had returned to normal, but the words were spoken with deep ridicule. He knew what he was doing. He swaggered his bulky self around my stool.

"No," I said flatly, gripping the beer bottle as tightly as I could.

"No?" He mimicked me this time. "No what? No political beliefs? Or no, I shouldn't assume that includes Ireland? Which is it?" He enjoyed himself, toying with me, almost with a giggle in his voice.

"Neville," Norm called out, finally breaking a silence that seemed would never end, "you're not here to solve the Irish problem. We both know that. We all know that." He waved his arm around to take in Wayne, Sonia and myself. "Take care of the fuckin' business at hand, it's getting' late." He settled back in his chair. "He's told the truth to everybody, what's your gripe?"

Cluny poured another drink and swallowed it, then filled the glass again. I noticed a slight shaking of his hands and hoped it was from the drinking and not anger. He gulped from the full glass and turned to face Norm, his back braced against the bar. After taking two clumsy steps forward Cluny pulled his old revolver from its holster.

"Fuckin' Yanks think you know everything," he was mumbling his words, but his voice was loud. He shook the hand with the revolver in it at Norm and then at the room in general.

The two Indians raised their M-16s and moved toward us. "I 'ave no idea why you are 'ere," he said to Norm. "Because you are running 'im?" He pointed the gun at me. It looked like an old thirty-two caliber revolver. "No great loss to anyone if 'e disappears. Fuckin' Irish are not fit to be on this earth anyway. This one," he whacked my shoulder with the barrel of the gun, "or any mother's son."

"You're drunk, Neville," Norm yelled at the Englishman. "This is all bullshit and you know it. Permission to talk with him came from higher up than me." He kept his voice sharp. "Are you done?"

"No. I am not done," he squawked back, hitting me aside the head with his revolver.

"I shoot this Irish shit and what are you going to do? Huh?" He looked toward his two armed men. Rapidly he said something to the two men, in what sounded almost like Spanish, but I couldn't understand it. It must have been an Indian dialect from Central America.

The two men said nothing, but slowly moved their attention from Cluny and me, to Norm and Wayne.

"You try to stop me, you are dead," he almost laughed, but held it back and sipped more vodka.

"So are you," Norm said very casually.

I looked at him, surprised by his calmness and noticed his 9mm automatic in his hand.

His rule was to always keep a bullet in the chamber so all you had to do was quietly pull the trigger to shoot

Wayne had a Tec 9 automatic pistol in his hands, resting on the bar. Sonia was back against the wall. I was sweating.

"You would die for this shit?" he said, hitting me again on the side of the head with the barrel of his revolver. He didn't hit hard enough to cut, but hard enough so I was jolted each time the barrel whacked against me.

"How would it look if I walked away and let someone like you kill one of my researchers?" Norm sat back, looking relaxed as he spoke, but kept his automatic trained on Cluny. "Christ, no one would go on assignment for me." He smiled, but it was not a friendly one.

Cluny poured more vodka into his glass. His left hand, the one he held his gun in, was shaking badly. He was scared and he was drunk, a dangerous condition. Doubly dangerous as I considered he was a scared drunk who wanted to kill me.

"I do not believe you would shoot," he said, moving away from the bar and me.

"You're wrong," anger replacing calmness. "You're drunk and I'm willing to bet Wayne can get your two cowboys before they can get me. That, Neville old man, leaves me all the time in the world to shoot you, after you kill Murphy. You a gambling man?" he sneered.

I can only imagine the expression that must have been on my face as this went on. If the shooting started and Cluny somehow didn't kill me, the cross fire between Cluny's Indians and Norm and Wayne would certainly do the job.

I felt perspiration run down my side. I am not a brave man, but have held my own a number of times when I was so frightened all I wanted to do was hide.

Maybe it's back to fear of the unknown again. It is better to do something that will cause a reaction, then to wait and leave it up to others. Especially in the situation I found myself in.

The two Indians watched Norm and Wayne. Cluny watched Wayne. No one was watching me. Cluny fumbled around, pulling the hammer back and forth on his revolver and sipping vodka. As soon as the alcohol gave him the courage I knew he would turn and shoot me, not caring what else happened. There's a lot of courage packed in those liquor bottles.

Cluny kept passing close, his revolver almost in my face as he played with the hammer.

"I do not believe you," Cluny mumbled, standing in front of me.

I believed Norm, but didn't figure I'd be around to testify to it. Fear of death, my death, and not bravery, made me reach out and pull Cluny's gun from his hand. I pushed his heavy bulk away as I grabbed the gun and then shoved the barrel of it into the flabbiness of his large belly. As I did it, I yelled in Spanish for the Indians to drop their guns or I would shoot Cluny. I hoped they understood my frantic Spanish. Somehow, in the panic of the moment, the barrel of the gun slipped behind Cluny's belt and got stuck in his pants.

"I'll blow your fuckin' brains out if they move," I yelled into Cluny's blotched face.

He said something in the dialect again and the Indians lowered their rifles.

"Put them on the floor," I yelled.

"You are crazy," Cluny moaned. "They will kill you."

"Put your hands behind your head," I said and Cluny hesitantly obeyed.

"They won't do that, Mick," Norm said calmly.

"Right," Cluny mumbled, a trembling in his voice.

"Why not?"

Cluny didn't move. He smelled and his breath was rancid. I couldn't pull the revolver out, since it was stuck, so I pushed against his flab. He moved back slightly as I did it.

Norm rattled off something quickly in the same dialect Cluny had spoken and one of the Indians answered him. I had never heard Norm speak anything but English or Spanish and wondered why anything he did surprised me? A startled look came over Cluny as Norm and the Indians spoke.

"What are you goin' to do now, Mick?" Norm said quietly. He spoke to me, but I noticed he watched the two Indians. My back was to Wayne, so I wasn't sure what he was doing. "You're aiming too low to blow out his brains," he grinned, and this time there was a small amount of satisfaction in the smile.

"There aren't any brains between his ears," I said, forcing my voice to sound firm, "so they must be down here." I heard Wayne's soft laugh and watched Norm's smile grow. "What did you say to those two?"

"I told them to remain calm and everything would be alright."

"What did they say?"

"To tell you he was drunk and stupid and not to shoot him. I told them you wouldn't," his smile stayed. "But, of course, that's really up to you."

Cluny sighed when Norm finished. He kept his hands behind his head and continued to sweat and smell. Perspiration marks stained the underarms of his bush jacket.

"You know why this asshole is so gung ho, don't you?" I rambled on since I couldn't free the gun and didn't know what else to do.

"Why?" Norm didn't move to help me he just sat there smiling.

I turned and glanced at Wayne and Sonia. Wayne's Tec 9 was still aimed at the Indians and Sonia was sitting again.

"He doesn't give a good God damn about any terrorist. He wants Seámus because he's an Irish Catholic Priest. The same reason he wants me dead. Dumb Limy." I jabbed the gun barrel against Cluny's flab and he winced.

"At least he's got a reason," Norm joked. "Bet he's killed others for less. What about it Neville?"

"I thought we 'ad a deal?" he mumbled, his voice rickety.

"You broke the deal," Norm said.

" 'Ow?" Cluny asked, his arms beginning to quiver.

"You were about a minute away from shooting, Mick," Norm said flatly.

"No I wasn't," he lied. "I was 'aven me some sport, is all."

We all heard the front door open. Both Indians raised their M-16s, one aiming toward us and the other turned to cover whoever entered. Norm kept his attention on the Indian watching us, while Wayne studied the other one. Tension filled the already restless room.

"*Que pasa?*" Rául Vargas asked as he entered from the front.

He didn't stop there, he kept walking, his service revolver held down at his side. Two plain clothes detectives I'd seen with him at other times, followed.

"Neville," Rául called out as he advanced, ignoring the armed Indian, "you and Mick getting close?" He stopped about ten-feet away. "There a problem here?"
The two detectives stopped by the bar.

"I think Neville's a little drunk," Norm said and pushed out a chair for Rául. "Sit down and I'll explain it."

Rául walked passed us, smiled, and sat with Norm.

"Seems Neville wants to shoot Mick 'casue he's Irish," Norm began.

"And, of course, Mick doesn't want to be shot," Rául said.

"Correct," Norm smirked. "Right now we're kind of at a stand off."

"Mick has a gun in Neville's pants?" Rául tried not to laugh.

"Yeah, something about trying to find Neville's brains. I don't understand that myself."

"The Indians"

"They're with Neville."

"So you and Wayne . . ."

"Tryin' to keep things even."

"In American movies they'd call this . . . what? A Mexican standoff?" They were both enjoying themselves and took some of the tension out of the dilemma.

"Yeah, but . . ."

"They're not Mexican."

"Neville's British. Mick's an Irish American."

"Then there's two Central American Indians."

"Wayne's Brazilian and God only know what mix I am. What kind of stand off would you call that?"

"Mongrel," Rául said without missing a beat. They both laughed and were joined by Wayne and Sonia. Wayne must have translated all this for her.

"Neville," Rául said, "you were not really going to shoot Mick, were you?"

"No," Neville said, his sour breath killing me. "We 'ad a deal. Maybe I got a little upset, 'is being Irish and me 'aving a little to drink."

"You are going to live up to the deal, right?"

"Of course." Neville was getting some strength back in his voice.

"Are you finished with him?" Rául said.

"Yes. You told me 'e would be 'ere until after the bullfights, so if we need to talk with 'im again, we will." He was threatening me, that's the way he meant it and that's the way I took it.

"You will be here till Monday, Mick?" Rául said.

"Till then or for as long as you need me, Rául," I said.

Rául stood up and looked into the restaurant. "Seems the party's over." He turned and stood next to Norm. "I think Alfonso and everyone went with Luis back to your hotel. Should we join them?"

Norm stood and was joined by Wayne and Sonia. No one put their weapon away. "You comin', Mick?"

I stared at Cluny. I hated him. I hated all the men like him that ran freely in small death squads throughout Central America. I knew he hated me.

There may have been a peace treaty signed in El Salvador, but there would never be peace with people like him. I slowly reset the hammer on the old revolver and left it dangling in his pants, covered by his drooping stomach. As I turned my back on him and walked to my friends, I wondered what it would have felt like to shoot the fat pig.

May 4, 1995
    11:05 p.m.

chapter NINE

"You're one fuckin' crazy Irishman," Norm
laughed when we walked out of *Alfonso's*.
Cluny and his two Indians were inside and I hoped
he somehow shot himself as he tried to untangle his
revolver from his pants. Rául had left the two
detectives behind to wait for someone to lock up and
the young bartender had scurried from the room as
soon as he was told to go, leaving everything
untouched.

"Why wouldn't the Indians drop their
weapons?" I said to Norm, and then looked at Sonia.
She hadn't said a word. As we left, Wayne made
sure she followed.

"Honor," Norm said.

The street was cleared of whatever had
happened earlier. Late night traffic darted by, adding
to the eeriness of dim streetlights and shadowy,
imageless sidewalks.

"Honor?" I repeated.

"Many of the men of their village work for Cluny. Their job, one of them, anyway, is to protect him. It would have been dishonorable to allow you to kill him." We had all stopped on the top step. "They would've died before bringing dishonor to their village," he added.

"Jesús," I mumbled into the cool night. "How do you know that?"

"I just know it," he said. "Like I know you're crazy. You okay?" he spoke to Sonia.

"Yes," she said.

"We can go in my car," Rául said and started toward the street.

The five of us got into the unmarked police car, Norm in front, Sonia, Wayne, and I squeezed in the back. Rául seemed quiet, considering what had just happened. Without comment, he drove the short distance to the hotel.

"Where'd you learn their language?" I said to Norm, the quiet beginning to bother me.

"Around," he said without turning. "I handled a fighter who spoke that kind of Spanish."

"Are you joining us?" I asked Rául as he parked the car.

"I think I will," he said after I caught him glance into the rearview mirror at Sonia.

"I have to ask you," Norm said with a wide grin, as we stood by the car.

"Yeah?"

"What were you thinking when you put the gun in his pants?" He couldn't hold back a quiet chuckle. "You weren't really lookin' for his brains?"

I laughed and felt the tension escape as I did. "No," I said.

Norm laughed too. "Damned strangest thing I ever saw."

"I stuck the gun in his stomach and it was swallowed up," I laughed and remembered the scary moment. "I guess his fat pushed the gun barrel down and then the hammer stuck on something so I couldn't get it out."

"You couldn't pull the trigger?" Norm laughed louder.

"I tried," I lied.

Even Rául smiled. Wayne quickly translated for Sonia, who smiled.

"I didn't know what to do, so I held on to it."

"I'm beginnin' to understand why they call you Mad Mick," Norm grinned, slapping me on the back. "You're nuttier than a Christmas fruit cake."

"God takes care of drunks, fools and Irishman," I confessed, glad to find some humor left between us.

"And you're batting a thousand," Rául said, but his tone lacked wit. He glanced toward Sonia again, tried a thin smile, and said, "Mick, as your friend, let me give you some advice. Go home. Now, right this minute." He stared at Norm. "You could get him across," he said sternly.

"Good advice," Norm said.

"I could drive you to the border," Rául said seriously, "no one would stop me. Consider it a deportation," he grinned.

For a moment, it sounded reasonable. Of course, it was reasonable, only it wasn't possible. I surprised myself as I thought that. It had to do with more than Padre Seámus, or Sonia or my own fears. I couldn't explain it to them, as they all stared at me, waiting for my answer.

I was frightened of Cluny because of the quiet threat he had made earlier, but I had my honor to uphold too.

It didn't make sense to me, left me confused as to why I honestly thought that, but that's what went around and around in my mind as we stood there. I feigned a lack of concern, or hoped I did, put my arm around Sonia, pulled her away from Wayne, and headed toward the hotel entrance.

"I haven't missed the opening of the bullfights in ten years and some dumb shit Limy isn't gonna make it happen," I bellowed, turned and waited for them to catch up.

Norm shook his head in bewilderment as he stared at me, a thin all-knowing sneer forming as he spoke. "Rául, would you escort Sonia, I need to talk with Mick."

"A pleasure," he smiled politely and held his hand out to her.

A look of terror crossed Sonia's face and she did a good job of hiding it from the others with a wide smile. But her eyes lost their brilliance and turned cold. Her soft grip of my hand tightened.

"*Esta bien,*" I whispered and kissed her cheek. "It's okay," I repeated.

She kept her forced smile as she took Rául's hand and they walked into the hotel. She didn't look back.

"I'm not leaving," I said hurriedly. "I'm not here because of the priest and that's that."

"I almost believe you, Mick," Norm said. "Now it doesn't matter. I want to explain somethin' to you, so later you don't come back and say you didn't understand."

"I'm listening," I said.

"Cluny ain't done with you, you know that, right?"

"I guessed that's what he meant," I said, remembering the quiet threat he made while I held the gun on him. My stomach knotted as Norm reminded me of my vulnerability.

"The best chance you have is when the priest, or anyone he sends, contacts you, you let us know. Keep it all above board, okay?" It was dark in the parking lot and I couldn't tell if he smiled or frowned.

"I don't expect Seámus to contact me," I lied, hoping that the darkness helped hide my expression.

"You're already lying, Mick," Norm said angrily.

"I am?" I figured he was bluffing, or at best taking a wild shot.

"Sonia's not some naive, Mexican flower girl," he said, anger still in his voice. "Tell him," he said to Wayne.

"She was ready to fight," Wayne said without emotion.

"What?"

"At the restaurant, while you had the gun in Cluny's pants, she wanted my extra pistol," he said. ""Told me she knew how to use it and I believed her"

"She was scared," I said.

"She isn't Mexican, Mick."

"No," Wayne agreed. "She's from El Salvador"

"She told you that?" I said nervously.

"In a round about way," Wayne said.

"Get to the point," I said. It was chilly standing there, lying.

"You're not fooling us and for damn sure, you're not fooling Cluny. You're also placing Rául in a bad spot. We want to help keep you alive and away from Cluny, but you gotta help us, Mick." Norm sighed and took a deep breath. "It's a waste of time talking to you, isn't it?"

"I'm staying," I said.

"Everything's bugged, remember that," he said. "Whatever you got to say to her, say before you're in the room. Explain that to her."

"I will." I began to walk slowly toward the hotel.

"You're a damn fool, Murphy," Norm said with a quiet chortle as the three of us entered the hotel.

Sonia stood by a large window and looked out at the lighted pool, a glass of something in her hand. Rául sat at a table with Alfonso, Natale, and Luis. There was no one behind the bar. I looked at my watch and it was already past midnight.

"Something to drink?" Luis walked behind the bar and waited for us to answer.

Norm and I took a beer, Wayne asked for a soda and Luis brought fresh drinks to the table. Sonia turned, glanced briefly at us, pushed loose strands of hair back in place, and then returned to stare at the pool.

"We must go," Alfonso said, taking his fresh drink from Luis. "From what Rául says my restaurant needs to be locked," he smiled. "I am glad you are alright." We shook hands.

"Will we see you tomorrow?" Natale asked, sipping his drink.

"If I am welcomed," I said, wondering what was really going through their minds. After all, this was their country and they couldn't run North.

"A long time ago, we told you," Alfonso looked at Natale, "that our place was your home . . . that we are family. You are always welcomed," he smiled.

"As are your friends," he nodded to Norm and Wayne. "Tonight is over and we are all well." We shook hands – *abrazo* – and said our good byes.

Luis excused himself and walked the three of them outside. Norm and Wayne sat at the bar.

"You think she sees something in the pool?" Norm asked quietly.

"I don't know," I said and looked at Sonia.

Norm laughed. "Mick, poor Mick. She's watching everything goin' on through the glass. She ain't lookin' at the damn pool," he sneered and drank some beer.

"Big deal," I whispered.

"We're goin' to our rooms. Talk to her about the bugs and go to yours." He drained his beer.

"I didn't see anyone unusual at the front desk," I said, not wanting to give into his orders.

"You don't see cockroaches when the lights are on," he said, stood, and walked away.

Luis bid them good evening as they passed. He looked nervously around as he walked to me. A flimsy smile greeted me as I stood there not knowing what to do.

"You know you are family to me also," he said, the smile almost gone.

"Yes Luis, and I appreciate it." I said.

He looked back around again, toward the front of the hotel. "I did not . . . What should I say?" The smile gone, replaced with a frown. "There are people here . . ."

"I know," I said. "There's nothing any of us can do. Be honest with them, Luis. I am hiding nothing," I lied with a smile of my own.

"In your room . . ."

"I've been told they have placed listening devices in my room."

He nodded and sadness came over his lively face.

"Good night, Luis." We hugged – *abrazo* – and I said, "Thank you for your friendship."

May 4, 1995
11:55 p.m.

chapter TEN

     I watched my image grow in the dark window as I walked to her and knew Norm had been right. She was not looking at the pool, but the reflections from within the bar.

     "See anything interesting?" I asked Sonia as I stood behind her. She shook here head no. "We have to go," I said, my voice low, not knowing what to expect.

     She placed her untouched drink on a table and followed me out the back door to the pool. Luis locked the door behind us and in a minute, he had the lights off. The window now reflected the bouncing pool light and our images.

     "We have to talk," I said. We stopped by the pool, not too far from the back stairway to my room. Sonia nodded and sat on a bench.

     "I don't know how much you understand about what's happening," I said slowly and sat next to her. "We're being watched."

I expected her to look around the darkness, but she didn't. "They have listening devices in my room. My friends said you are safe as long as we stay together. Tomorrow, maybe something will happen and you can get away. Get lost while we're on the streets. But tonight," I paused, not sure what to say.

"I understand everything," she said clearly, looking at me. Her eyes were large and alive again. Her smile was honest. "The Brazilian translated everything that happened in the bar. I know who Cluny is. I did not know his name earlier, but now I do." Her English was accented, but correct. She must have seen the confused expression on my face because she smiled wickedly and then laughed softly. "I speak your language," she laughed. "Sometimes you learn more by pretending ignorance, than you would if you tried to argue."

"You fooled me."

"You were easy," she snapped back. "You saw an ignorant flower girl and that is all."

"No," I said. "I saw a pretty young lady Padre Seámus sent. The green carnation told me I could trust you, because Seámus trusts you."

"Maybe," she said after a silent moment.

"You told Wayne you're from El Salvador."

"No, he guessed. He is good with accents. When I thought you would shoot the fat man, I asked for his extra pistol. Told him I would use it, knew how to use it. He would not give it to me. Like most men, he thought I needed protection. I can protect myself," she said.

"Is that what I'm doing now? Protecting you?" I was beginning to wonder about her.

She smiled and the coldness of her words was gone. "Maybe you feared what I would have told them, if they had arrested me? You still do not know what those documents were. We are . . . protecting each other," she said, finally agreeing to what we were doing.

"It's not over," I said. "We're supposed to be together . . ."

"Lovers?" Her words filled with curiosity.

"Something like that. You'll be okay," I said.

"I know," she smiled.

"When we get to the room, we must not talk about any of this. You understand about the listening devices?"

"You have told me once. Is that not enough?"

"I'm trying to be safe. To protect both of our interests."

"Yes. I understand," she said.

"Are you tired?"

"Yes," she smiled. "There is a big bed in your room?"

"Yes." I think I blushed and it surprised me.

"I miss, so much, my big bed," she sighed.

"You came here with Seámus?" She piqued my curiosity.

"Yes. I was assigned to come with him."

"Assigned?"

"It is a long story," she said.

"I love long stories."

She lay back on the bench, placing her feet over my lap and smiled her wicked, know everything smile. "Like lovers would sit?"

"No."

"No? In El Salvador, yes." She sat up, pulling her feet away. "How do Americans lovers sit?"

"You would rest against my shoulder or lay your head on my lap, but not your feet," I said.

She stood and sat close to me. Then she arched herself over my lap and rested her shoulders against the armrest of the bench, a compromise to my suggestion. "Better?" she smiled.

"Yes," I said.

"My father was a professor at the university and my mother taught at the primary school. My two older brothers and I attended the university. Our family crime was that we were educated. My father asked his students to think for themselves and this was his crime." Sometimes she had to force the words and I wasn't sure if it was because they hurt, or she was having trouble with the English. Maybe a little of both?

"My father did not come home one night. Later his body was found at the volcano. You know the volcano?" She looked at me, her eyes almost wet.

The volcano she mentioned was where the military death squads dumped bodies. It was not far from their main headquarters. If your body was there, it was understood you died slowly, tortured.

"Yes, I know about the volcano," I said, wondering if she would ever believe the likes of me could really know about the volcano.

"My mother did not come home. It was months later. She had done nothing. A primary school teacher. They murdered her with machetes." Tears fell from her eyes. She wiped at them.

My brothers and I ran away. We hid with neighbors and friends. But it was not safe for them or us. My oldest brother, Paco, did not return one night. My other brother, Ernesto, and I stole a car and headed to the east . . . the mountains, where the guerrillas were.

"We left the car at a small, burned out coffee plantation and walked for two days. The guerrillas welcomed us. I knew first aid, so I attended the wounded and fought. Ernesto died during the assault on San Salvador."

She twisted about, uncomfortable with remembering her past as much as from the bench.

"Now there is peace." Her words were filled with contempt.

"The murderers of my family are free. Maybe I will never know who did the murders, but we all know who ordered them . . . who approved them. I made some of the *comandantes* uncomfortable with my words, so they sent me with the priest. We had given him passage before, when he traveled from Guatemala, so I knew him. The peace, if it works, is important to the people; I know this, so I came. But I will never be at peace," she moaned softly, fighting tears.

"I know saying I understand sounds foolish and maybe it is. But I try to understand. I want to do something that will help. Maybe that's why I'm still here? I want Padre Seámus to have the items he says he has and I want to publish them." I told her this with my arm around her. She had stopped crying. Her smile was warm and I hoped it meant she believed me.

"He has them," she said without moving away. "Your friend who speaks the dialect, is with your government?"

"I think so, but he denies it."

"He speaks the dialect, so he has worked in Central America." It was a statement, not a question. "He is my enemy."

"Not today," I said.

"Today he is Cluny's enemy. The enemy of my enemy, is my friend," I quoted her, though I had no idea whom it was I quoted.

"The Brazilian?"

"Him too."

"I hate them," she said, her voice low but tough.

"Hate consumes a lot of energy"

"You sound like the *comandantes*," she grinned. "I miss the mountains, my friends. So many of them have returned to the city. I no longer like cities," she said, acknowledging the fact to herself as well as to me. "Do you live near the mountains?"

"No. I live by the ocean."

"It is a big city?"

"A small community."

"If I do not die, I would like to see your community," she said.

"I'd like to show it to you. We'll get across," I said. "I'm not ready to die," I whispered, not sure if I spoke to her or myself.

"You are afraid to die?" She twisted around and looked at me.

"I try not to think about it." I was ready to squirm.

"In the bar, you were brave." She seemed puzzled.

"In the bar I was scared."

"The policeman and your friends would have taken you to the border, why did you not go?" She studied me with her Bamby brown eyes.

"I can't answer that. But it has more to do with anger, than it does with bravery. That I know. Sonia, I am the furthest thing from a brave man you will ever meet."

"You are Irish, like the priest?" She sat up.

"Yes," I said, wondering what it had to do with anything.

"Your people fight the British?"

"Yes, for centuries."

"All the time, when we were bored, the priest would tell us stories about Ireland and the rebels. He said the Irish were not afraid to fight or die."

"Some of us are not so brave," I said.

"I do not understand," she mumbled, as if talking to herself, and stood up. "You are not brave and you are afraid to die, but you do not leave?" She smiled, as if she knew a secret. "You joke. Yes?"

"Maybe the joke is on me," I said.

"Your humor is different." She took my arm.

We walked slowly to the stairs and up the three flights to my room. I stared into the darkness on each landing and saw no one. If they were watching me, they were doing a good job of hiding.

Of course, I wasn't supposed to see them. If Norm hadn't warned me, I wouldn't have known they were around.

For a fleeting second the thought that Norm had lied about the surveillance, ran through my head. A cold shiver shook me as soon as the image of Cluny tossed the thought out. Surveillance was the least of my worries.

"Cold?" Sonia said.

"A little." She must have felt me shiver. "We're here . . ."

"Do not tell me again," she said sternly, in a hushed voice. I took it to mean about the listening devices. I only smiled and opened the door.

I looked around. The light by the television was on. It hadn't been when I left that afternoon. Sonia switched the main light on. I wouldn't have known anyone had gone through my room. From one drawer I pulled the hidden bullfight tickets and counted them. Two were gone. Norm had them, I told myself, but it didn't make me feel any better.

"Let me use the bath," Sonia called out from the bathroom.

I turned to look at her but she wasn't in the room.

"Please?" she said, a chuckle in her voice. "Are these for the bath?" She held a small bag of bath salts the hotel provided.

"Yes," I grinned back at her. "The hotel provides them."

"You wanted to use them." She shook the small bag of bath salts.

I got a clean pair of running shorts and a sweatshirt for here. "Use these," I said and handed her the clothes.

"What?" she said, taking the strange outfit.

"To sleep in."

"And you," she smiled, but in her eyes I saw some concern.

"These." I pulled the sweatpants from the drawer. "Okay?"

"Yes," she smile. "I can wash some items in the sink?" She backed away so she didn't have to look at me.

"*Por que no?*" I said as she closed the bathroom door.

I turned the television on to a cable station and watched an old black and white cowboy movie with Gary Cooper.

Sonia was busy washing her personal things in the bathroom sink and the loud sound of splashing water suggested the tub was filling fast. I shut the lights off and double locked the door, remembering to put on the chain lock. It all seemed humorous to me as I did it. Back on the bed, the flickering light from the TV dimly lit the room. The sound of pouring water had stopped. A small sliver of light showed from the bottom of the bathroom door.

I saw images and sounds coming from the TV, but I didn't pay attention to them. My mind raced with morbid questions that formed their own ghastly answers. I was scared. This time my fear was for me, not Seámus. I'd told Sonia the truth; I was not a brave individual. Why was I there?

Years ago, while working on a story, I was in Fort Lauderdale, Florida. I don't remember why or what it was about. But I do remember meeting a beach bum, who lived on an old barge at one of the many marinas that dot the Florida cost.

I arrived at his party in the middle of a conversation about how to do the right thing in a tough situation, a bad situation, something like that. I remember the beach bum took a quick drink and said, "You can always tell the right thing to do in any situation," he smiled, a smile that told us he knew many of life's secrets, "because it's the hardest thing to do. The easiest thing to do is only that, the easy thing."

I don't know why, maybe because of the ring of truth to it, but I've always remembered it. I haven't always abided but it, but it has always rung true.

I lay there and tried to think of what I would've been like if I had grown up in Sonia's place.

I took a lot of wild guesses that turned me into a super human, but I finally accepted them as lies and honestly doubted I'd have ended up as strong she had. The thought of what I would do if I found a loved one hacked to death by a machete only heightened the fear I felt.

Light suddenly shot into the room as Sonia opened the bathroom door. It startled me for a moment, until I realized where it came from.

She stood there and smiled. As she walked away from the door, I could see her more clearly. Long, thick black hair cascaded over her shoulders. My sweatshirt hung loosely over her, too big for her small frame. Dark, firm, shapely legs, half-hidden by the bottom of the sweatshirt, stopped at her small, calloused feet. I gave a soft wolf-whistle and stood up. She smiled shyly in the shadows.

"My turn," I said, taking my sweatpants from the bed.

"You need the bathroom?" She turned to look into the bright light.

"Only for a minute," I said.

"My things," she half whispered, still looking at the bathroom.

When I came out, the TV was off, the room was dark, and Sonia was under the covers. She returned my wolf-whistle, but followed it with a soft laugh. I slid in next to her and wondered what sin I was paying for? The fragrance from the bath salts engulfed her and made my heart cry. It was going to be a long night.

"*Buenas noches,*" she whispered.

"*Buenas noches,*" I said.

I felt her turn and was surprised when she kissed me on the cheek.

"I have many questions for you, tomorrow," she whispered in my ear and turned away from me.

My mind played more games with itself and sometime during those games, I realized Sonia's breathing had relaxed and she was sleeping. She slept like a baby, unafraid of tomorrow or death. I tossed and turned, unable to sleep, afraid of tomorrow and death, whenever it came. Maybe she had the secret to life. It didn't help, I was still scared. Scared of tomorrow and what untold horrors it might hold for me.

Before I fell asleep, I realized it was already tomorrow and as I turned and looked at Sonia, I told myself, So far tomorrow hasn't turned out too bad.

May 5, 1995
7 a.m.

chapter ELEVEN

It was seven o'clock when the hotel coffee was delivered. With less than five hours sleep, I faced another 20 hours before I could possibly fall onto a bed. I sipped coffee, while Sonia took a shower. Beginning late that afternoon, friends from around Los Angeles would arrive at the hotel and then find their way to the *Hotel Caesar*. The stragglers would arrive the next day, Saturday, and do the same. I had no idea of what to do with Sonia – not really, anyway. If she left, I wasn't sure how safe she'd be. I doubted I could keep her against her will and wasn't sure I wanted to. Another night like that, with her in my bed, would have left me restless and weary. How much of it could I have taken?

Seámus McGillicuddy was a whole other problem, though I knew Sonia and he were connected.

Would Seámus try to contact me again? He must be wondering what happened to Sonia. Or did he know?

The sun was up and bright, a new day had begun, and all I had were questions I couldn't answer.

Sonia came out of the steamy bathroom wrapped in a large towel. Her long, dark hair hung down, still damp, and the vampy smile she greeted me with, melted my spirit. Sassy black eyes shone clearly from her freshly washed face. A light blush came as she spoke.

"My blouse is still damp," she said, looking past me.

From the closet I got a denim shirt, almost the faded color of her jeans. "This'll be a little big." I handed her the shirt, "But baggy's in, in L.A."

"It is soft," she said with mild surprise, taking the shirt.

"It's old," I said. "There's coffee." I pointed toward the coffee pot and cups. "I'm going to shower." I looked into the still steamy bathroom. "Did you leave me any hot water?" I teased.

She walked past me, picked up her hand washed clothing and the clothes I'd put together for her last night. With a clever smile she said, "I thought a cold shower would be best for you, this morning," and let me into the bathroom.

When I came out, she was sitting on the bed, dressed in her jeans and my shirt, her hair still down and sipping coffee.

The television was on a Mexican news program. Her smile was warm and she was beautiful. How could that be? I wondered. There was no make up here and she didn't have any with her last night.

She'd placed some of my clothes on the bed. "What's this?"

"I think you will look good in those," she said, referring to the clothes. "There is nothing on the news about last night."

I looked toward the television and frowned. I had known there wouldn't be, but she didn't. "I'm sure they did their best to keep it from the media," I mumbled and poured the last of the coffee into my cup.

"Your friends?" She stared at me.

"Cluny," I said her, offering a smile up for forgiveness.

"Rául too," she said. "They could not keep the news people away without his help."

"You're right," I said and picked up the clothes on the bed and went into the bathroom to dress.

She had chosen clothes that had us nearly dressing alike. I put on faded jeans, a denim shirt, and an old tan sport coat with patches on the elbows. I decided against the loafers and put on a comfortable pair of tennis shoes. I had a feeling there'd be lots of walking ahead of me and they were much more comfortable. While I dressed, the phone rang, and I heard Sonia's soft voice answer it.

"Dick called," she said as I came out of the bathroom. "He said he is waiting at his place for you," she smiled wickedly, "and told me to come too."

"Thank you," I said. "Well?"

"You look good," she grinned. "Who is Dick?" she said as I sat to tie my tennis shoes. She frowned when she noticed what I was doing.

"A friend who lives down here," I said, ignoring her pout.

"Tennis shoes?"

"When my other friends come this afternoon, we'll do a lot of walking," I said. "They'll want to shop and bar hop. If you're going to stay with me for the weekend, we'll have to get you a few things too." I looked toward the ceiling, hoping she understood my meaning.

"You want me to stay?" A soft blush came to her.

"Yes," I smiled and stood up.

She came to me, hugged me and kissed my cheek. "Does Dick know all your girlfriends?" She looked toward the ceiling and winked at me.

"I've never brought anyone to the bullfights," I lied with a warm smile. "You're the first," I told her, wondering if we were playing a game or not.

"Do you think I will be the last?" she said, as we were ready to leave.

"I hope so," I said with a smile and a kiss to her cheek. "I really hope so."

The hotel lobby was cluttered with people checking out and others waiting to be seated at Luis' for breakfast. I was supposed to meet Dick here and wondered why he wanted to meet at his place? Five taxis were outside, hoping for a fare to the airport. If anyone was in the lobby, waiting for me, I couldn't tell.

We taxied to Dick's. The early morning was cool, though the sun was beginning to brighten the sky. Shop owners were out washing down the sidewalks in front of their businesses with a hose and broom, cleaning off the unending soot and litter. I fought the temptation to turn and see if anyone had taken the next taxi and followed us. It didn't matter at this point. Since the phones were bugged they knew where I was going, but it didn't mean they weren't keeping tabs on me.

"Is Dick like your other friends?"

"No," I said, without looking out the back window. Curiosity was eating me alive.

"No?" She seemed surprised. "What is he?"

"He's an American who has a bar and restaurant here in Tijuana. I met him about five years ago," I said, knowing she had a right to that answer. Especially after my friends she'd met so far.

We were dropped off in front of Dick's. I paid the taxi driver and gave him a decent tip, since the fare was much less than the fare to the airport. He muttered a *gracias,* and I was sure he wished we'd taken another taxi or the bus.

Dick opened the door as soon as the taxi pulled away. We walked in and he locked the door behind us.

This early in the day, the bar's staleness was gone, replaced by a light, un-offensive pine scent. The lights in the bar were brighter than I'd seen them before and noise came from the kitchen, along with the aroma of fresh brewed Mexican coffee.

"You're the young lady I talked to earlier?" Dick said and extended his hand. "I'm Dick."

"Sonia," she said softly, and shook his hand.

He led us to a small table near the bandstand. We sat and welcomed the pot of fresh, hot coffee and the assortment of Mexican sweet rolls. Sonia ate politely and I caught her staring at Dick. Did she see him as handsome, as other women have told me, or was she trying to place him somewhere within the puzzle my friends had created for her?

"You were with our friend here, last night?" He asked, not making it sound like anything but small talk.

Sonia nodded and glanced at me. "Yes."

"You know about that?" I should have known he would.

"In certain circles, it's the talk of the town," he smiled and bit into a sweet roll. "How'd you two meet?" he said, washing the sweet roll down with coffee.

Sonia looked at me, her black eyes accusing me of something I didn't want to think of.

"Be careful, okay?" I mumbled between bites. "She's already had a run in with Norm and Wayne," I said, hoping he remembered who they were from last year. I knew I had discussed them long before he ever met either of them.

"Sounds as if you don't like Mick's CIA friends," he grinned at both of us. "Don't take them too seriously," he said.

"Let me explain," I said and watched Sonia's expression change with my words.

She went from looking confused, to frightened, back to confused as I explained to Dick about Raúl's warning, meeting her and the killing outside of *Alfonso's*. He listened intently, a smirk on his face, as I told of Norm's demonstration and the arrival of Cluny. A small chuckle came from the smirk as I retold about the revolver being caught in Cluny's pants. He looked to Sonia for agreement, but all he got was a cold stare. Being a gentleman, he made nothing of the fact that we had spent the night together in the bugged room.

"You're in a shit pot of trouble, boy," he said casually, as he went behind the bar for a fresh pot of coffee. He refilled all our glasses. "I'm on your side," he said, trying to get Sonia to smile. She didn't.

"We're being watched," I said to break the silence.

"About a half hour after I called your room, two jokers pulled up outside," he said. "Two cars, covering both one way streets, so whichever way you go, they go. I'd say you're being watched," he grinned.

"How do you know this?" Sonia said, suspicion in her voice.

"I'm the guy that's gonna get the priest across the border," he said, the smirk gone, a hardness taking its place. "If you're going with the priest, I'd like to know."

His frankness caught me by surprise, as it did Sonia. Thursday evening, Dick had told me I'd need him to get Seámus across, but I hadn't given much thought to it.

"You've got a way?" I said.

"I'm working on it," he said. "Is Sonia staying or going?".

"I'm staying."

"She's going." We both spoke at the same time and then looked at each other, puzzled expressions on our faces. "Even if Padre Seámus gets across, you won't be safe," I said.

"Neither will you," Dick said. "Even with the priest across the border, as long as Cluny's here, neither of you are safe."

"The first problem to solve is Seámus," I said. "Get Seámus and Sonia across."

"You figure Norm will take care of you?"

"I suppose so," I said, but wasn't too happy with the thought.

"Can you get in touch with the priest?"

"I can try," Sonia said, nervously. "Not from here."

"From where?"

"I cannot say," she said with a confused look to me.

"I understand," Dick said with a nod. "And I respect your caution. We must get you out of here, without allowing anyone to follow."

"Yes." Sonia almost smiled. Her black eyes were intense and she was toying with the loose strands of hair on her forehead again. "Can you do that?"

"I don't see why not," he grinned. "What about you?"

"First Sonia," I said.

"Let me make a couple of calls," he said and left for the seclusion of his office.

"He says your friends are CIA," she sarcastically murmured across the table. "Can I trust him?" she said, her tenebrous eyes wide with worry.

" I do."

"To me," she whispered tautly, "you seem to trust everyone. Maybe you are CIA?"

"No," I whispered back, though I didn't know why we were whispering. "I trust people I know."

"You trust me?" A thin, wicked grin came with her question.

"Yes," I said without thinking about it.

"You do not know me," she said. "How do I know you *know* Dick?"

"How do I know you don't really work for Cluny?"

"Did Cluny know of the green flower?"

"No," I said. "I trust you, Sonia, because you came with the green flower and that tells me Seámus trusts you. I know Seámus."

"If anything I do, reveals Padre Seámus . . . I am not unlike Cluny's Indians," she said sadly.

"Seámus trusts me and he trusts you," I said.

"Yes," she said softly.

"Then trust me, as Seámus would."

"There seems to be little choice," she smiled, and reached across the table to take my hand. "Thank you for last night."

"What did I do?"

"Nothing," she smiled and blushed, pushing away the loose stands of hair.

"If anyone can get you across, it's Dick," I said, wanting to change the subject from last night.

"Is he a coyote?" She held onto my hand.

"All I know," I said, "is that he owns this place. It's none of my business why he doesn't cross the border."

"You have interesting friends," she said and pulled her hand away as Dick came and sat back down.

"A water truck will be here in a little while," he said and gave Sonia a piece of paper. "There's a very small and narrow space between where they store the bottles, that I think you can fit into," he said and glanced at her thin frame. "You'll have to give the driver a general idea of where to take you. Okay?"

"Yes," Sonia said without emotion.

"When you've contacted the priest, call me at that phone number."

Sonia looked at the paper. "This is not a Mexican phone," she said, confused.

"No," Dick said. "It a San Diego number for a cellular phone I have in my office. Call collect, if you have to."

"I call San Diego and the phone rings in Tijuana?" she said, not able to hide a smile.

"Exactly." Dick returned her smile.

"You have a way to help?" She still whispered.

"I'm working on a couple. They're not fool proof," he said. "And they're both dangerous for the priest. If American Immigrations catches either of you, they'll deport you."

"We know. There is danger wherever we go,"" she said.

A shrill whistle came from the kitchen. "Trucks here," Dick said.

We stood up and Sonia looked nervously at me. I took some American money from my pocket and handed it to her. She went to say something and I shook my head. We followed Dick into the kitchen and out into a covered shed. A large green water delivery truck was parked there, hidden from view. Two men, one white, the other black, neither Mexican, were helping unload water cooler stands from between the A-frame shelves that were racked with water bottles. The two men had military style haircuts. Dick talked with the Mexican driver and money exchanged hands.

"He will make a few deliveries," Dick said, standing next to Sonia. We followed him to the back of the truck where he showed her the small passage between the A-framed shelves. "It's small, but you'll fit. You slide all the way to the back window," he pointed down the narrow passage, "and when he's finished with the deliveries you can tell him where to take you. He'll take you as close as he can to where you want to go, but he needs to be careful too. Understand?"

"Yes," she said.

"When you call that number, either Mick or I will answer," he said. "Probably me, but don't talk to anyone else but us. Okay?"

"I understand," she said with a half smile. She looked nervous. She glanced around at the two men who helped unload the coolers and at the Mexican driver. She had every right to be worried. She hugged me and kissed my cheek. "I trust you," she whispered in my ear.

"I'll see you soon," I said and kissed her.

She smiled at me as Dick helped her up onto the back of the truck. He was too large to fit down the narrow passage. The two men restacked the coolers in the open passageway. I couldn't tell she was back there. While the truck slowly pulled away, we backed into the shadows to remain unseen from the street.

The two men closed the large doors to the shed as Dick and I walked through the kitchen and into the bar. When I checked my watch, I was surprised it wasn't much past 10.

"She'll be okay?" I said as we sat and poured fresh coffee.

"Nothing's without risk, Mick," he smiled. "She'll be fine," he said as he read my worried expression. "Can she handle herself on her own"

"She got here from El Salvador with Seamus," I said

The two men who helped in the shed stood in the doorway, their broad bodies requiring more room then was available. Dick waved them to the table.

"Gentlemen, I'd like you to meet a friend of mine. Once you get to know him, you'll understand why he's called Mad Mick Murphy," Dick chuckled. "Mick," he smiled, "meet two of the finest U.S. Marines this side of the border."

"Rob," the white Marine said, as we shook hands.

"Jeffrey," the black Marine said. We shook hands and sat down. "This the guy you told us about?"

"That's him," Dick said, the soft chuckle still there. "Mick, these gentleman and a few of their friends," he looked at his watch, "who should be here within an hour or so, are gonna keep your crazy Irish ass safe from Cluny."

The three of them laughed loudly, while I asked, "What the hell are you talking about?"

May 5, 1995
11 a.m.

chapter TWELVE

"You ask too many questions," Dick said with a grin to the two Marines. "You know that?"

"It's how I make my living," I said. "You want to explain what's going on?"

"We got things to take care of," Rob said and stood. He was six foot, about 190 pounds, with weathered outdoor skin and sharp blue eyes.

"Anything else?" Jeffrey said. He was taller than Rob, a good six three, 200 pounds, and all muscle. He was very black, with a thick nose that showed signs of being broken more then once. Lively brown eyes stared at Dick.

"Give us a few minutes," Dick said. They both walked toward the kitchen and were gone.

"What the hell's going on?"

"Good soldiers," he said, nodding toward the kitchen. He stared at me, as if thinking about what to say. A small grin appeared on his handsome face, followed by a quiet laugh. "Can I talk to you, without playing twenty questions?"

"I doubt it."

"Me too," he said, still grinning. "Okay. At least let me say what I got to say"

"Begin."

"Let's sweeten the coffee," he said and went to the bar. He brought back a bottle of Jameson's and poured a little into each of our coffee cups. He left the bottle on the table, along with the pot of coffee and the Mexican sweet rolls. "I keep aware of things in this town. I got friends in high and low places . . .," he said with a smirk pasted on his face.

"And that keeps me ahead of trouble. I pay good money to be informed and everyone knows it. That's how I knew about Cluny and his friends, when you asked yesterday.

"I didn't know you were gonna be involved. Anyway, last night I got a call and was told about the shooting at *Alfonso's* . . . and about you.

"From what I was told, I figured Norm and Wayne were there. I had a couple of locals keep tabs on you, knew when you left *Alfonso's* . . . safely . . . knew who was at the hotel bar with you . . . and knew when both of you went to your room. Since Norm's your friend, I'm assuming you know the room's bugged?"

"I know," I said. "What's your interest in all this?"

"Mick." He looked hurt. "You're my friend . . . am I right?"

"Yes."

"So, I want to help a friend."

"Because we're friends, you're keeping tabs on me and you're willing to help Seámus get across the border?" I said, my skepticism not hidden.

"Yes," he said and sipped his spiked coffee. "You can't understand that?"

"What's in it for you?" I sipped my coffee, enjoying the taste of Jameson's.

"Jesús Christ," he blared. "What's in it for me?" He mimicked my words. "I'm gonna make a million bucks off saving your asses," he sneered. "That what you want?"

"I could understand it better," I said. "This isn't a game, Dick. If you know about Cluny and these people, you're aware of the tough spot you're going to be in. And you're willing to do this because we're friends?"

"Yes," he said, his hurt expression still there.

"Okay," I said, figuring I'd have time to work it out the truth later. "What about the Jarheads?"

"Over the years, I've had a good rapport with the American military that come here," he said, more relaxed. "I've done them some favors . . . they've done a few for me. Rob and Jeffrey have been friends for a long time. They came in last night, we discussed your situation . . ."

"They know about Seámus?" I cut in. What kind of favors had they done for each other, I wondered.

"Not by name," he said. "They're aware of the situation. They have more to do with keeping you out of trouble, than with getting Seámus . . . and Sonia across."

It didn't seem as if I had much choice. I either accepted his help, or I didn't.

If I didn't, my only hope was with Norm and Wayne, and that didn't leave me with much, since they were personal with Cluny – somehow they were connected to the government. I had no doubt they'd turn Seámus over to whomever they felt were the proper authorities. That knowledge left me cold.

"What's your plan?" I said, putting aside misgivings I felt.

"I have two things in the works, but I have to meet the priest first."

"Why?" I had my own paranoia and lack of trust.

"Photos for papers," he said, "to begin with. I have to see if I can match him and Sonia up with a couple in San Diego."

"I don't understand." I sipped my coffee.

"If I can match them up, close anyway . . ." He paused, thinking about how much to tell me. Why the secrecy between us? Was he afraid Cluny might get me and make me talk?

"There's a ship that sails to Ensenada from San Diego and back each day. When you book passage you get to stay at a hotel in Ensenada and sail back the next evening, or sail back the same night and stay at a hotel in San Diego."

"I've seen their ads," I said.

"What if the couple that spends the evening in Ensenada drives back and the priest and Sonia sail back in their place?" He smiled to show me what a good time he was having. "A trivial check by Immigration in San Diego and they're across."

"Can you do it? Can it be that easy?" I said.

"All I can do is try. But you see why I have to meet the priest?"

"Yes." But my paranoia was still there. Was I missing something?

"When she calls, will they come in?" He poured more coffee and Jameson's into our cups.

"I guess it depends on Seámus and his paranoia," I said, hoping he'd used the time to rest. "He may want to talk with me."

"That might be impossible. You have to go about your business, meet your friends, bar hop . . . all the shit you do every first bullfight. Norm and Wayne with you again this year?"

"Yeah, I wonder about that," I frowned, thinking about the coincidence.

"You do?" he said, almost laughing to himself. "They'll know if you change habits."

"You're right," I said, wondering how to handle Seámus's paranoia.

"I'm open for ideas," Dick said..

"I'm thinking," I said. "What's your other option?"

"Still gotta get the priest to Ensenada. A fisherman friend will take him offshore and someone I know with a seaplane will pick 'em up . . . and fly 'em to where?"

"My place," I said automatically. "Rockport Beach."

"That's the end of my plan, so what happens in Rockport?"

"Haven't gotten that far," I said.

"I guess that leaves us with wait and see time on our hands." He looked at his wristwatch. "She should be dropped off by now."

I looked at my wristwatch, it was a little after eleven. "I should be going," I said.

"Give her till noon," he said, freshening our coffee. "When they see you leave without her, they may wonder and we don't need 'em remembering the water truck."

"I can have lunch at *Caesar's,*" I said, accepting his advice. "Noon's okay."

"I want you to take Rob and Jeffrey with you."

"How do I explain two Jarheads tailing along?"

"Bullfight fans. You met 'em last summer and they've come to join you," he said, already having thought it out.

"What about tickets?"

"I'll get you two private booths, mix and match the tickets and no one will be the wiser," he said, keeping ahead of me.

"Shady side," I said, not able to put everything together yet.

"I'm going too," he said. "Has to be the shady side."

Rob came in, followed by the young bartender, placed a small brown paper bag on the table and unlocked the front door to Dick's, open for business. The bartender busied himself with glasses, ignoring us.

"Gotta open," Dick said as Rob sat down. "Here." He handed me the bag.

I opened it and saw a 9mm Ruger automatic, a holster, and three loaded magazines. "Loaded?" I asked without touching anything.

"Yes," Rob answered, his voice softer than I'd expected.

"I told 'em you know how to handle it," Dick said.

"Yes," I agreed. I assumed that Rob had something like it hidden under his thin jacket. "You?" I asked him.

He nodded yes. From the kitchen, I could smell the aroma of spicy Mexican cooking. I put the three magazines into my sport coat pocket, pulled the automatic from the holster to make sure the safety was on.

The automatic felt light, but I knew that was the way they made them. I slipped the gun into the holster and felt a cold chill run through me. I attached the holster to the inside of my pants in the back. The day had begun so promising, Sonia in my bed and now I sat in a bar with a couple of Jarheads, all of us armed to the hilt and for what?

Jeffrey entered from the kitchen and another older Marine followed him. He was shorter too, but carried himself with authority. I could see him studying me as he approached, his walk slow, deliberate, using the time to his best advantage.

"You made it Benny." Dick said, standing as he greeted the new arrival. They shook hands.

I stood up, the holster and gun uncomfortable in my back. I knew I'd get used to it before too long.

"Benny, Mick," Dick introduced us, "Mick, Benny."

We shook hands and said hello.

Benny was better dressed than the other two Marines. Even so, his haircut told you he was military. I was sure his holster was hidden by the cut of his sport coat. The five of us sat down, Dick pulling a chair from another table.

Three drinkers came in and sat at the bar, away from where we were by the small bandstand. Noise came from the restaurant side that suggested an early lunch group had arrived. Benny's cold blue eyes scanned around us. I wondered what he was searching for.

"Jesse and James," Benny began, "are outside. They'll move ahead . . . I'll pick up the rear," he said, thinking I understood what he was talking about.

"Jesse James?" I said, fighting back a smile. I looked to Dick for help.

"I haven't gone through everything with Mick," Dick said. "Rob and Jeffrey go with you," he said, "Jesse and James – not Jesse James, smart ass – will be covering you from a distance. Benny, here, will keep all of you in sight. You're well covered, Mick."

He was going to a lot of trouble out of friendship, I thought. What was he really up to, I wondered. Guilt slithered up on me as I sat there, a doubting Thomas.

"Is it necessary?" I said, exposing some of my curiosity.

"I think so, " Dick said. He ignored the questioning glances from the Marines. "Mick, you're gonna have your usual good weekend. You and all your friends," he said. "I promise and while Cluny's keeping tabs on you, I'll see Seámus and Sonia get across . . . to Rockport Beach, right?"

"Yes."

"Sometime this weekend, Cluny – or one of his henchmen – is gonna figure something's wrong and try to pick you up. From what I understand, they were within minutes of getting the priest. You butt in, the priest gets away. They have to grab you, Norm or no Norm." He was explaining their plan and the reason for it, no longer sounding like a saloon owner who liked small jazz groups. He was beginning to sound like Norm.

"These guys go after you, they ain't gonna care about who else is around. So, in our own way, we're protecting you and the others. What the hell good does it do to get them to Rockport, if you're here? Maybe planted here?" A cold stare greeted me as he finished.

"Jesse and I have radios," Benny said, "we can watch you from two different locations. Rob and Jeff know how to get our attention," he nodded at the two Marines. "Where do you go from here?"

"*Caesar's* for lunch, maybe run into a few friends. If they're not there, I sit outside, drink a few beers, and talk with Juaquin and wait. Once they get here, we bar hop up and down *Revolucion,* shop. We usually come back here late in the afternoon." As I explained my afternoon plans, I wondered how safe any of us were going to be that weekend?

"Who do you expect?" Dick said.

"Norm and Wayne were supposed to meet me today."

"CIA," he said to the Marines.

"Howard Bolter and Jim Breslin are supposed to be here around noon. Five others tomorrow," I said. "Nine in all from the States."

"If we count the CIA guys," Benny said. "Do you think they'll be there?"

"How better to keep tabs on me?"

They all smiled. Benny looked at his wristwatch. "It's already noon," he said. "You go and don't worry if you don't see us," he said, a devilish grin clashed with his ice-cold blue eyes. "We'll be there." He stood up, shook my hand, and left through the kitchen.

"I think you should call Sully," I said.

"The cop I met last year?"

"Yeah. Tell him to come directly here tomorrow."

"Why?"

"He has to be the contact in San Diego or Rockport Beach," I said. "You can reach him at home, after four."

I wrote his home number of a paper napkin. "Tell him I'm in trouble and he'll understand." To keep my mind from erupting with fear, I was putting together a plan and who better to help me than Sully? On the downside, he was lugging along his partner, a Cuban American named Juan, who didn't really like me.

May 5, 1995
12:30 p.m.

chapter THIRTEEN

A luminous sun welcomed us to the beginning of a hot Mexican afternoon as we walked out of Dick's dim establishment. We wandered silently up the dusty, old street and turned on to a congested *Revolucion* before my eyes fully adjusted to the light. I missed spotting the cars that would follow me and couldn't help but wonder what they thought when Sonia didn't exit. Would it be reported?

"Either of you ever been to a bullfight?" I asked, as we turned onto the busy main street, afraid of what they might answer.

"I've been goin' for the last four years," Rob answered.

"Me too," Jeffrey added. "Mostly on the sunny side and mostly drunk," he said with a smile.

"We don't get drunk when we're workin'," Rob said quickly, turning as he spoke. "We'll keep up appearances, but we won't be drunk." He assured me and turned back to watch the street traffic.

"Do you know where Benny is?" I said to make conversation.

"We don't have to know where Benny's at," Rob said. "He's gotta know where we're at."

"Relax," Jeffrey said lightly, "Benny's the best. He ain't gonna let anything happen to you."

"That's good to know," I said, unable to spot Benny on the crowded sidewalk, and kept walking. I didn't know what either Jesse or James looked like and wondered who, if either, was responsible for a car? Rob walked about a step or two in front of me, to my right and Jeffrey was an arm's length behind, to my left. When the sidewalk became crowded, Jeffrey moved in behind me.

It was almost one p.m. when Juaquin greeted us at *Caesar's*. His smile was friendly, but his eyes questioned my company. I introduced them as friends of Dowly's.

"No lost *gringos?*" I said as we sat at my regular table, next to his shoeshine stand. There were six chairs at the table for four, early afternoon drinkers, locals and tourists already took most of the remaining tables.

"*Tomarse tiempo,*" he said. "Soon," he smiled toward the two Marines. "First *Corrida?*"

"No. Been comin' for years," Rob said, his voice almost lost in the street noise.

"You want a coke or something?" I asked Juaquin as he stared at me. Chuy, the waiter, was busy serving another table, but he nodded hello. It was his way of saying he'd be with us next.

A Mexican man called to Juaquin and sat in his shoeshine chair. Juaquin excused himself and went to the chair.

"Beer for you," Chuy said, sliding up next to us, ignoring calls from another table.

"Too busy for Friday," he said, waiting for Rob and Jeffrey to order, his harried eyes glanced over the unusual early afternoon crowd.

"Three beers," Jeffrey said and Chuy left to take orders from the other patron.

"How long do you hang around here?" Rob stared at the street.

"I'm expecting two friends anytime now. Then there's Norm and Wayne, they're already here," I said.

"The CIA guys. Who're the other two?"

"Howard Bolter, a TV director and Jim Breslin. Jim owns a couple dive shops."

"They know anything about what's goin' on?"

"Not a thing," I said as Chuy delivered our beers. "Run a tab?"

"Need you ask?" he said quickly and rushed away.

"Are you gonna say anything to 'em?" Rob held the cold beer bottle, but didn't drink.

"No," I said, not understanding when I'd made that decision.

"Will the other two say anything? Do they know each other?" Jeffrey said.

"They know each other," I said and then admitted, "I have no idea what Norm will do or say."

"Dick said they're your friends. I don't understand whose side they're on. Are they here to help you?" Rob said.

"It's a love hate relationship," I joked and told them the little I knew about Norm and why I felt he worked for the government, CIA or whomever.

"So he pulled your ass out of the fire in Panama and then it was your turn to help him in Nicaragua, right?" Rob said, still holding his untouched beer, Jeffrey took sips from his bottle.

"That and the fact that we live close to each other," I said without telling them about personal favors we'd exchanged over the years, to find Juaquin standing by us.

"*Amigos,*" he said, pointing across the busy street and into the crowd waiting to cross.

In the mixed crowd of locals and tourists, stood Howard and Jim, waiting for the light to change. A few Mexican youths dashed between traffic, ignored by the policeman on the corner. They did not worry about jay walking tickets.

A new law in California allowed certain Tijuana traffic citations to be filed with the Department of Motor Vehicles and until they are cleared, your driver's license and auto registration are not reissued.

This was done to cut down on corruption in the police force of Tijuana. It was still better to ticket a tourist, but now it was done when the law was broken, not when an officer's palm was itchy.

It was a tribute to Joaquin's memory, as well as his eyesight, that he recognized my friends from across the street. He hadn't seen either since last year.

"Thank you, *gracias,*" I smiled. "Nothing to drink?"

"*Nada,*" he smiled. "*Alli,*" he pointed, this time toward the Fifth Avenue Bar.

I had to stretch myself out over the crowded sidewalk to look past the corner of the hotel to the bar and there, waiting for the light were Norm and Wayne. As Howard and Jim crossed the street I could see Norm signal them, waving. They waited for Norm to catch up.

Howard Bolter's five-ten and slowly losing the battle with gravity and drink. Sharp brown eyes stared out from his ruddy face and thick black hair, specked with gray, flopped around as he walked. He began directing television sit-coms twenty-odd years ago, progressed to one-hour television, and now directed made-for-TV-movies. He worked hard, was an award-winning director and liked to party. His casual style of dress fit in for that weekend. He wore a loose fitting, light blue sport shirt, dark blue baggy pants, and penny loafers without socks. Mister Hollywood.

Jim Breslin stood an erect five-foot eight and was as athletic as he looked. His tanned face and shaggy blonde hair made him look younger than his 35 years, until you sat across from him and saw the toll his outdoor lifestyle had creased into his blue-eyed smiling face.

He lives near me in Rockport Beach and owns two dive shops, one in Rockport and one in La Paz, Mexico. We met in Rockport and again in La Paz. I introduced him to Dino at the Caribe West and since then we've been traveling in the same circles. That Friday, like most days, he wore a bright print shirt outside his loose white pants and old floppy sandals.

Howard and Jim first met Norm two years ago in Tijuana. They were invited to his gym by the airport, but neither ever went.

Howard should've and Jim got more than enough workout during business hours.

Norm and Wayne greeted Juaquin in Spanish. They were dressed alike, jeans, loose fitting sport shirts, worn outside, and well-worn tennis shoes, with socks. You couldn't tell from looking that either carried a gun holstered in back.

I introduced Rob and Jeffrey to everyone while Juaquin pulled an empty chair to the already crowded table and somehow we all managed to sit. Norm's cold blue-gray eyed stare told me he wasn't buying my story on the two Jarheads. I smiled in return. Howard ordered more beers for everyone but Wayne, who asked for a coke, and Chuy rushed back into the bar, ignoring requests from other tables. He remembered Howard as a good tipper from last year. The drinks weren't going on my tab. Rob finally sipped from his beer. Jeffrey was about half done. Both gave their old bottles to Chuy as he delivered fresh, cold beers for everyone.

"You're getting a little grayer." I pointed out to Howard as we all drank.

"Makes me distinguished looking," he laughed.

"You should grow a beard," I said catching a glimpse of Norm's forced smile as I spoke.

"It would probably be white," he continued to laugh. Howard enjoyed himself wherever he was.

"Contrast," I said. "Maybe it'll stay dark as your hair turns gray."

"Good point. Contrast, you say?" He pretended to give it some thought. "I could begin growing it today," he said. "But then by Sunday I'm going to look shabby and in need of a shave. What do you think?" he said to no one special and took a long pull on his beer.

"I think on Sunday you're gonna look shabby anyway." I told him and everyone laughed.

Juaquin shined a few shoes, Howard's loafers included, and kept unwanted sidewalk peddlers and street urchins away from the outdoor bar's patrons. Howard insisted on paying for each round, telling everyone it was only residual money and then he'd laugh, keeping the joke private. He tipped Chuy as expected.

"Where's Sonia," Norm finally asked. He had to be reading my mind.

"Gone home to change," I said and drank.

"Home?" Norm smiled at me. "Really?"

"She'll meet us later," I said, returning his grin.

"Sonia, Mick?" Jim said a puzzled expression on his face. He, and others in Rockport Beach always considered Mel, my accountant and friend, to be my only love.

"A local young lady," Howard said with a wide grin. "Does she have an older sister?" He took another long pull on his beer. He was ready for another one. "Chuy," he called out as the waiter slid between tables at the other end of the patio, *"mas, por favor,"* he raised his empty bottle into the air. Rob and Jeffrey shook their heads no, tapping their almost full bottles to show him they didn't need another. *"Cuarto, mas, Chuy."*

"One more," I agreed, finishing my beer, "and then we have to get going," I said. "There's a few taco stands and bars we've yet to hit."

"Have either of you been on Mick's Tijuana tour?" Howard asked the two soldiers, a sinister grin on his face.

"No, sir," Rob said, "but we've heard of it."

"Hell of a tour," Jim said. "You have something to look forward to, right?"

"Hell of a tour," Norm echoed. "Got a feelin' this year's will be the best," he grinned. "Unforgettable, even." He kept grinning and drained his beer.

Chuy brought four cold beers and took away the empties.

"Time for the john," I said and stood up. I quickly shook my head toward Rob and Jeffrey as I saw them begin to stand.

"I'll join you," Norm said. "Be right back," he said and pushed his way through the tables to the hotel's entrance, leaving me behind.

Inside, the narrow bar that led to the famous restaurant was dark and only half filled. A TV over the entrance showed a Spanish soap opera that most everyone seemed to ignore. Norm waited for me half way up the aisle.

"Dick's Jarheads?" he said, putting his arm around my shoulder. His hand quickly felt the holster beneath my jacket. "You planning a war?" He almost laughed.

"I told you I met them at Dick's," I said and began walking toward the men's room.

"Christ, Mick. I thought last night we decided to cut the shit?" His voice was low but the words were strained. "They're carryin', you're carryin'. That supposed to be protection?"

"I just want the asshole to leave me alone," I said, pulling away and entered the men's room. "I won't be caught by surprise again."

"And the three of you think you can do that?"

I didn't answer. I used the urinal and tried to seem unconcerned.

"Maybe you're figuring on Wayne and me helping?" he said, washing his hands. His cold stare watched me in the mirror as I came up to the sink. "What about the girl? Has she gone to the priest?"

"She went to get a change of clothes and she'll meet me later." I washed my hands and tried not to look into his mirrored eyes. "Whatever comes down, if anything," I said wiping my hands, "all I really want you to do is keep the others safe. Okay?"

"That I can do," he said as we walked back into the bar. "If the priest contacts you, are you gonna let me know?" He stopped by an empty booth and waited for my answer.

"This the beginning of my bullfight weekend?"

"Supposed to be," he said, the expression on his face blank.

"Are you on this weekend with me?"

"Supposed to be," he said with the same blankness.

"You're with me, Wayne and whoever are with me, with us . . . if the priest contacts me, you'll be there. Right?"

He leaned against the empty table and leered. "Answer the fuckin' question, Mick. Yes or no? And, Mick, don't shit a shitter."

"I don't expect Seámus to contact me . . . and if he does . . . "I paused and stared back at him. " If he does, I don't know what I'll do. Okay? Cluny scares the bejesus out of me. You must know that?"

"You should be scared," he said, his expression still cold.

"I am," I said and walked toward the patio bar.

Once again, the glaring sun blinded me for a few seconds, but finally I fumbled through the crowd to our table. Rob and Jeffrey had worried expressions that faded as I sat down.

"We need to get Cuban cigars," Howard said.

"What do you mean we white man?" I joked and drank some cold beer to dampen my parched throat. Whose side was Norm on? "Maxim's," I said after I swallowed. "They sell them. I still say you should try the better Mexican cigars."

"I will, promise, but these are gifts," he said and toyed with his empty bottle.

"My birthday's coming up," I said and drained the beer from the bottle.

"I'll send a card." Howard applauded.

"You leave?" Juaquin said, his hands stained from shoe wax and polish.

"Yes. This is everyone, until tomorrow," I said. "What time will you join us?" I slapped Howard on the shoulder so he wouldn't think I missed his quip.

"Seven?" he said. "That is good?"

"Seven, if we haven't come by here for you, we'll be at the *Café Américan.*" I glanced at my wristwatch, it was almost 2:30 p.m.

"Not too much beer, *amigos,*" he warned. "You tell them?" he said, his stare going toward the two Jarheads.

"Tell us what?" Howard said.

"*Cinco de Mayo* weekend," I said, and smiled at Juaquin, knowing he'd understand or at least try to. "Cops are just extra careful with American drunks, that's all," I lied.

"We do want to be careful," Norm said with a sour note in his voice and stood.

"Street vendor tacos and cold beer," I said and led them out of the patio and onto the sidewalk.

"And Cuban cigars," Howard said, already sounding a little tipsy.

"I'd like a Cuban cigar too," Norm said and fell in with Howard.

"Everything okay?" Rob stayed a little ahead of me.

"Fine," I lied.

"You shouldn't go anywhere without one of us," Jeffrey said, taking his place behind me. "It ain't safe."

"They're on our side," I said and hoped I was right, as Norm and Howard climbed on a donkey cart to have an old-fashioned photograph taken. They put on large, *sombreros* and it didn't seem to bother them that the ragged donkey had been painted with stripes to look like an even uglier zebra.

The old photographer and his young assistant tried to get the rest of us to join them. None of us did. Finally, the photographer placed his primitive pinhole box camera in position and exposed the film. Each paid five dollars and was told to return in thirty minutes to pick up their black and white photo.

"I have a hell of a collection of these," Howard said and we moved on.

"I hope you're right," Rob said as we moved onto a small street vendor's taco stand.

"Right about what?" I said, getting in line to order a few pork soft tacos.

"That they're on our side," he said flatly, cutting in front of me.

May 5, 1995
    4 p.m.

chapter FOURTEEN

Sonia had chosen a light cotton sport coat for me to wear during the cool morning. It was comfortable then and hid my holstered automatic, but by noon it helped the harsh Mexican sun punish me as I walked along the congested streets.

We munched on soft pork tacos, applying our own condiments, making them as spicy hot and plump as we liked. We sucked on paper cups of cola as we ate and walked. Everyone followed me, our mouths full of food, our hands trying to hold napkins, cola and the second taco.

The first bar we entered was a small dark room, smartly placed within a short distance of three taco vendors and a multitude of tourist shops. It was cool, clean and inviting to parched shoppers and adventurous eaters who didn't know how powerful real Mexican hot sauce can be.

And, of course, there are those of us who know, but never seem to learn. Wayne sipped a cold coke at the bar; the rest of us swallowed the first iced bottle of beer in two, maybe, three-long gulps. The second beer we sipped.

Norm backslapped his way to me at the end of the bar. My tacos were gone and my second beer was almost drained. Howard ordered another round for everyone. It was going to be a long afternoon. Norm forced himself between Rob and me, keeping his back to Rob. Jeffrey sat at a table near the door, talking with Jim while he kept an eye on the entrance. Wayne entertained Howard and Rob with stories of the Brazilian rainforests and headhunters.

"You're not cut out for this shit, Mick," Norm said quietly, holding his fresh beer.

"What?"

"Look around you," he said. "Your Jarheads, Wayne, me, everyone carryin' is dressed for comfort as well as to conceal," he laughed. He was enjoying himself. "Now look at you." He pointed his beer toward the shadowy mirror behind the bar. "What do you see?"

"Nothin' much," I said.

"Buy yourself some comfortable shirts, Mick. You want to play this out, you can't be sweatin' like a stuffed pig," he laughed.

"Funny," I answered and tried to look past him to where the others sat. "Mind moving?"

"I'm amazed by your composure," he said, ignoring my request to move.

"Why?"

"Why?" he mumbled, almost choking on his beer. "Here you are, walking down the middle of a busy Mexican street," he glared at the street from the bar, "protected by two Marines?" His puzzled look quickly turned to an all-knowing simper. "You do this, knowing a man like Cluny is gonna try and grab you. And here you are with friends and protectors, drinking beer and throwing caution to the wind. I'm impressed." He swallowed more cold beer. "Cluny's the kind of guy . . . drunk or sober . . . could eat dinner and watch someone stick a cattle prong up your ass. And that's before he asks you anything."

"I'm supposed to run and hide?" I said, unable to hide the anger in my voice.

"I would," he whispered. "I figure Dick has about five men on you. Two here," he nodded toward Rob who still stood behind him, "so that would leave the other three outside giving back up. Am I right?" he said, staring again toward the street. Was he looking for Benny?

"Maybe I'm counting on you and Wayne if something happens," I said halfheartedly.

"Dick wouldn't do that." He tried to hold back a grin.

"I'm not Dick." I drank.

"Cigars. Cuban cigars." Howard bellowed from his seat, his last empty beer resting in front of him. "Mick," he called as he stood.

"That's what we're discussing," Norm lied, his voice high and almost excited. "Mick?"

I finished my beer and tried not to think of Cluny or cattle prongs. A chill ran through me.

Jeffrey stood and went to the door. Norm greeted Howard with a handshake and smile.

"I was just telling Mick, before we go anywhere else; we have to get those cigars." His arm went around Howard's shoulder, pulling him closer like a co-conspirator.

"Damn right." Howard agreed and gave me his *I'm the director* growl. "Lead us," he said, gesturing with an arm sweep toward the busy street.

Jeffrey led the way. Maxim's was across the busy street. I pointed to the left and Jeffrey walked in that direction. Rob walked close to me.

"Everything okay?" he said as we pushed through the crowd.

"Yeah."

Salesmen and saleswomen called out to us, and other tourists, as we passed, promising us the lowest prices on their merchandise. It didn't seem to matter that most everyone dismissed their pleas. Their products hung out over the sidewalk, impossible to ignore. At the stoplight, we waited for the walk signal.

"What's a good Cuban cigar?" Howard said as we walked with the light.

"For my birthday I want *Romeo and Julieta*, Churchills," I told him.

"Good choice," Norm said.

"The best?" Howard asked Norm as we walked into Maxim's.

"Yes," Norm said. "I get them whenever I can."

Maxim's is a three-story department store catering to the duty free shopper and unlike the small shops that lined the street you did not barter at Maxim's. In their lower level, they have a large selection of liquor and cigars.

The seven of us walked down the short flight of stairs and as soon as Howard saw the large tobacco display, he and Norm rushed past us. It was like seeing a kid in a candy store. I could hear Norm pointing out different Cuban cigars. His years of travel in Central America had made him an expert on Cuban cigars as well as their exported revolution.

"What are you buying?" Howard held three boxes of cigars.

"Nothing," I smiled. Norm had one box of cigars.

"You goin' back to the liquor store?" he said as the young clerk rang up his order. It was more than $200 and he paid it happily. Contraband. It always makes things better.

"They carry my cigars," I said. "Their liquor prices are better too."

Jeffrey led the way up the stairs and out. The sidewalk and street more congested than before.

"Let's go to that *toro* place," Howard said. "I wanna smoke one of these suckers." He beamed, a kid holding a bag of candy.

"To the left," I said.

"Is he talking about E*l Torero?*" Rob said.

"Yes. He likes sitting out on the balcony."

"Must have some Marine in him," Rob joked.

El Torero is a second-story restaurant-bar that indulges the military and any stray tourists that stagger in. Their prices are high, but the drinks are strong and the food is edible.

Colorful bullfight posters and photos are displayed on the brightly painted walls. Multicolored tables fill the balcony that overlooks *Revolucion* with its belching vehicles.

Not a place to eat, considering all the fine restaurants Tijuana has to offer, but as good a place as any to pollute the air with cigar smoke and our livers with cold beer. Not to mention clean rest rooms.

El Torero's entrance is in an alley that runs all the way through to *Avenida Constitucion*, and is lined with stalls filled with discounted goods for the tourists. As we entered the wide alley, it was already crammed with servicemen and tourists, the vendors all busy pushing their wares.

The brightly painted stairway is windy and narrow. It opened into a large room with a circular bar and many small tables. Glass doors opened on two sides to the balcony. The bar was filled with servicemen, all making passes at the young, attractive Mexican bartender as they happily downed her concoctions.

A few couples sat out on the balcony, sipping drinks and holding hands. Howard pushed past Jeffrey and led the way to the where he wanted to sit. We pushed two of the larger tables together and ordered our drinks from a slim Mexican waitress, her huge brown eyes taking each one of us in.
Looking down we watched the traffic putter along. The weekend rush hour had begun. It was after four p.m. An hour and a half it had taken us to make the six blocks. At this rate, we'd get to the bullring by Tuesday.

Howard unwrapped one box of cigars and with a small Swiss Army knife pried open the top. The box held twenty large cigars. He handed one to each of us. The cigars were fresh, their aroma pleasing as only a fresh cigar's can be. Unfortunately, if you are not a cigar smoker, it doesn't matter. But I am and I enjoyed myself.

"Damn you, Howard," Jim said, as he opened the end of the cigar with a small knife. "You got me hooked on these. When I'm at the shop in La Paz, I always buy a box and smoke the damn bunch of 'em." He carefully lit his, making sure the whole end burned brightly before putting out his match.

"They are wonderful." Howard agreed and lit his. "Of course we should have brandy or something stronger than beer," he said as the young waitress delivered our beers, two bowls of hot sauce and a basket of freshly fried tortilla chips.

We all smoked, even the two Marines and Wayne. Norm blew thick white smoke off the balcony and smiled wickedly at me.

"We have a long night ahead of us," I reminded everyone. "Beer until dinner," I said. It wasn't a rule, but it was something I tried to live by when I dealt with this many guests on a long bullfight weekend.

I excused myself to use the rest room and Rob came with me. When we returned fresh beers had replaced the ones we left. Mine had been almost gone, but I doubted Rob had drunk much of his. Jeffrey smoked and watched the street below. Could he see Benny?

It seemed, to me, that Norm was staying close to Rob and Wayne close to Jeffrey. If something came down, was it their job to see I was vulnerable? Is that why Norm wondered how many others there were?

Nothing eventful happened while we were there. Howard asked some questions about the bullfights, as if he were really interested in them and not there for the party leading up to Sunday afternoon. Jim was more honestly interested in the *matadors* and their history, something I was able to offer a little information on. We smoked and watched the traffic along the street. As we sat and talked, the evening began and soon the cars and trucks had their lights on and the noise from their blaring horns broke our phantasm.

"I need a taco." Norm said as he drained his beer. "Anyone else?"

"Yeah," Howard said, the last small end of his cigar finally placed in the old ashtray.

It was almost six p.m. and a six-pack or two into the evening, so the idea of something solid, even soft tacos, sounded good.

"About a block down the street there's a side walk stall that's good for tacos," I said, the last of my beer remained in the bottle. My cigar was out and in the ashtray with Rob and Norm's.

Howard paid the bill, again, and the rest of us dropped dollars on the table for the tip. We moved through the crowded bar and carefully made our way down the long stairway, trying not to bump into the customers working their way up. Most of the customers looked like service men and all the waitresses were bright-eyed and winsome. A hell of a combination.

The second taco stop was not a vendor's pushcart like the first, but a large open window that faced into an alley and offered three small tables with chairs for their clients.

We ordered tacos and cokes and sat watching the man and woman behind the glass cook and chop the meat. They placed each order in a little rattan tray and we filled the small tortillas with cilantro, onions, peppers and both green and red hot sauces. Tiny ventilation fans blew heat and smoke from the modest stand and carried the spicy aromas from within out onto the street. As hot as I was, inside the scanty kitchen had to feel like hell.

"This mean we won't eat at Dick's?" Norm said, licking his fingers. Both his tacos were gone and he was drinking his second cola.

"See where we're at when we're hungry," I said, finishing my last taco. "It's still early."

"Sonia supposed to meet you at Dick's?" he said matter-of-factly, looking more at Rob than at me.

"Yes," I grinned.

"I need a beer." Jim yelped, returning the rattan tray to the window. "Hot." He fanned his mouth and drained the cola from his cup.

"Hell of an idea," Howard said.

I led the way, Rob and Norm beside me, to *La Bolear* an old bowling alley turned into a monstrous bar. We were off the tourist path and in a real Mexican bar. No one behind the bar has ever admitted understanding English, though they don't seem to have a problem accepting the dollar. Mexico is their country and we were guests, the least we could do is attempt to speak their language.

Norm ordered and paid for beer and Tequila gold shots for everyone but Wayne. "To an unforgettable weekend." he toasted with the Tequila and drank a shrewd grin in my direction. Everyone followed suit, even Rob and Jeffrey.

"I have to meet Juaquin," I said to Norm, loud enough for everyone to hear. "Finish and go to Dicks?" I wasn't a Tequila drinker and he knew it, so I was overly concerned why he'd be buying Tequila shooters that early in the evening.

"Think we can get Dick to spring for a big bowl of fresh, hot shrimp?" Norm said, looking around for everyone's approval. "With that sauce?"

"He's going to be so glad to see you, I think you can get him to do most anything," I said, staring him down.

"Sometimes I don't think he likes me," Norm moaned as we walked out of the bar. "Do you think he likes me?"

"I don't think it matters," I said, annoyed at his foolishness.

"What do you think?" He turned and asked Rob.

"He likes everyone," Rob said back without seeming to pay much attention to Norm.

Late afternoon twilight was quickly turning to evening darkness. Friday night traffic filled the streets as we made our way toward Dick's, car lights splashing wherever you looked. The opened shops had lights on that eerily swept out the old dusty windows onto the sidewalk. Streetlights flickered, some came on, and some didn't. With the sun gone, a cool ocean breeze worked its way through the old streets.

"I can't remember," Howard yelled at me from behind, "does Dick smoke? I mean . . . can I have another cigar?"

"Yes," I said. "That box will be gone before the evening's over," I laughed thinking of the money he'd spent for them.

"I'll buy more tomorrow," he yelled back.

The streetlight outside Dick's *Café Américan* worked and the area was brightly lighted from his neon signs as well. Rob opened the door to the bar entrance and we walked in. The bar was crowded and many of the tables were already taken. The service men were easy to spot, their haircuts gave them away, but there were Latin males too.

Down at the small stage, Dick was busy talking with two men. The bartender waved to Rob and pointed to the end of the bar where there were a few empty seats. Howard and Jim grabbed two; Wayne sat next to them as soon as Jeffrey sat. It looked more and more like Wayne was glued to Jeffrey. I didn't take that as a good sign.

"I'm gonna say hi to Dick," Rob said and walked away.

"Report in is more like it," Norm bitched with a smile as we sat at a small table. "Want a beer?"

"No Tequila," I said. "Kind of early isn't it?"

"I felt like a shot," he grinned. "I bought one for everybody, what's wrong with that?"

"Don't buy me any more, okay?" I said. "But I'll take a beer," I grinned to match his.

"What's she drinking?" Norm asked, his smile broadening.

I looked up and saw Sonia standing there. She had on a red summer dress that showed off her shapely legs, her long black hair ran down over her shoulders a beautiful contrast, and she carried a large, colorfully designed, pull string bag. She looked at Norm, her large black eyes expressionless, but then her smile came and she walked to me. I stood and hugged her, kissing her cheek.

"What would you like to drink?" I said, holding the chair for her.

"*Cuba Libre,*" she said to Norm, "*doble lima, por favor.*"

"I should've guessed," Norm grinned back and went to the bar for our drinks.

"Is everything okay?" I said, keeping my voice low.

"In some ways, yes," she smiled, but her pretty black eyes looked sad. "Your friend is a good man," she sighed.

"Norm?"

"No, I mean Dick," she tried the smile again.

"I have to talk with him. We just got here."

"I know. I have been here. You look very hot . . . uncomfortable," she said, tenderly running her hand across my brow.

"Too hot with my sport coat," I said, sorry when she pulled her hand away.

"Take it off."

"Dick gave me a gun. I'll have to buy a couple of shirts like Norm's," I said, not wanting him to sit with us, but wanting a drink badly.

"Tonight I have clothes," she said, indicating the bag. "I do not know what is happening." Her lonely eyes searched for an explanation.

"I'll find out," I said and was about to ask for Seámus.

"One *Cuba Libre*, double lime and two beers," Norm said as he delivered the drinks and sat. "To friendship," he toasted and we all raised our drinks.

"And honesty," I added and Norm nodded as he drank.

"What's friendship without honesty?" he said. "You look very pretty," he told Sonia. "I'm glad you were able to get home and change."

"I am also," she said, her voice soft.

"You are with us for the weekend, I hope," he said with one of his brightest smiles.

She looked at me and blushed. "I look forward to the weekend," she said, her voice still low, uncertain. "You have more friends?" she asked, looking toward Wayne.

"Gentlemen," Norm called to the bar and Howard, Jim, Jeffrey, and Wayne turned. "You know Wayne from last night," he said pointing at Wayne, "and you must know Jeffrey," he went on, "but these two gentlemen, and I use the word loosely, are Mick's friends from the beach. Right?"

Howard and Jim stood and came to the table. Norm introduced them and they sat down with us. Sonia looked nervous, but she held her own. Rob came, followed by a waiter who carried two large bowls of hot sauce and chips.

"Let me guess," Norm said, "Dick would like to see Mick?"

"Yes," Rob said.

"Go ahead, Mick," Norm said, "we'll keep anyone from stealing your girl," he smirked, knowing I would understand the double meaning. I wondered if she did.

"Check on the shrimp." Norm called after me as I left the table.

May 5, 1995
8:15 p.m.

chapter *FIFTEEN*

Dick Dowly sat in the small windowless office, his feet on top of his antiquated wooden desk, along with an empty wire basket and a cordless phone. He greeted me with a relaxed smile and, "Shut the door, Mick."

I held onto my beer, closed the door, and sat on a folding chair. The office was neat, two four-drawer file cabinets were off to my left, a small table top copy machine to my right, a long comfortable sofa behind me and the white washed, stucco walls were covered with photos, mostly black and white of Dick with jazz musicians and Mexican politicians.

Somewhere on the wall, there were a few pictures that I had been included in. I didn't know where he'd put them, or where he'd put the ones to be taken in the future.

"The boys behaving themselves?" he said without moving.

"Yeah," I mumbled and drank. "No problems."

"Good. Sonia sure is pretty," he grinned and pulled his feet from his desk. "I've talked to Seámus," he said, his tone hardened as his voice lowered. "He came in with Sonia in a bakery truck," he grinned, proud of his cleverness. "Under the circumstances, I think that's all you should know."

"You and Norm have circumstances on the brain," I said. "Is there anything I should know?" I placed the empty beer bottle on his desk and told myself to get the facts from Sonia later.

"Cluny's the circumstances, Mick," he said, his smile gone. "That and I'm not sure where Norm fits into the whole picture. You still think he's on your side?"

"It's hard for me to think different."

"Think hard, Mick." he said and it sounded a lot like a warning. "We knew he'd make Rob and Jeffrey. Does he know about Benny?"

"No. He asked about others . . . guessed you put five men on me, but I denied it."

"Why do you think he cares?" His voice tinted with sarcasm.

"He needs to know the difference between friend and foe if it comes to that," I said, wanting to believe it.

"If that's what you want to believe," he said and twisted in his chair, not a believer.

148

"How's Seámus?" I said, unable to keep from wondering.

He glared at me and twisted some more in the chair. "Christ. You won't let it be, will you?"

I didn't say anything.

"Okay, let's see what I can say without endangering Seámus."

"Hold on." I returned sharply. "He came to me for help, he's my friend, remember? How the hell am I going to endanger Seámus?"

"Calm down, *amigo*," Dick said, raising his hands in surrender. "I know all that, but you seem to have missed the big picture." He said nothing for a moment and then pushed away from his desk, as if he needed more room to continue. "Cluny gets what he's after and he's after Seámus . . . and you're in his way. If he wants you . . . and I think we agree he does . . . he'll attempt to get you. Since he needs you alive . . . for a while anyway . . . ." He stood and walked to the file cabinets, looked down at me while he continued, "There's a chance he'll get you." His voice became villainous. "And Mick, anything . . . *anything* . . . you know, you'll tell him. You'll tell him to keep from hearing Sonia scream again . . . or you'll tell him to end your own pain." He stood there, his expression ghastly, his green-gray eyes stared deep into me, and his scorn was as warped as his words.

As lurid as his words were, they were not said in anger, but with concern and the limited patience of someone dealing with a novice.

"You're right," I said and hoped the fear that ate at my stomach stayed hidden. "He's okay . . . physically?" I asked, but really wondered how he knew so much about Cluny?

"He's resting, he's eaten, and he's safer than he's been in months." A smile returned to his pale face. "Sonia wants to go and she wants to stay," he said, returning to business. "I don't know why she can't make up her mind." He sat down. "I don't think it's you, champ." A sparkle gleamed from his eyes.

"She should go with Seámus," I said, without thinking about it. If I were in danger, she was in twice the danger.

"You talk with her," he grinned. "She doesn't know any more than you do, but she sure is nicer to look at. I talked with Sully," he said, getting back to business.

"And?" I wondered how much he told Sully.

"He'll be here tomorrow, late morning. Juan's coming too," he said with a smirk. "Who's Juan?"

"Sully's partner," I said. "What did you tell him?"

"About Seámus. You didn't tell me they'd met."

"They've met," I mumbled. "You tell Sully everything?"

"Basically. He said to tell you not to worry about Juan. Why?"

"He's Cuban-American and we don't agree on much," I said, remembering how he'd saved both Mel and me from being murdered while my condominium burned around us.

"Sully told me a little about him," Dick said with his smirk. "Thirsty?" He stood and as he stretched, I noticed the holster under his shirt.

"Yeah." I said and stood. I wanted to ask him his honest opinion on my chances, but didn't. I fought the thought of how Norm offered to take me across the border and I turned him down. "You joining us for dinner?"

"Here or *Alfonso's*?" He opened the door to the loud bar.

"Probably *Alfonso's*," I said and stared into the crowed room. "We'll come here tomorrow after the party at the bullring. You're coming, aren't you?

"I'm part of the weekend, starting now," he said boisterously and we walked into the bar.

"How about a platter of shrimp?" I said before he closed the office door.

"Norm," he laughed. "Shellfish is gonna be the death of him."

"A big platter," I said, "when Juaquin and you join us there'll be nine to feed."

"On the house, I suppose?" He walked to the bar.

I went past him to our table. Juaquin sat with the others, his hands almost free of shoe polish stains. He looked freshly showered and wore blue dress pants with a white oxford shirt and spit-shinned black shoes. This weekend was a reason for him to dress up and for the rest of us to dress down. Even without the soldiers, you could tell the *gringos* from the locals without a scorecard.

I kissed Sonia on the cheek, told myself I did it to keep up appearances in front of Norm, but knew better, and then greeted Juaquin, who drank coffee. Two tables had been put together, along with ten chairs.

"My shrimp?" Norm said before I sat.
"Ordered."

"Can I smoke?" Howard said, surveying the crowded bar.

Along with three ashtrays, there were an assortment of hot sauces, sliced, pickled peppers and three baskets of fresh tortilla chips on the table. Everyone had some form of drink in their hands or on the table and as I sat next to Sonia, all conversation stopped.

"I don't mind," I said, "but first offer one to Dick and then light up."

"What if he doesn't want one?"

"The hell with him," I said playfully and pointed out the clean ashtrays.

Howard placed an opened box of Cuban cigars on the table and looked anxiously around for Dick. Sonia's *Cuba Libre* was half-gone. Rob and Jeffrey held their beer bottles by their long necks, but didn't drink. Wayne ignored his full glass of coke, while Howard and Jim seemed to be collecting empty bottles of beer. Joaquin's coffee cup was empty, but he didn't care.

"What have I missed?" I said, wishing I had a beer. I turned to the bar, but couldn't get anyone's attention. "Is there a waitress?"

"Drinking and bullfights." Norm placed his empty bottle on the table. "That's what we were talking about," he said when he saw my puzzled look, "and the waitress is real busy right now."

"You too?" I kidded Sonia. "Bullfights?"

"No. I listen," she said, brushing the loose strands of raven hair back from her forehead. "I have never tried to understand so much English."

"You doing okay?"

"Yes," she said and blushed, her large black eyes opening wide as a smile slowly formed on her lips.

"I understand," Wayne told her. "When I first came here everyone spoke too quickly."

"To Mexico?" Sonia said turning away from me.

Wayne chuckled. "I forgot where we are," he said. "When I first arrived in the United States."

Norm tapped my shoulder and I turned to him. "Walk me to the john and we'll get a couple of beers," he said and stood over me waiting.

"Gee," I said foolishly, "I feel like a school girl."

"Why?" He pulled the chair out for me.

"High school girls always go the bathroom together," I told him, forcing a grin. "What's up?"

"Women, in general, go to the bathroom together," he said. "Wayne won't steal your girl," he laughed, not too loudly, but loud enough for everyone at the table to hear. They all got a good chuckle out of it.

We pushed through the crowded bar to make our way to the men's room. Norm seemed to enjoy keeping Sonia and me away from each other. He began to make me nervous and Dick's doubts were becoming my doubts.

"What's up?" I said as we washed our hands.

"What do you know about Dick?" he said and we walked back into the noisy, crowded bar. "You seem to trust him with a lot."

He had a point, but I didn't tell him that. "He owns this place." I looked around the packed room.

Norm stopped and I thought he wanted to order our beers, but instead he put his large hand on my shoulder and helped me drift to the empty bandstand. "You honestly believe this is it?" he said and spread his arms to take in the whole place.

"Yeah," I said, puzzled with what he was doing.

"You think I'll turn your friend over to Cluny, don't you?" he said, his expression as blank as I'd ever seen it. "Yeah," I said after a moment. "I think you made that clear last night and earlier today."

"Mick, I'm here because you're my friend. I don't *have* to be here. There's nothin' in this for me." He must have seen my unbelieving look because then he said, "I'm on my own time."

"So why the speech last night and this afternoon?" He always left me curious.

"I hoped you'd cross the border with me last night," he said, a look of disappointment on his face. "When you didn't, I tried to figure a way to keep you from Cluny . . . and yes, if it was the only way to keep you safe, I'd give him to Cluny. There are others who might do it for money."

"Anyone I know?" I said, cynically.

"Dick's taking care of you, right? Protecting you, with his Marines? Did you ever think that maybe, just maybe, he was your jailer?" He looked at me and waited. I didn't say anything. "He's got you covered, he's got the girl covered . . . does he have Seámus covered? Don't answer me," he said, backing off a little. "I've known Dick a long time, you must know he does more than run this café?"

"I've thought about it," I said, still running his words around my head. "He's too close to the border to be any kind of drug smuggler. The DEA would cross and get him. So, maybe he's wanted for something that isn't important enough to chase him across the border. What do I care?"

"First of all, your concept that he doesn't cross the border is wrong. It's an image he likes to project, but it isn't true. Can you believe that?"

"How do you know this?"

"Why is it, you always have a hard time believing I know things, when you know I do?" he said. "What Dick is Mick, he's an arms merchant. This is his cover." He looked around the room.

"Arms merchant?"

"Which word didn't you understand?" he said joking, but his expression was too serious. "Fact is he works . . . sometimes he works for the government. This is off the record, Mick, off-off the record."

"Go on."

"Sometimes, as you know, means not all the time," he tried the joke again, but couldn't pull it off. "Other times he sells to whomever can pay . . . and that whoever has been Cluny in the past. Probably, Dick is the personification of a mercenary. He hasn't any politics. His loyalty is bought and paid for and fluctuates like the price of gold. If he can, he sells to both sides. Some of the Jarheads you see here are no longer in the service, they work for Dick. They demonstrate his equipment. They train his buyers. Hell Mick, he sold to the Contras. He was one of the middlemen the Administration used back then. What do you think Seámus or Sonia would say if they knew their protector sold to both sides in El Salvador? What would they say if they found out Dick sold to the Guatemalans when the Carter Administration stopped U.S. Aid because of human rights violations?"

"What interests me," I said, and hoped my confused feelings went unnoticed, "is how you know all this?"

"Don't be an asshole," he said, shaking his head.

"So, what do you want from me?"

Norm looked at me and for a moment I thought he was going to laugh but then he frowned and shook his head as if in disbelief.

"If I get her a visa to cross with you, would you leave right now?" His voice was low and had an edge to it.

"Do you think she'd leave Seámus . . . run away?" I said, and wondered the same. Could he have gotten her a visa that quickly? It didn't matter, because I knew she wouldn't leave Seámus.

"Mick, I don't think about her, except where you're involved. I don't care if she stays or goes . . . I care whether you do," he said, the edge gone from his tone.

"She won't run away," I said, sorry that I believed my own words. "Me," I forced a smile that neither of us believed, "I'm here for the bullfights."

"What is it about you that makes it impossible for common sense and women to mix?" he said. "Do you know?"

"It must be the failure of higher education," I said and put my arm around his shoulder. "How about that beer?"

"You buy," he said and pushed me away with a mild shove. "Do you feel okay with Dick's help, or do you want me to stick around? It's *your* bullfight weekend."

"Stick around," I said and looked to see if I could locate Dick. "You're part of this weekend," I said.

We walked to the bar and I bought us each a beer. Then I wondered about both Dick and Norm. Was either lying? Maybe both of them were lying. Maybe they were really out to help me. Norm had come through for me any number of times in the past, so if that counted for anything I should believe him.

"You lookin' for the *camarones*?" Dick called from the kitchen's double doors. A waiter slipped by him, carrying a steaming bowl of pink shrimp. Dick pointed toward Norm.

"Show him our table," I said to Norm, "I need to talk with Dick."

His crumpled expression told me all I wanted to know, as he led the waiter away. "You comin' right back?" he said, his back to me.

I didn't answer, but grabbed Dick by the arm. "Can we talk in your office?" I said, a nervous tension taking over my voice.

May 5, 1995
9 p.m.

chapter SIXTEEN

"You look pissed." Dick said as he closed the door to his small office. "Norm?"

"Yeah," I said, holding back, as best I could, the hostility I felt. "I want to talk with Seámus."

Dick sat, his old chair squeaking. I didn't want to believe what Norm had told me, but there were more reasons for believing Norm, than there were for not believing him. The thought that I may have turned Seámus over to a mercenary that would sell him to Cluny frightened me. That Dick not only knew Cluny, but had done business with him – business that established him as a representative with not only my nemesis, but with the enemies of both Seámus and Sonia – angered me. That, at least, explained how Dick new Cluny's operation so well.

"What did Norm say to piss you off?" Dick said, sitting back in his chair, watching me.

When I didn't answer, he forced a thin smile and nodded his head as if he now understood without my having to speak. "Something about me?" he said, but he wasn't guessing or asking a question.

"Two things concern me, Mick. How much he told you . . . and what you really think." He sat straight and rested his elbows on the desk. "You want to talk with Seámus . . . because you think he isn't safe?"

"You told me he was safe."

"Now you have your doubts," he said, "I can't blame you. You think because I've done business with the Guatemalan government I'd turn Padre Seámus over to Cluny?"

"The thought crossed my mind."

"I can understand that," he conceded with a smirk. "Before you judge me, Mick, where do you think I got the weapons to sell? People like Norm come to me . . . Norm himself more than once. They come to me to do what they want to, but can't . . . for one reason or another."

"Like it's unconstitutional?"

"Sometimes," he said without showing any guilt. "I work for the same government Norm does. The elected officials, Mick, they're temporary. The people we work for, they'll be here in four years, eight years, hell, they'll still be here in twenty-eight years. Without these people, the government wouldn't run. You think the action of elected officials tore the Berlin Wall down. Hell no. You think some congressman or senator was responsible for the end of communism in the Soviet Union? You can't be that naive.

"Hell, I like Seámus. And I think you and Sonia make a great couple . . ."

"You like him so much, how about I talk to him?"

"I'll go you one better. Let's go see him." He stood and took a deep breath and then sighed. "I don't know why Norm's here, but me, Mick; I'm trying to help you get Seámus across the border. The joke's that no matter what he thinks he's got, or you think you can do with it, nothing's gonna change," he sighed to keep from chuckling.

We walked silently through the bar and into the kitchen, then out into the loading area where Sonia had been hidden in the back of the water truck. The large doors were closed and the room was dimly lighted from over head.

"If what you think is true," he said slowly, as we entered the dark storage area, "Seámus would be history by now."

"I've thought about that."

We stopped in front of a shelving unit that was almost as long as the storage area and went to the ceiling. Cartons of canned and boxed goods filled the shelves. Using a remote control device Dick had a section of shelving open like a door, quietly revealing an obscurely lighted, narrow hall.

When I hesitated to follow him, he turned and laughed passively. "Damn you," he chuckled, "if I didn't know better I'd think you were paranoid. One of three things is at the end of this hall, Mick. Seámus, Cluny or nothing." He was enjoying himself and continued to laugh. "No reason to bring you all this way for nothing."

"Where are we going?" I said, and knew that the weapon holstered against my back was as useful as a twig.

"You want me to trust you with my secrets, but you can't trust me, is that it?" He stopped laughing and stared hard at me. "You comin'?"

I moved slowly toward the narrow hall and wondered if it was smart to do so?

"I'm not in business with the Mexican government, Mick. You ever notice the three story apartment building behind my place?" I didn't say anything. "I own it . . . not on paper," he went on, waiting for me to reach him. "This is my private escape route or hiding place. Hell, Sonia's not the first person I've had to sneak out of town or across the border. I do more than sell weapons," he said as I reached him.

I didn't want to think of what else he did for those he considered to be *the government*. When I entered the hall it was not as narrow as it had appeared. The large shelves dwarfed the entrance. A few steps in a staircase began and I followed Dick as he climbed.

"I put up a few of my employees and a couple of the soldiers in these apartments," Dick said as we slowly climbed the shadowy stairs. He tapped the plain walls as he spoke. "You can't tell there's a door on each landing, can you?"

I walked along in silence, too afraid of what might be waiting ahead to speak. I told myself, if I really thought Cluny would be there, I wouldn't have followed. Even as I thought that, anxiety tore at my stomach.

"I use this route to set up meetings between people who can't or shouldn't be seen together. It serves its purpose," he said and turned to make sure I was still there.

The hall was quiet, but the spicy aroma of Mexican cooking seeped through the walls. "Sound proof?" I said nervously. How was I supposed to interpret his statement?

"Of course." Dick stopped on the top landing. "We're here," he mumbled. "Still worried?"

"Too trusting to be worried," I lied and did my best to put a thin smirk on my lips. "You first," I motioned with my right hand.

Using the remote control, he opened a section of the hallway wall. Dick went in, leaving me alone with my anxieties. A warm light flowed from the opening, bathing the once dim hallway, allowing me to see the raw wood walls and floor. From where I stood, frightened and nervous, I could hear the faint tone of conversations, but couldn't understand more than it was English.
Gathering what little courage I had, I marched into the light and hoped there was a clean bathroom real close.

I walked into a nicely furnished bedroom, a large queen size bed against the wall, covered with a print comforter and four oversized pillows. Colorful throw rugs covered sections of the waxed hardwood floor. A large wardrobe cabinet angled away from the wall that, when it was in place, covered the entrance to the hidden passageway.

Seámus walked into the room and startled me. He wore clean clothes, his ragged shaved head from my hotel had been neatly done in a GI haircut, and his beard was gone. He still appeared fragile, but looked relaxed.

"Thank you," he said calmly and grinned.

"You look good," I said. "Everything okay?"

He laughed quietly. "I'm deloused, fed . . . what else could there be?" He walked to me and hugged me. He smelled like baby powder and whiskey. "Come on," he said and I followed him into a living room.

Dick handed me a large coffee mug filled with strong Mexican coffee and a shot of Irish whiskey that I smelled before I tasted it. Seámus picked up his mug off an end table and sat on a blue sofa.

"We'll be in the kitchen," Dick said, telling me we were not alone. "You can talk," he smiled and walked away.

"Is there something wrong?" Seámus said.

I sipped my coffee. "I was worried about you."

"Your friends are taking good care of me," he said and sipped at his coffee. "I owe you. I really do," he said. "Who would have thought you'd be my savior?"

"I'm glad I could help. You remember Sully?"

"Yes. He's the policeman, right?"

"Yes." Looking out the window behind Seámus I could see the night lights of Tijuana and a star filled sky. I took a long swallow of the hot coffee and relaxed. "Wherever you enter the States, he'll meet you. He'll be here tomorrow and work things out with Dick."

"Dick told me. We leave early Sunday morning for Ensenada," he said. "I think I'm the last one," he said cheerlessly.

"Last one?" I said, not understanding.

"The others who were going to try and cross," he mumbled, "no one has heard from them. None," he cried. "I must be the last one," he repeated. "They all died because of me."

I didn't have anything to say. He was probably right and he still wasn't safe as long as he was in Mexico. I looked around and hoped Dick had left us alone.

"Take this," I said and, as I sat next to him, tried to give him the automatic I had holstered under my coat.

He stared sadly at me and shook his head. "I couldn't take a life, Mick. Not even to save my own. It's a mortal sin," he said. "Don't miss understand me. I know you would only use that to protect yourself, or others and I don't believe that would be a mortal sin for you. But for me . . . I fear that if I could use it, I might not know where or when to stop. Anger and hatred . . . and grief has had control of me before," his eyes watered as he remembered, "when I've come upon massacred Indians, a village . . . men, women, children . . . I could have taken up a weapon with the guerrillas then, but I didn't. I'm a man of God, of peace . . . I'm supposed to be, anyway. If I give in to the anger and fear, then I become like those I oppose. I would rather die," he said stubbornly. "I'm not passing judgment on you or your friends, but on myself." He took a long swallow of his whiskey-tainted coffee.

"Dick had Jameson's," he smiled, looking tired again. "I suppose it's yours?"

"He takes good care of his friends," I said and knew Norm was right about Seámus' reaction to finding out the truth about Dick and his politics.

"He's taking good care of me," he said as I holstered my automatic. "Thank you for worrying."

"Seámus, Sonia has to go with you. She's not safe with me," I said and finished my coffee.

"Yes, I agree. Dick said there's room for her."

"Dick." I called toward the kitchen.

He walked into the living room with a pot of coffee in one hand and the bottle of Jameson's in the other. "Refill" he asked.

"No," I said, as Seámus held his mug up and took the mixture. "What about Sonia?"

"Tomorrow, when you come for dinner," he sat and placed the coffee and whiskey down, "we'll bring her in here and Seámus and she'll be gone before your group moves on. Will you be able to explain it to your friends?"

"I'll come up with something," I said, not knowing what I had in mind. "Speaking of my friends," I looked toward the bedroom. "I think we should be getting back."

"If you're ready," he said.

"I'm ready." We all stood. Seámus hugged me his eyes were still damp. "Pray for me Padre Seámus," I whispered to him.

"Until the day I die you will be in my prayers," he said and put as much strength into his hug as he could. "Pray for me, too."

"I will," I said. "I'll see you in Rockport Beach on Monday." I walked out with Dick.

"I'm sorry," I said as we walked down the stairs. "I . . ."

"Don't be sorry for being cautious," he said before I finished. "Which brings me to another unpleasant subject," he mumbled in the dim light. "What about Norm?"

Yes, I told myself, remaining quiet as we walked. What about Norm? "He's my friend," I said after a moment's hesitation and left it at that. I needed a bathroom again.

May 5, 1995
   11:05 p.m.

chapter SEVENTEEN

Rául sat and talked with Norm as Dick and I pushed our way to the table. Dick held up two fingers to a perky waitress who smiled her reply as we sat with the others. She returned quickly with our beers and took refill orders from the others. Nothing beats sitting with the owner of a saloon.

"I was just telling Norm that *los aficionados* wait for you at *Alfonso's*," Rául said as we sat. He looked at his watch and his face took on a quizzical expression, which only added to the confusion I felt.

Sonia stood and walked to my chair. "We go?" she said, putting her arm over my shoulder. "The papers," she whispered to me with a soft kiss to my ear. She hadn't forgotten the papers we had hidden beneath the cushions in the bar.

"After my beer," I smiled up at her as the waitress returned with a tray full of drinks.

Dick got up and offered his seat to Sonia. As she sat he nodded to Rául, who stood and they both excused themselves, saying they'd be right back.

"We leaving?" Rob said, his full bottle of beer swung in his hands.

"After this drink," I said to assure everyone at the table. "Did you have enough shrimp?" I said for Norm's benefit, noticing, finally, that the large basket of shrimp was gone.

"He who hesitates . . ." he smiled, but watched Dick and Raúl walk away. "You work things out?" he said, his voice low, almost lost in the din of the busy bar.

"Yes," I said, unable to keep a grin from forming as I spoke.

Jeffrey and Wayne kept Jim and Howard busy in conversation, never seeming to drink while the other two gulped theirs. Juaquin sat quietly, observing. Rob's concentration was portioned between Norm, Sonia, and me.

"You two missed out on the cigars." Howard called out loudly from his seat. "No one complained," he grinned and went back to his conversation and drink.

"I think we should go back there," Norm mumbled, nodding his head toward Dick's office. He kept from looking at Sonia.

"A conspiracy?" I joked, beginning to feel more confident with Dick's loyalty.

"Raúl wants to talk with the four of us," he continued to mumble. "Excuse us?" he said to Sonia. "We'll be right back."

We both stood. I put my hand on her shoulder. "I just talked with Seámus," I whispered, using it as an excuse to kiss her ear. "Everything is going to be okay," I said and gently squeezed her shoulder.

"I will be okay," she smiled and turned to Rob.

"You want me to come along?" Rob asked, a cold stare directed at Norm.

"We're going to talk with Dick and Raúl," I said to assure him and walked off with Norm.

They waited in Dick's office, the door open, each with a new drink. We walked in and Norm closed the door. The suddenness of it frightened me for a second and I couldn't figure why, since closing the door was the natural thing to do.

"According to Norm, you've had an uneventful day," Rául said, his tone half way between official and friendly. Not the tone he had greeted me with when I sat at the table.

"No Cluny, if that's what you mean." I wished I had a drink in my hands. "Right?" I turned to Norm.

"Right," he said.

"No terrorist either?" Rául said.

"Nothing to report," I tried joking and again directed myself to Norm.

"Cluny hasn't found him either," Rául said, his voice exhausted, his expression rigid. "You're falling in deeper every minute," he said, almost sounding frustrated, with his stare fixed on me.

"Why?" I said. "I've told the truth and Norm's been with me most of the day. Isn't that good enough?"

"For a rational person, possibly, but I doubt it's enough for Cluny. There are too many unanswered questions and they all seem to revert to you and when you entered the picture." He explained, as straightforward as he could, the official things he knew, without feeling he had compromised his office.

"These people work best at night," Norm said to break the silence that followed Rául's statement.

"Meaning?"

"Meaning," Rául cut in, "that you are thinking like a *gringo,* Mick. Your civil rights do not exist here. You of all people must understand that?" he said. "You know American history, right? Not high school history, real American history?"

"I think so," I said, wondering what he knew about real American history.

"Think of where you are now . . . Tijuana, as Mississippi and the year's 1945 . . . you're a black tenant farmer and Cluny owns the plantation . . ." his puzzled expression stayed fixed on me.

"Or, if you prefer, think of yourself as an illegal Mexican migrant worker in Orange Country in the early 50's."

"Or a Chinese coolie in the late 1800's in California," Norm said, no jest in his voice. "You getting the picture?"

"I don't have any rights and my life isn't worth squat. Is that it?" I really wanted a drink. "Cluny scares me. Okay?"

"I think he understands," Dick said, defending me. "Mick, everyone in this room has your best interests in mind."

"I appreciate it."

"But you won't leave," Rául said as Norm nodded in agreement. "Even if you can take Sonia with you?"

"I won't leave," I said and hoped my nervousness stayed hidden.

"Safety in numbers, maybe?" Rául smirked.

"Then let's go eat." I turned to the door.

"You and the girl ride with me," Rául said. "It's safer and less likely Cluny would try taking you from me."

"I'll join you," Norm said. "But don't think Cluny cares about local cops."

"Rob should go too," Dick said quickly before Norm could add the last person to the carload. "The rest of us will taxi there."

"Howard and Jim are on their way to passing out," Norm said before I opened the door. "How much more can they drink?"

"They might black out," I said, remembering how they typically drank, "but they don't pass out."

"Two falling down drunks aren't gonna make this any easier, if it comes to that," Norm said, his tone stern. "The sooner we can get back to the hotel, the better."

They all agreed. Even I saw their point.

"Okay," I said. "But first we eat. *Alfonso's* and the *aficionados,* then the hotel. Luis is at *Alfonso's?*"

"Yes," Rául answered and put his empty glass on Dick's desk.

We left the office and entered the crowded bar. Someone was playing the piano, warming up before the band for the evening started. Dick stopped and watched the piano player for a few moments. As I passed, he caught my arm.

"They don't know," he whispered and stared toward the kitchen and then followed me toward the table.

"They know about the Jarheads?"

He nodded yes, as we joined the others. Sonia hugged me and I told her we would be going with Rául and Norm.

· · ·

The evening remained uneventful, in the sense that no one tried to kill anyone and all we did was eat and drink to excess.

The barroom at *Alfonso's* was too crowded for Sonia and me to search for the documents we hid Thursday evening. After dinner, and a prompt from Norm, I suggested we all retire to the hotel for a nightcap and *los aficionados* couldn't have been more agreeable. Images of the past evening must have played around in their heads long before I had arrived.

Sonia and I slipped away from the pandemonium and sat quietly by the hotel pool. The old sport coat that had caused me discomfort earlier that day now draped Sonia's bare shoulders, keeping the evening chill away from her. My holstered automatic rested in her colorful over night bag.

One of the four, Norm, Wayne, Rob, or Jeffrey, always had us in their view. At the time, I'd completely forgotten Benny, Jesse and James. Where had they hidden themselves?

"Your *toro fiesta,*" Sonia said, sitting close to me, her voice soft, "reminds me of *futbol.*"

"Soccer?" I said, knowing she didn't mean American football.

"Yes. When I was in school, with my brothers . . ." Her voice saddens for a moment and then picked up. "We always attended the *futbol* parties. What a celebrations. *Festividad,*" she laughed and then added, sadly, "*diversion,* a diversion from what horrors surrounded us. You would have enjoyed my brothers. After the games, especially when we won, what parties.

"I understand you and how you relate to your Mexican friends and appreciate the *corrida,* but your friends . . . they do not care as you do," she said.

"They are good people," I said, meaning Howard and Jim.

"I like them," she said, both of us knew who we were talking about. "They party without really caring the reason?"

"Yes," I said. "But I think they believe they're here for the bullfights. We all came because of the *fiesta* at the bullring tomorrow and the bullfights just happen to come next."

She hugged me as if she were cold and kissed my cheek. "I remember the first time I drank too much," she whispered, almost giggling. "My *Tio Paco's* birthday. I was only sixteen and my brother gave me a rum and coke."

"*Cuba Libre,*" I laughed, remembering Norm's expression when she asked for that drink earlier.

"Yes," she smiled, "but in El Salvador, you do not call it that." Her expression saddened. She held me tighter for a moment and I felt her sob. "I have no more uncles, or brothers," she cried meekly, "or parents . . . or family," she mumbled and without looking, I knew there were tears on her cheeks. "I have no past to give my children," she mumbled bitterly to herself. "They have destroyed my past, what kind of future can I have without a past?" she said and moved away from me. "What future do I have?"

"The one you make for yourself," I said, not knowing what else to say or if it made any sense. "That's all most of us have."

"You have a past," she said. "Family? You can look at old photos from childhood?"

"Yes." I felt bad for her and all those like her that terror has left behind.

"In the United States I must work on my future so I can have a past for my children," she said firmly, again almost forgetting she wasn't alone. She moved closer and held my hand. "You do not need to tell me again about the hearing devices." Her words came lightly, a small argument settled within her. "I am tired," she yawned and stood, still holding my hand.

As we stood, I signaled Norm by pointing up and he nodded. Dick said something to Rob and I watched as he left toward the front of the hotel. At that moment, I felt safe.

We walked quietly up to my third floor room, aware of the shadowy hallways we passed. The sky was clear and filled with stars. I carried her colorful cloth bag, the top open so I could see the black handle of my automatic.

The room was cool and when I went to put the wall heater on Sonia asked me not too. I didn't. I gave her the handbag as she hung up my sport coat. I placed the holstered automatic on the end table and pulled the window blinds closed and then put all the locks on the hotel door.

"Here," I said to Sonia, handing her the shirt and shorts she'd worn the last evening.

"No thank you," she smiled, her sadness diminished. A small blush came to her face as she slithered out of her dress and carefully folded it over a chair.

She didn't look at me as she pulled the covers back and slipped into bed. I stared at her, taking in the beautiful copper tone of her skin and the attractive contour of her small breasts.

"Please shut the light off and come to bed," she whispered, not looking at me.

I shut the lights off.

May 6, 1995
  8:45 a.m.

chapter EIGHTEEN

An abrupt knocking startled me awake. Filtered light slipped from the drawn curtains, aggravating my hangover and oversensitive eyes. The knocking turned to banging and I saw the blurred image of Sonia sitting up, her small breasts uncovered, wild raven hair rambled over brown shoulders, her arms outstretched, aiming my automatic toward the door. Cautiously I reached out and gently placed my right hand at her elbow. She looked at me, tired, frightened eyes questioning.

"Those people wouldn't knock," I said.

Slowly the tension went out of her arms and she lowered the gun, refusing, for the moment, to let it go.

"Murphy," Norm yelled from the other side of the door. "Get your ass out of bed."

Sonia handed the automatic to me and, without saying anything, slipped naked from the bed. I watched her bronzed body walk through the dimness and couldn't stop thinking about the passion we'd shared. Begrudgingly I stood, placed the gun on the night table, and opened the door, hiding my nakedness behind it. Sonia closed the bathroom door.

"You know what time it is?" He had an inane grin on his face. Through the open door, he handed me a pale yellow guayabera shirt, similar to the one he wore. "Don't embarrass us again," he said, and meant dressing properly to carry my gun. "You can buy some others in the lobby."

"What time is it?" I mumbled instead of thanking him.

"Almost nine," he said and sipped from the glass in his hand.

"Bloody Mary?" I asked.

"Miguel's bloody Mary," he said and sipped again. "Couple of pitchers sitting on the bar. Best thing you ever did for me," he said with a wide smile and handed me the glass. "You look like you need it," he smirked and began to walk away. "Ten minutes?"

"Half hour," I said and closed the door.

Years ago, hung-over, ready, and willing to die, I followed Juaquin to a local *farmacia*, where I purchased a small bottle of local painkillers. I was assured they'd remedy my hangover, sour stomach and diarrhea. I fumbled through the hotel dresser, found the current small bottle, an annual gift from Juaquin, and swallowed two pills with a mouth full of the best bloody Mary anywhere. I stood there, eyes closed and felt the pills slide down and then drained the glass.

When Sonia called my name, I opened my eyes. The bathroom door was ajar and I could hear the shower running. I was feeling better already.

After showering, I dressed in the yellow guayabera, jeans and tennis shoes. My automatic was hidden beneath the loose shirt. Sonia slipped into a pale orange summer dress that she pulled from her cloth bag and hung up the night before. She stretched the elastic top of the dress over her shoulders so it appeared as a peasant blouse. I don't know where the wrinkles went, but the dressed clung to her nicely and made me think of last night and why we'd overslept. Thin black sandals, good for walking she promised me, adorned her feet.

We entered the hotel's restaurant about an hour after Norm's wake up call. Howard and Jim held out there hands and I quickly put the magic painkillers into their palms. They just as quickly gulped them down. Three empty pitchers sat on the table, an empty or half-empty glass in front of everyone but Wayne. Rob, Jeffrey, and Wayne had coffee. Dick Dowly smiled and pulled a chair out for Sonia.

"Breakfast?" he said.

"Coffee?" The young waiter said as we sat.

"Please," I said. "*Dos vasos, tambien*," I said when Norm refilled his glass with Miguel's bloody Mary blend.

He returned with two cups of strong Mexican coffee and two glasses for the bloody Marys. "Breakfast?" he said in clear English.

"*No gracias,*" Sonia said, drinking her coffee. "*Y tu?*" she said and watched as I filled her glass with the thick bloody Mary mixture.

"Nothing," I said to the waiter. "Best bloody Mary in the world."

"*Por que?*" she smiled and drank more coffee.

"*Porque,* he drank too much last night," Norm said for me.

"Pills and this?" she said, her look of puzzlement shared between us.

"It works," I said.

"Oh, yes it does." Howard agreed as he finished his drink.

"What time will you be at *Caesar's?*" Dick asked, ending the trivial morning tête-à-tête.

I forced my hung-over mind to function. "Paul, Bryan, and Mike are supposed to meet us there around noon," I said, not one hundred percent sure. "Rául's suppose to meet us at the bullring a little after one. I think," I finished with a grin.

"Close enough," Dick joked. "Sully and Juan?" His smile did not hide the roguish glint in his eyes.

"Yeah," I muttered, "if they can make it." I ignored the stare from Norm. He still didn't know Dick had Seámus hidden, but he let on that he guessed we were up to something and never let me forget Sonia was not a naïve Mexican flower girl.

Dick looked at his watch. "If you're not going to eat, we should be going," he said innocently.

I gulped the nectar of Miguel's famous bloody Mary, Sonia sipped hers, and said, "We ready?"

Luis Morales, the owner of the restaurant, and *aficionado*, walked to our table as we all stood. "You are not leaving?" he said, a look of sadness on his face. "You have not eaten."

"You will be at the *fiesta?*" I said, taking Sonia's hand.

"Of course," he smiled. "Everything is okay?" His eyes glanced away from us and took in the outside pool area and then he gazed upward.

"Fantastico." I said and looked at Sonia so he would understand. "It always is, Luis."

"And Miguel's bloody Marys?" he said as his eyes took in the empty pitchers on our table.

"Non better in the world."

"I know a bartender in La Paz," Jim cut in, "who says he knows Miguel, but he can't match the drink."

"A Mexican bartender using Vodka," Luis smiled to Jim. "I should consider myself lucky none of you like *menudo*. A better cure for what ails you," he grinned to me. *"Este tarde,"* he said and walked to another table.

"Before I forget," I said loudly, so everyone would stop, as we entered the hotel lobby. "Here." I pulled the folded invitations to the afternoon *fiesta* from my back pocket. "You won't get in without this."

"Two years ago you lost them," Howard laughed.

"And the tickets for Sunday," Jim reminded me.

"But we got in."

"Yes," Dick said. "Of course, if I recall, it's because Manuel Ruiz was at the gate."

The standing joke of last year, of how I'd lost both the needed invitations for Saturday's private party and Sunday's tickets for the bullfights the year before, had not been forgotten. I had them Friday night as we began drinking at *Alfonso's*, but they were gone when we met Saturday morning. Maybe next year it would be forgotten. As we piled into taxis I had a feeling it would be something only I would forget.

Norm, Sonia, Rob, and I got into a taxi, Dick took one by himself to his restaurant and Wayne, Jeffrey, Bryan, and Howard followed in another. The driver and I discussed Sunday's *matadors* as he navigated through the old residential side streets, slowing at stop signs and finally speeding down a one-way alley, the wrong way, to drop us off at the less busy side entrance to *Caesar's Hotel.* Rob paid for the taxi, relieved to be out of it alive.

"That guy could scare me," he said with a nervous grin.

The sun was high in the sky and strong. Cool shadows dotted the busy sidewalk as we wandered toward the outdoor café, where Juaquin waited. Traffic belched along, jamming the *avenida* that was already congested with foot traffic.

Juaquin had three tables pushed together, their twelve chairs tilted forward so everyone knew the spaces were saved. He smiled his friendly stained grin as we turned the corner. The patio was filled with tourists, using the late morning shade as a respite from the crowds and sun. Chuy plied between the crowded tables, his small round tray held high, filled with glasses and bottles, taking drink orders verbally. With his free hand, he pointed toward our saved tables, deserted the other patrons, and waited for us.

"Beers," he smiled, proud of his memory, "and coffee or coke?" he said to Wayne.

"Coke," Wayne said.

"*Yo tambien,*" Sonia added before Chuy could walk away.

"*Por que no?*" he said, picked up his full tray and headed toward the inside bar.

"Can we buy Mexican cigars today?" Howard asked as he stretched away from the table.

"On the way to the bullring," I told him.

"I guess I'll get some too," Bryan said, watching for Chuy to return.

"Me too," Norm chirped in.

"Mexican cigars are good?" Sonia asked.

"The best," Juaquin said.

"I agree," I said.

Heat from the sun and autos wafted into the shaded patio from the choked street. At each of the tables, tourists drank and talked and pulled their purchases from bags, to glance at them again, making sure they hadn't been cheated after all. Others talked of what they would go back and buy, while couples argued over who paid the lowest price, who had the best deal. Small Indian children sauntered the busy sidewalk holding a multitude of wares for sale: gum, colorful paper flowers, small cloth animals that swayed from wooden posts as the children drifted and worthless jewelry; those that did not offer items for sale begged for money. Older men and women hawked American cigarettes at bargain prices, heavy Mexican blankets, and an unlimited selection of multicolored paper flowers, exotic string hammocks, and shoddy jewelry. Brown skinned men, wrinkled from the sun, strolled with guitars and offered a tune for one American dollar.

"Do you have a favorite song?" Norm said to Sonia in Spanish, when one of the strolling guitar players stopped at our table.

"No," she smiled and the man moved into the crowded patio.

Chuy slipped the full tray of drinks onto the table and passed them out.

"Keep the change," Norm said as he handed him a folded American bill. "To the *fiesta*." Norm raised his beer in toast.

We all clinked glasses and mimicked his words. The first beers went quickly, the hair of the dog, as they say. Bryan swiftly caught Chuy's attention and almost as quickly, Chuy returned with another round of cold beers. Half way into the second beer, the small talk began. Howard discussed cigars with Norm and Juaquin; Jim talked diving with Rob, Jeffrey and Wayne, leaving Sonia and me to stare at each other, afraid and unable to talk freely. I showed her the small program for Sunday's bullfights and told her a little about the two *matadors* I knew. Jim ordered a third round before most of us were finished and when Chuy delivered the cold beers, he brought two baskets of chips and two bowls of hot Mexican salsa.

"There's three lost souls." Howard laughed to himself as he stared into the busy street.

On the other side, waiting for the light to change, were Mike Collins, Paul Hamphill and Bryan Fahey, the remaining members of our weekend party. Mike stood above the others, his bushy, dirty blonde hair easily spotted in the Latino crowd. He enjoyed drinking, making him one of Howard's pals. His lively blue eyes made up for a large nose that seemed malfunctioning with his thin build. Mike wrote for television, where he met Howard and looked younger than his 40 years.

Paul was the oldest of our group, late 50s, over weight for his five foot eight frame, deaf as a rock without his two hearing aids, smoked two packs a day and had a cough to prove it.

Bryan his full head of thick white hair was a result of not caring if he had it or not. Since it never looked groomed, we all believed him. He was a studio scenic artist and worked when he wanted to. When he worked, he lost weight and because of this, he took to using colorful suspenders, that way he avoided buying clothes for his varying weights. Paul turned more work down from Howard than he accepted, but they remained close. He loved to sketch and whenever he joined us for the weekend, he left us with bar napkin characters we all treasured. He told some of the corniest jokes ever heard and laughed at every one them.

Mike and Paul wore jeans, tee shirts, and tennis shoes. Bryan wore a white dress shirt; open at the neck, with a pocket full of pencils and bright red suspenders held up his baggy chino pants. He shuffled across the street with the others, scuffed old loafers on his feet.

After a quick introduction of the Marines and Sonia, we all sat and when Chuy came for our orders, he brought more salsa, chips and a plate filled with strips of pickled chilies, onions, and carrots.

I gave them their passes for the afternoon at the bullring and they joked about how I'd lost the tickets two years ago. Wasn't anyone ever going to forget that?

"Do you know what Jeffrey Dahmer asked Lorraine Bobbet?" Paul said, crushing out his cigarette.

We stopped talking and looked toward Paul. I whispered to Sonia about Dahmer and Bobbet. Norm tried to explain the question to Juaquin.

"What?" Howard said, already laughing.

"You gonna eat that," Paul said with a burst of laughter.

Sonia and Juaquin stared at us, not understanding. We laughed and drank beer and ate chilies.

"You heard about my uncle turning one hundred?" Paul said. He was still laughing from his first joke. Between coughs, he lighted another cigarette and when no one answered, he continued.

"We threw him a party and my brother and I got him a twenty-five-year-old hooker, honest," he said to us, a wide grin on his weathered face. As he spoke, he sketched on his bar napkin. "After we finished the cake and ice cream I introduced him to her. I said, Uncle Stan this is Bamby. He smiled his toothless smile and she said, I'm gonna offer you super sex and when she smiled I was jealous. My uncle looked at her, thought for a moment, and said, I'll take the soup."

We all laughed. Paul slid the napkin to Sonia and she looked at it and then at him. She showed it to me. It was a sketch of her and he had captured her perfectly.

The salsa, chips, pickled chilies, onions, and carrots were gone and we were well on our way into a six-pack of beer each. Rob and Jeffrey seemed relax and sipped slowly, so it never seemed they weren't drinking. Sonia, Wayne, and Juaquin drank Cokes.

It was hot out and the sidewalk and street were congested and noisy. Guitars strummed all around, people argued and those that weren't arguing yelled to be heard over the arguments.

"If I came upon this group in Rockport Beach I'd bust them," Sully yelled from the sidewalk.

We all turned and greeted Sully and his partner, Juan. Sully stood there laughing at himself and us, his overweight frame covered with a loose fitting shirt. His red face and thin white hair made him resemble Paul. Juan was younger, short and heavy with raven black hair like Sonia's. His brown eyes were hard and he quickly took in Sonia, Juaquin, and the two Marines. Everyone else he'd met or seen with me in Rockport Beach.

"Where we sittin'?" Sully said as he and Juan pushed their way to our table.

There wasn't a free chair on the patio and every table had more people at it then was supposed to be. Juaquin looked at me and shook his head in helplessness.

I introduced Sully and Juan to Sonia, Juaquin, Jeffrey, and Rob. Chuy took their drink order not caring that they had to stand.

As we toasted the *fiesta* for the hundredth time, Dick Dowly exited a taxi and joined us.

"I hope this group's coming to my place and spending money tonight," he said and shook hands with Sully.

"Think it's time we head to the bullring," I said and finished the last of my beer.

"We're gonna need three or four taxis," Howard said.

"We'll walk," I said and everyone stood. "We've time," I told them and we all snaked onto the sidewalk. I wanted to walk off the alcohol.

"More back up?" Norm spitefully quipped as we approached Sully.

"Naw," I said and slapped Sully on the back. "Here for the weekend?"

"No," Sully said dully and then a thin smiled formed. "Told Juan about the Saturday party and we figured, what the hell, let's drive down."

"You're not going to let me down, are you Murphy?" Juan said, only half joking, as we pushed our way along the crowded sidewalk.

"Not Murphy," Norm cried out. "This is gonna turn into an unforgettable weekend. Right?" he said looking at me with a heavy slap to my back. "Unforgettable. Who are we following?" he laughed as he realized we were in the back of the slow moving group.

Sully winked at me and stared into every dark bar we passed.

May 6, 1995
3 p.m.

chapter NINETEEN

As we strolled along *Avenida Revolucion,* the afternoon sun blazed down on us. Cactus Liquors is located off a side street that was a dirt path when I first came to Tijuana, but is now one of many businesses on a paved, three lane, one-way street. The price and selection of liquor and cigars is cheaper than where we'd walked from. Paco, the owner, and I have known each other for sometime. His son, Jorge, runs the store, while Paco socialized with old friends. Paco and his wife had six children, but only Jorge showed an interest in the family business. After graduating from business school, he returned to Tijuana and began to build up his father's establishment. A few adventurous *gringos* found their way to the store, mostly because of advertisements for Mexican cigars and the large selection of Mexican beverages. Others found it by word of mouth.

We purchased more than we could legally cross into California with, but it didn't seem to bother anyone. As one of Jorge's added, free services, Cactus Liquors delivered to your hotel. We left the hotel's name with him. Few Americans took advantage of this service, afraid of being cheated, Jorge told us with a sad smile.

"Tomorrow, at the plaza." Paco called as we left. "Box six," he said, proud of the small private box Jorge bought for him each season. "Free beer," he said with a laugh and went back to socializing.

Howard sniffed the Mexican cigar as he walked along. Smiling, he lighted it. "Good, Mick," he said and blew thick white smoke into the busy street. "Should've taken the box with me."

"Beer break." Bryan yelled.

We were half way to the bullring and the street had changed from tourist shops, to Calimex supermarkets, candy stores, small restaurants, gas stations and modest businesses that made Tijuana a busy metropolis. Small taco stands sprouted from windows and alleys, offering many inexpensive foods and cold drinks. Here, few, if any, spoke English.

There's a small park where *Revolucion* turns away from Tijuana and becomes *Agua Caliente*. The park is called *Parque 18 de Marzo*. Probably named after some battle. Two pushcart vendors serviced the park and took advantage of the small benches placed there. We took over most of the benches while we ate tacos and drank beer.

"There's tacos and beer at the bullring," I said, and then sat and ate.

"Have you spotted your tail?" Norm said, his taco gone.

"No," I said and looked around. I hadn't given it much thought since we began our walk.

"You got one, maybe two," he said between gulps of beer.

Sonia glanced into the busy street and then around to the side street. "How do you know?" she said, not looking at Norm.

"I know," he said flatly.

"He knows," I said, though I'm not sure there was any assurance in the knowledge.

"They have to keep an eye on him," Norm said quietly to Sonia. "Tomorrow, noon, they're no longer welcomed in Mexico. Mick's the only living person they know that's seen the priest."

He put a little extra emphasis on *living* and his squinty stare let me know he hadn't bought her story. When he said it Sonia's expression saddened and just as quickly hardened again. Was she remembering the murdered friends she'd lost on the journey?

"I understand," she said pleasantly with a deceiving smile. "I expect they will do something before tomorrow," she continued softly, but the words were spoken firmly.

"I wish your boyfriend were as smart as you," he grumbled.

"Sunday?" I said, as his words finally caught my attention. "I thought Cluny was here till whenever?" We continued to sit.

"Last night the Mexican Attorney General's office flew someone in and they changed the rules," Norm grinned. "Too much shit goin' down and it's makin' them a little nervous." His words trailed off, slowly and only his silly grin stayed.

"Sunday at noon?" I said again, not knowing if I should be excited or nervous.

"Sunday at noon a plane will be here to take them back to Guatemala. If they're not on it, they'll be arrested," he said flatly and sipped from his beer. "Cluny's gotta come up with somethin', Mick, and my guess is it's you," he groused and left us alone.

"Great," I moaned and finished my beer.

"Damn good cigar, Mick," Howard yelled out from the taco stand, where he, Jim and Bryan were getting another beer.

Paul and Mike walked around the stone tower that stood in the center of the park, stepping gingerly around the mothers and children who lay on blankets eating. Paul touched the large stones, feeling their texture, as he talked to Mike. Sully and Juan sat with Dick, while Juaquin talked with Wayne and Jeffrey. Howard, Bryan, and Jim walked through the park smoking cigars, lost in the haze of their own world.

I looked around for Rob and noticed him at the opposite end of the park, waiting at the taco stand. When I located Benny in the same line, adrenalin rushed through me and my mind rapidly tried to identify some danger, but couldn't. I looked toward Dick, who had joined Norm at the taco stand.

"Something is wrong?" Sonia said, staring at me.

"No," I lied, poorly. "I have to talk with Dick," I said and took her hand. I suggested she stay with Jeffrey and Wayne she refused and followed me.

"Another taco?" Dick kidded.

"No," I said abruptly. "I thought maybe we should try that stand," I said, looking toward the other end of the park. "Rob seems to like them."

"Am I missing something?" Norm said, noticing the urgency in my voice.

"No," Dick said. "One of the back up men is talking with Rob."

We all stared toward the other taco stand and watched as Rob and Benny ordered tacos and beer. When their orders were delivered, they walked away, like strangers. Rob walked toward us. We met him half way into the grassy park.

Rob looked at Sonia and then Norm, while he munched his taco and sipped beer. Dick nodded his head.

"Cluny has the bullring surrounded," he said and ate. "About twenty people outside and another six or eight inside."

"He can't expect Seámus to show up there," I said, mostly to myself.

"There's three cars following us. One is using side streets zig, zagging our walk. There's one stayin' a block or so ahead of us and the other's behind us. Two men in each car and they're using radios to keep in touch." Rob wiped his mouth on the small white napkin the vendors gave out and then sipped his beer.

"This is crazy, Mick." Norm said directly into my face. "You're the target, shit for brains. You've got friends who shouldn't be here right now."

He looked toward the benches. Of course, he was talking about Howard, Bryan, Mike, Paul, Jim, and Juaquin. "I'm guessing Sully and Juan are part of your scheme? You don't have the right to put them in jeopardy," he said as a reprimand.

Dick touched Sonia softly on the shoulder and smiled at her. "As right as you are, Norm, it's a mute point now," he said. "They're not safe if Mick leaves. It's not safe if we all turn around and head back to town. They'll pick us up for sure if we do something they don't understand."

"The bullring?" Norm said, but knew it wasn't a question.

"The safest place," Dick agreed. "Lot of influential people there."

"Rául's there," I said. Sonia was holding tightly to my hand. I wondered if she could feel my nervousness. "What about afterwards?"

"Kind of late to be thinking about that, isn't it?" Norm snarled and walked away. He whistled loudly and like the Pied Piper of old, he led the way and we followed.

We had to look like the lost brigade of Tijuana as we paraded along, a mixture of sizes and colors. Sonia walked holding my hand, Rob and Norm led the column, Wayne and Jeffrey brought up the rear, leaving Dick with Sully and Juan and the others sandwiched in between. No one but I noticed.

As we neared the bullring, we passed through a section of street that was lined with large, old Chinese restaurants. Years ago, I learned the role the Chinese played in the development of Baja. These days, with the profit made in smuggling Chinese from the mainland to the United States, Mexico is often a first destination. As we came upon Tijuana's Bob's Big Boy Restaurant and the circling red and white bucket of Kentucky Fried Chicken, we saw the top portion of the bullring grandstand.

"Do we know this one?" Howard said as we passed a four by eight foot poster advertising the bullfights and naming the matadors.

"Two of them," I said, tapping the wood poster.

Traffic flowed along the four-lane road, old drab busses putted along, belching their toxic fumes, while station wagon taxis stopped at waving men, women and children until they were so full there was no more room and went on their way. Short, portly Indian women moved along, bulky packages balanced on their heads, a child tugging at their vibrant skirt or holding their hand. The sidewalks were active with men and women and children, skinny and fat, young and old, tall and short and some in between, in business suits, bright summer dresses, mixed amongst faded worn outfits, brown skinned, white skinned, all moving, noticing us without comment. We moved around and through all this, talking and smoking, only a few of us aware of the real danger that circled us.

Tijuana motorcycle police kept order as cars and trucks plied their way into the large dirt parking lot of the bullring.

"Hey, Mick." Bryan called to us, as we were about to enter the parking lot. "Are they women?" he said, pointing at two of the helmeted police who rested on the small wall that enclosed the parking lot.

"Sure are," I said.

"You don't see that in LA," Bryan said.

"Women's lib in Mexico." Paul snarled. "The whole world's gone to hell," he grumbled.

"If I put a female motorcycle cop into a script about Mexico no one would buy it." Mike laughed along. "Maybe I'll do that?"

Ahead of us, across the dirt parking lot, we saw the recently white washed outer adobe wall that surrounded the bullring. Fresh bright red trim highlighted the entrances and ticket windows. The same bright red was used to stencil *sol* and *sombra*, sunny or shade, seating over the entrances. Towering above us was the exposed top section of aged metal scaffolding, fitted with wooden planks for seating.

We walked across the parking lot, dodging cars and trucks, whose drivers ignored the directions of parking attendants, causing them to signal the police, who in turn blew whistles and ran into the pointless quandary to take control.

"This is something even I couldn't draw," Paul laughed as we slipped into line at the entrances.

"Christ," Howard yelled along, "I'd give anything to get this show on film. Maybe next year?"

"I'll write it," Mike said.

We all turned for one more look at the vaudevillian attendants and whistling police before showing our passes as we walked through the gates.

Uniformed police, appearing far removed from the whistle blowers outside, checked invitations of those that enter. Today, for the only time during the Tijuana *Gran Inauguracion de la Temporada* designated guests could enter the arena and enjoy the privilege of walking the *callejon*, a moat like area behind the small arena wall and between the opening of the private rooms that were below the general seating. This was where the press, sword handlers, and special guests stood during the bullfight. Everyone would be allowed to walk the dirt arena. The air was filled with the aroma of spicy cooking and I could almost taste the beef and pork tacos that were grilling on the inside.

People filled the entrance plaza and a loud band played Spanish bullfight music. Freshly white washed walls had murals of beautiful Mexican women wearing wide brimmed, colorful hats. Men walked through the crowds handing out cold bottles of beer from buckets of ice.

Alfonso and Natale waved from the patio, where they sat at a filled table. Luis Morales talked with Manuel Ruiz at the crowded bar. When Luis waved and said something we couldn't possibly make out, Manuel excused himself and walked toward us.

"Mick," he said shaking my hand as he nodded to Dick and in the general direction of the rest of our group. He might remember their faces later on, but their names were lost from last year.

He greeted Sonia in Spanish, his smile as welcoming as ever. "Rául would like to speak with you," he grinned, even though he had to know if Rául requested me away from the crowd it couldn't be conversation he wanted. Manuel pointed toward his two-room office complex where a fence that separated the sunny and shady sides of the arena entrance began and divided the plaza areas.

"Thank you," I said. "A good turn out?"

"Very good," he said happily. "All the *matadors* for tomorrow and others."

"Jesús Glison?" I asked as we walked toward his office.

"Yes and he asked for you. I will talk with you later. Please enjoy yourself," he said and nodded toward Sonia. "The food is good and the beer is cold," he said shaking my hand again. "There is also Mexican wine," he said to Sonia as he turned to leave.

Rob, Jeffrey, Dick, Norm and Wayne had followed us as Manuel, Sonia and I walked. Sully and Juan stood a short distance away, while everyone else hurried for the cold beer and tacos.

Rául stood in the doorway, wearing a light sport coat over a white dress shirt, opened at the collar. He looked hot. As we approached, he said something to the three men in the room with him and they left.

"Why don't you invite them all in?" Rául greeted us sarcastically as he looked into the crowd and kept us from entering. "Come in," he finally said and moved into the room.

The walls were freshly painted and the tile floor scrubbed. Transparent curtains covered the two large windows that looked toward each side of the arena plaza. Two old sofas and four uncomfortable chairs took up the small waiting area of the first room. Behind the closed door was Manuel's office. We all stood.

"Close the door," Rául said and closed the door that led into the sunny side of the arena entrance as he left. Rob closed the door. Rául nervously paced, looked at each of us and then out the windows into the crowd.

"Cluny is here," he said coldly. "He has less then twenty-four hours left . . ." Rául glanced toward Norm, who nodded his head. "You know?"

"Yes," I said. Sonia moved closer.

"I wish you hadn't come here."

"Cluny has more people outside," Dick added.

"I know."

"This is why I'm here," I said, pointing out the windows. "No other reason."

"That's irrelevant," Rául said.

"Not to me." I said abruptly

"Forget the other night at *Alfonso's*," Rául said, catching me by surprise. "Right now my concerns are the people out there . . . . innocent people, who you are putting in danger. You should've crossed the border the other night with Norm." His stare was cold.

The room became very quiet. The frivolity from the plaza vestibule cascaded through the walls and filled the room with an eerie oddness that made me uncomfortable. Cluny was out there, amidst the laughter and revelry. It didn't seem right.

"That was then, this is now," Dick spoke up, forcing the eeriness away. "Mick should've crossed and he shouldn't be entertaining his friends out there." He pointed toward the window without taking his eyes from Rául. "He didn't cross and he has innocent friends out there."

"And some not so innocent," Rául added, looking at Rob and Jeffrey.

"We don't want any trouble," Norm said after an odd moment of silence. "With the police here, yourself and whoever else is runnin' around, we thought it would be safest to be in a crowd. If we're wrong, we'll leave. Just tell us."

"How many people do you think he has outside?" Rául said and walked back to the window. He stared out. Was he looking for Cluny?

"He had three cars following us," Dick said. "Six men total. We think he has about 20 people surrounding the bullring and six or eight inside."

"Ten people, counting Cluny," he mumbled with his back to us. "It could be more. How many of them are my cops?" he said to himself and walked away from the window. "How many are you?"

"What you see and three on the street," he said flatly.

"You?" he said to Norm.

"The two of us in this room." He nodded toward Wayne.

"Didn't I see Sully out there?" Rául looked at me.

"Yeah," I said not wanting to be caught in a lie. "But he's just down for the day with another cop."

"If you count Sully, the other cop and everyone else you've mentioned, you're still out numbered . . ." he paused and looked at Wayne and Dick . . . "out gunned too?"

They both nodded their reply.

"I can't help you," he muttered and rubbed his tired eyes. "My responsibilities are to those people out there. If stopping Cluny is going to get any of them hurt, I won't do it. Do you understand?" he said, moving toward me.

"You're the chief of police," I grinned nervously, hoping my anxiety was hidden. "You'll do what you have to."

"If you cause it to come to a stand off, like the other evening, I don't know how many of those uniformed officers will be on Cluny's payroll and how many will obey me," he said. "Mick, I think you've just trapped yourself. Give him the priest." His voice was low from exhaustion.

Sonia squeezed my hand. Her black eyes were large and anger radiated from them, her expression was defiant.

"He's not mine to give," I said.

"That's too bad," he said and opened the door for us to leave.

May 6, 1995
7 p.m.

chapter TWENTY

People entered the plaza as we walked out of the small office. Sully pointed in the direction of the bar and, without talking, we followed him. Over in a far corner, Juan had somehow occupied a table and saved it for us. Two tables away Juaquin sat crowed in with the rest of our party, babysitting *gringos.*

Sully, Juan, and Rob stood, while the rest of us sat tightly packed at the small table. Giving up, Jeffrey finally stood. A waiter brought us a tray with paper plates filled with grilled pieces of spicy meat, yellow rice, refried beans, a stack of hot corn tortillas and a small tub of peppers, radishes and onions. Before the waiter finished a man delivering beer stopped and served us.

Wayne asked the waiter about a soda for Sonia and himself. We began to eat before the sodas arrived.

"Rául didn't look too happy," Sully said between bites of food and sips of beer.

"Cluny's here," Dick said, "but we already knew that."

"Is Mick safe?"

"Not as long as he's in Mexico," Dick said.

Sully looked down at Sonia and then at Norm. "Isn't there anything you can do?"

"Not today," he said. "The window of opportunity is gone." His stare going from Sully to me. "How are you keeping in touch with the men outside?"

"I'll mingle," Rob said and left the table.

"Okay," Norm grinned at Dick. "How do you suppose all of us get from here to your place?"

"Taxi," Dick said. "But we should stop at *Alfonso's* first."

"Why?"

"It's closer. It's also, what Mick does every year. We know it, they know it," he pointed toward Juaquin, "and Cluny's gotta know it by now."

We sat in shadows of the overhead bleachers, protected from the hot afternoon sun. Our beers were gone before we'd finished eating. Bryan pushed his way to our table, a smoldering cigar in his mouth, and a tray filled with beers in his hands.

"You need a refill?" he grinned and put some of the beers on our table. Biting on the cigar, he smiled and continued to where the others sat.

"Behind you, to your right, by the stairway, there's a guy staring at you," Jeffrey said quietly, as he reached past me for a bottle of beer. "Got a brace on his leg," he said as if he doubted his own sight.

"Long hair in a pony tail?" I said without turning.

Jeffrey nodded yes.

I turned and off to my right, where Jeffrey said he'd be, stood Jesús Glisen, a young matador, surrounded by fans. I waved at him and he waved back. He excused himself and walked toward us. He walked proudly through the crowd, accepting acknowledgement from friends and admirers as he passed.

On his right shoe, running up to his knee, was a brace for his leg, a childhood legacy.

He wore the brace honorably and when it came time to kill the bull in the arena another brace was placed over his right arm, for strength, and he killed as bravely and as well as any matador in Mexico. He was young and handsome and with his youth and abilities, the brace became his badge of courage.

It was his second year as a matador. I met him two years ago when he was a *novillero* and we'd been friends ever since. Maybe he was five foot ten, thin with light brown eyes, almost yellow, and thick, long brown hair. His skin was fair and a small band of reddish brown freckles ran across his long lean nose. He worked so close to the bull that every time I'd seen him he'd been tossed, leaving me to wonder if the blood that soaked his clothing was his or the bulls. He showed no fear and laughed at his exploits in the arena. To see him work was to see the true essence of the bullfight, something that time had all but eroded.

"I am glad you came," Jesús said, lightheartedly.

I stood to meet him. We shook hands, hugged - *abrazo* - and I introduced him to everyone. Joaquin's table emptied immediately and I did another round of introduction.

"When do you fight?" I said.

A waiter quickly came and brought us tacos and beer. It's always good to party with saloon owners and celebrities.

"Two times in *julio,*" he said and gulped beer. "Maybe two in *augusto* and the golden sword in *septiembre.*"

"But the golden sword matadors aren't decided until the end of August," I said, unable to hide my amusement.

"He doubts me," he smiled amorously at Sonia. "I will give you the golden sword," he pledged.

"First you must win it," she smiled chastely back.

"Unless I am killed, I will be here and if I am here, I will win." He toasted us with his words and beer and drank. "Is it not true?"

"Yes," I said. "If you are not killed and you draw good and brave bulls, you will win."

"And you will all come." He cheerfully toasted again.

Jesús enjoyed himself wherever he was and if there wasn't a party, he'd begin one. Howard, Bryan, Mike, and Paul quickly fell in and told of how we'd all seen him last summer. Mike promised to make all his fights that summer. Bryan sat with them and I could see his green eyes feed all the details to his sponge-like brain. Paul quickly sketched Jesús and passed the napkin vignettes around.

"I think I should've saved a bigger table," Dick said.

"Damn Mick. We don't need to add to this group." Norm joined in agreement.

"You let somethin' happen to this kid," Dick nodded toward Jesús, "and the Mexicans will kill you before Cluny can."

"I get the message." But it was hard for me to think of Cluny and the fear I'd felt at *Alfonso's* Thursday night. The fiesta was what I came for, these were the people I wanted to be with and Seámus was a phantom, almost gone, until I looked into Sonia's coal-black eyes and a chill ran up my back.

"We may have a problem," Rob said, carrying a tray of cold beers. "There are no taxis outside."

"Taxis should be double parked," I said, coming back to what was happening around me.

"They want us to leave the way we came," Norm said.

"Why?"

"Damned if I know."

"Benny said as taxis slow down or stop the local cops make them move on. They're not even allowed into the parkin' lot."

Bullfight music and festive chatter engulfed us, as the band played and people tried to be heard. Young women, in small groups paraded around the plaza, a fashion show of color and youth. Young men followed and tried to make conversation, all the time knowing that the protective eyes of mothers and fathers and brothers followed them.

Couples sat or stood by the far walls, some rested on the aged stairways. Others snuck into the small private rooms, closing the primitive wooden doors behind them. Police strolled through the plaza in pairs, others stood above, staring down from the upper sections.

"You will come to the arena?" Manuel Ruiz asked. He had come upon us quietly, hidden within the moving crowd that surrounded us.

"It is time?" I held Sonia's hand.

"Soon," he said. "You will take Sonia to the *callejon* and let her see all these *matadors*." He used his hand to circle the crowd. "Then tomorrow you will see honest *matadores*, not drunkards," he smiled at her. Manuel excused himself and was quickly swallowed into the crowd.

"With twenty people on the outside they have every exit covered," Norm said. He scanned the upper level of the bleachers. "Whose side are they on?" he said as pairs of police moved overhead.

"Will Juaquin stay with the Rockport Beach crowd?" Dick said. He looked toward the table they sat at. Jesús laughed and drank with them.

"He'll be the only sober one there," I said.

"Sully, you keep them in tow for as long as you can. When you can't keep them here, get them back to the hotel," Dick said.

"Tryin' to get drunks to do somethin' . . ." Sully began.

"If they won't go to the hotel, get them to my place."

"Okay. Juan comes with me?"

"Yes," Dick said.

"What's the plan?" I said.

"Not sure."

"We should let Rául know we're splitting up. Give him a chance to keep an eye of 'em." Norm nodded toward Juaquin.

"Good," Dick said. "Sonia . . ."

"I stay with Mick," she said, her voice low.

"For now," he smiled.

All this time I had not seen Cluny and I didn't think they had either, since no one spoke of him. No menacing men marched by or stood around eyeing our group. Policemen strolled by, but none had stopped or seemed to pay attention to us. The crowd grew and would soon leave the plaza and enter the arena or take seats above and watch the amateurish and intoxicated tyro bullfighters. There would be laughs and shouts of approval to those that appeared brave and boos to those who dropped the red-cloth cape and ran from the small calf placed in the ring.

Sully and Juan walked over to Juaquin and while they spoke to him, he turned to me. I nodded my head and he replied in kind. Sully pointed toward the newly opened gate that led to the arena and they all followed Jesús Glisen into the ring.

The crowd that filled the plaza slowly entered the arena or climbed the aged stairway to their seats. Only a few men stayed within reach of the free beer, talking and laughing amongst themselves.

"What do we do without taxis?" I said.

"Might be irrelevant, Mick," Norm said quickly.

I looked at him and followed his hard stare away from the table. Cluny, three uniformed Tijuana policemen and four Central America Indians stood six tables away peering at us.

Cluny was dressed in wrinkled jungle clothing again. Sonia squeezed my hand and I pressed back. Cluny had a petty grin on his puffy red face, the others were expressionless. None of the remaining guests of the fiesta seemed to notice anything unusual. At least they weren't carrying automatic weapons.

Rob and Jeffrey inched away from their sides of our table. Dick moved toward Sonia, while Norm and Wayne stood.

"Please do not move," Cluny mouthed, his words scarcely audible.

"You want something, Neville?" Norm said, as he pushed his chair away.

"Dick." Cluny chirped. "Why am I not surprised to see you 'ere?"

Dick said nothing.

"I believe it is time for me to take the terrorist," he said to me. "You will tell me where 'e is." His voice rose as he walked closer, followed by the Indians and police.

"I don't know where Seámus is," I said. "You've been following me."

"Yes," he said and inched closer. The Indians stayed a step or two behind and deliberately separated. Two policemen stayed to his right and the third to his left. "I believe you 'ave not seen 'im. But I believe you know where 'e's at."

"Wrong," I said, trying to hide my worry.

They stopped one table away. By that time, everyone was strategically dispersed, but it was still eight of them to six of us. At that moment, I realized I should have given Sonia a weapon, knowing it would have been more useful in her hands than mine.

"I think you should come with me," he smiled his shallow, sadistic grin. "No games. These policemen are 'ere to arrest you," he said and stopped moving. "It is all legal."

"Neville, this is bullshit and you know it," Norm yelled.

"Yes, bullshit. An appropriate term considering where we are." He laughed superficially. "I do not 'ave time for your silly games, Norm." He waited. The three policemen unclasped their holsters. "You come too, Norm. No one else. Of course, if the young lady wishes to join us . . ." he laughed.

Weapons were drawn on both sides. It happened so quickly I didn't have a chance to pull mine. Cluny hadn't pulled his old revolver either. The three policemen had 9mm automatics, the four Indians each held menacing looking short-barreled rifles. Later I would learn they were Heckler and Koch assault pistols.

"Where is this getting us, Neville?" Norm said, his voice cold, but controlled. "My people will have your balls."

Cluny chuckled, almost like it had all been a bad joke. "I should give a bloody fuck what the CIA thinks?" he said. "You people couldn't take Miami back if the Cuban exiles wanted it."

He stood at the table, looked past me at Norm, and then very carefully gave all of us a brief stare. "I get paid for results," he said, raising a foot onto a chair. "I always get the results I am after. You both know that." He glanced at Dick and Norm. "Does 'e know that?" Cluny nodded toward me.

"He works for me." Norm shouted in return. "Or are you deaf? You checked and know it's true."

"Yes, yes I did," he grinned.

"You know there'll be repercussions," Norm said.

The men who remained around the bar quickly became aware of the situation and, with beers in hand, slunk away from our direction. Small pockets of people moved about the plaza, heading to the rest rooms or the stairways, unaware of us. Policemen seemed to have vanished. Laughter and encouragement - *OLE. OLE.* - could be heard, along with blasts of reverberant music, coming from the unseen bullring, as the spectators enjoyed themselves.

"And what bloody repercussions wait for me if I fail this assignment? Do you 'ave any idea? No," he yelled. "You think I care about violating some Washington ethic? I care about finishing my assignment, successfully. Bottom line that is all the people I work for care about. Your people in Washington 'ave not been bloody supportive of my employers since Carter was president and my employers do not give a flying, bloody fuck about violations . . . if I get the job done."

Sonia hugged me briefly and while she did, she removed my automatic from its holster. She was armed and I wasn't.

"Couldn't the three of us go to the office," Norm said, and nodded toward Manuel's office across the plaza, "and talk this through? Avoid any decision that could come back and haunt us."

"If 'e's willing to tell me where I can find the terrorist that would be acceptable." He looked toward me, his expression told me he knew better.

"Can't tell you what I don't know," I said without barking in fright.

198

"I fear the methods required would not be available in that office," he said clearly. "You understand?" His crazed cackle sent chills through me and I felt Sonia shift behind me.

"And what methods would they be?" Dick said. He had moved close to me, his automatic at his right side.

"Are you CIA this trip, Dick?" Cluny said, removing his leg from the chair. He sat on the table's edge, relaxed. He was in his element, nurturing fear and enjoying himself. The only thing missing was his bottle of Mexican vodka.

"I'm trying to enjoy the weekend," he grinned back at Cluny, "this party and tomorrow's bullfight, with some friends. Your problem, Neville, is you're out of your element in civilization," he taunted. "I don't give a good god-damn about your terrorist or Murphy's priest. If I did, I'd be out looking for him. And imagine how your employers would respond if I brought him in and not you. I bet there's a big reward."

"You know there is," Cluny said, staring at Dick. He had to wonder if there were truths in Dick's words.

"If he was in Tijuana, I'd have him and if I had him, I wouldn't give him to you . . . I'd get the reward for myself. You know that," he said.

"That does sound like the Dowly I know." He stood up straight, took a step toward us, and stopped. " 'Owever, I 'ave always figured you a quixotic and believe you would put 'is friendship a 'ead of money. Sorry."

"*Tambien,*" Raúl called out as he walked down the stairway behind Cluny, his 9mm automatic firmly in his hand, hung down at his side. Three steps from the bottom he stopped and when he looked around black-garbed policemen, all holding Galil automatic rifles, appeared out of nowhere. Above, on the first level walkway, more armed police stood at the railing. "Now you will all put your weapons back where they belong." He walked down the remaining steps and continued until he stood between us.

There was a moment's hesitation, but then Norm and Dick holstered their automatics, followed by everyone on our side.

Sonia did not put my automatic back and when I turned to look at her she stared at her opened purse and smiled.

Cluny gawked at Rául and then peeked past him at the numerous armed police that out numbered the eight of them. With a nod of his head, the three police and four Indians put their weapons away.

"You," Rául said in Spanish to the policemen with Cluny, "who are you working for?"

"We are off duty," one said.

"You are in uniform."

"We did not have time to change."

"You have time now." With a short toss of his head, he ordered them to leave. "Be in my office tomorrow morning," he said as they hesitated to obey.

They backed up slowly and then turned and left.

"Like it or not, Mexican law rules here," Rául raged, as he paced between us. "What the hell were you planning to do? You are not in the jungles now," he yelled toward Cluny, "or Dodge City," he said to us. "This is a private gathering and no one . . . other than you," he waved his arm around, "are involved. There will be no violence here. Understand?" He didn't wait for anyone to respond. The exhilaration and revelry of the unseen crowd flowed out of the bullring and into the plaza. Laughter and jeers screeched between chanted *OLE. OLE.* "You want to kill each other, do it somewhere other than my city . . . my country," he shrieked. "Your terrorist is not here, at this bullring, so there's no reason for you to be here. You're not on holiday. Tomorrow, with or without your terrorist, you leave Mexico or go to jail. If I were you, I wouldn't spend valuable time chasing this dumb Irishman. Do I make myself clear?"

"I have authority . . ." Cluny began angrily.

"You may feel you have authority, Neville, but look around. I have twenty-five, Federal anti-terrorist police here from Mexico City and their orders are to assist me. Me," he yelled. "I'm chief of police. Who the hell are you?"

"May I leave?" Cluny said, his voice low, his face red with anger.

Rául gestured toward the exit without answering. The Federal police did not relax. We all watched Cluny and the four Indians walk slowly across the plaza and out the exit. Everyone knew Cluny had armed agents within the crowd that we would not recognize until they had pulled their weapons and then it would be too late. As Rául turned to us, I noticed that the black clad police were still ready to respond.

May 6, 1995
    8:45 p.m.

chapter TWENTY ONE

"I don't know if you've told me the truth or not," Rául said. "As your friend I want to believe you. As chief of police, I find it difficult. Too much against you. Maybe Norm is telling the truth?" He looked hard at me, his brown eyes large with anger. "CIA agents, Central American death squads . . . a terrorist Catholic priest . . . a left wing American journalist and you." He stopped pacing in front of Dick. "You of all people, Dick. You need my cooperation," he said, "I have enough problems with the local politicians and drug gangs . . . I don't need you assholes using Tijuana as a playground now that the Iron Curtain is down. Invade somewhere else," he said coarsely. "I should deport everyone. I should jail you. Armed foreigners . . . that's against the law," he snarled. "Where are the others?"

"With Jesús Glisen," I said.

Rául looked toward the thunderous bullring. "What are you going to do now?" he said, returning his attention to us.

"We were leaving."

"All of you?"

"No," Norm said. "We're going without them." He nodded toward the bullring. "They have nothing to do with this."

"And you think that matters to Cluny?"

"No. Sully's with them and we hoped you'd see they got back to the hotel."

"I don't baby sit foreigners. Once they're out of here, I can't be responsible."

"Okay," I said, unable to out stare him. "May we leave?"

I saw Rául the policeman for the first time and though I understood it, I didn't like it.

"I wish you'd never came," he said harshly. He took a two-way radio from his jacket and told someone at the other end to send two taxis to the front gate. "You know Cluny hasn't gone." His words were a warning, spoken with concern, not anger.

"We know," I said. "Will you be at *Alfonso's* later?"

"I don't know what later holds for any of us, Mick. I might, I might not. Hell, you might not either."

I didn't need to hear that.

We walked toward the exit, past the anti-terrorist police, who remained prepared to respond. Rául walked with us. The roar of the crowd applauded someone in the bullring and lively music blasted from behind the walls.

"As a courtesy to Sully, I'll see that they get back to the hotel," Rául said quietly when we reached the exit. "Be careful, Mick, this isn't over."

"Thank you," I said and we exited to the taxis.

. . . .

We waited at *Alfonso's* for more than an hour before people began to wander in from the bullring. We sat in the bar, by a window that looked out onto the main street.

"Can you do anything to stop Cluny?" I said to Norm.

"Not really and he knows it."

The waiter brought us our drinks, the Marines kept to beer, Norm and Dick switched to tequila, Wayne and Sonia stayed with soda, while I switched to rum and coke.

"What will he do?"

"He'll go back and recheck everywhere he's checked since he arrived and he'll hurt people doing it. If he finds the priest he'll leave quickly."

Sonia stared at him. She'd seen a lot of people hurt in her life and its meaning meant more to her than it did to me.

"If he doesn't find Seámus?" I said and took a long swallow of my drink.

"You. He'll come for you. He knows who you are and where you're at. You're the last person known to have seen the priest, he needs you. He doesn't fail and that's why his bosses like him."

I kept to myself, my theory on how he knew all this. How often had he and Dick worked with Cluny? The question troubled me and what I thought the answer would be sent quivers through me. It was not the time for Sonia to be more frightened of them than she already was.

"He thinks we're protecting you," Dick said.

"And that's bad?"

"Yes," Norm said. "He must think . . . or the generals think, more likely, that we want to get Seámus and his information across the border. We're not dealing with rational human beings and that's scary. He sees me here and thinks it's business. The only thing that makes sense to him is I'm here officially."

"Like I told you before, nothing Seámus has will affect anyone . . . anything that happened in the past. There's nothing new in what he's got," Dick said. "No one in the States is gonna care." "Why all this then?" I said, annoyed at their preaching.

"Some questions don't have logical answers, Mick. Paranoia, probably. No one will ever know," Norm said curtly.

"Is that true?" Sonia said. Her black eyes were deadened as she grabbed hold of my arm. "Everything is for nothing?" She stared at Norm.

"I've told him these things, Sonia," Norm groused, "but he thinks he can save the world. People don't give a damn." He sipped his tequila.

"I have to try," I said more to Sonia than to anyone else. "I can't believe no one cares."

Sonia released my arm and sighed.

"I have help coming for Benny," Dick said to change the direction of the conversation. "They should be here by now."

"How does that help us?" I said, avoiding Sonia's stare and wondered who the help was, but didn't want to ask.

"Us, Mick?" Norm growled. "Damn you. It don't help us at all. Maybe it helps you."

"Okay. Me," I said.

"I guess what it does, it gives us a fighting chance. When Cluny tries somethin', we'll have a little extra back up."

The gaiety of the fiesta came with the people as they filled the bar and overflowed into the restaurant. We moved back to our regular table in the main room. Many of the people I knew waved or came by, promised to see me at the bullring on Sunday and went on their way. Chuy and Luis stopped, drink in hand, sat awhile and then moved on. Natale arrived and wanted to know if we were going to eat. He had shrimp and would add all the garlic I wanted.

"Natale," Dick said, "You've had them here. Tonight's my turn."

"Of course," Natale laughed. "Maybe Alfonso and I will come too," he said and looked around the raucous restaurant. "I could use some quiet." He went to another table.

The few that knew what had happened there on Thursday seemed to have put it behind them or were too caught up in the carousing to care. A *mariache* group strolled through the bar and into the restaurant, playing and singing loudly.

"From me to you," Alfonso said, using *ustesdes* the Spanish plural for you, as he delivered a tray of drinks to our table.

"Sit," I said.

"Too busy," he smiled. "Natale said we may join you later."

"You can get away?"

He laughed happily. "When they get hungry and realize they have only taco change, they will go."

He left when a waiter came for him with a customer's charge slip.

"Where the hell'd you go?" Howard yelled as he led the others in through the rear entrance. Most of his holler was lost in the merriment of the crowd.

Jesús came with them, Sully and Juan were last to enter. The look on Sully's face told it all, he'd been unable to get them to go anywhere but *Alfonso's*. Even drunk, they'd been with me too many times not to know my routine.

"What are you drinkin'?" Bryan asked, looked at our drinks, and pushed his way into the bar.

"Sorry," Sully mouthed and pulled an empty chair to our table. "Rául helped get us out and into a taxi, but they wanted to come here."

"At least we tried," I said.

By the time Bryan returned with a tray of drinks, we sat squeezed in at a table for eight. Bryan passed out the drinks; he'd gotten them all right, and stood beside us.

"Salud," he toasted in Spanish and drank.

Mike passed around napkin vignettes Paul had drawn during the afternoon. Some were of us and others were of people who had caught his attention at the fiesta. The few of Sonia and Jesús were excellent.

"Where the hell'd you go," Howard asked again. "Can I smoke?"

"We lost you," I lied. "Everyone have a good time?"

They all talked at once. Juaquin sat quietly, an all-knowing grin pasted on his weathered face.

Jesús called the roving *mariache* band to our table and requested a love song. Sonia gave me a quick smile; I glanced at Jesús and knew it was for her. They strummed their guitars, plucked the large base, while the violinist vied with them, the trumpet player played loudly and when they were done, we were mostly deaf. Jesús paid them and because they knew who he was, offered another song for free.

"Would you like to choose?" he said to Sonia, his blood shot eyes focusing on her pretty face.

She asked for a song in Spanish and the musicians beamed their approval and began. She said something to me, but I didn't hear her.

"Excuse me," I whispered into her ear and got up.

She smiled, finally realizing no one could hear with the music on top of us.

I shook my head when Rob stared at me and stood. I mouthed the word: head, and pushed myself through the rabble and into the bar. The crowd was boisterous, but better than sitting next to a playing trumpet.

Shouts of recognition came from some of the men buried too deep in the crowd to shake hands or slap my back in greetings. What everyone agreed on was that we'd see one another on Sunday afternoon.

Two men I recognized, but whose names didn't come to mind, exited the men's room as I entered. One of them held the door for me and we promised to talk later, the evening was still young.

The chaos and music filled the men's room, even with the door closed. After using the urinal, I splashed cold water on my face and washed my hands. In the large mirror I saw a man come from one of the stalls. He was huge, well over six-foot, more massive than Norm. Long black hair was pulled straight back in a ponytail, a hooked nose was prominent on his weathered Native American face. He nodded to me when he saw I was staring. I smiled back and began to wipe my hands on paper towels. He wore faded jeans, old cowboy boots, and a worn black leather jacket. When he reached past me for paper towels, I saw white strands of hair mixed in his thick black mane. We tossed our wrinkled paper towels in the trash at the same time. I laughed quietly as I turned to him. The coldness of his black eyes caused me to end the chuckle.

"Mick." He said my name flatly, without changing his inert expression.

"Hi," I said and hoped someone would walk in. No one did. "Loud out there," I said and took a step toward the door.

"Crowded out there," he said and put his hand on my shoulder.

"Do I know you?" I stopped and he walked next to me. "No."

"Can I do something for you?"

"Yeah."

"What?" I said after a long anxious moment.

"You have to come with me."

"I do?"

"Yeah. Outside."

"I'm with some friends."

"You don't want them to come along."

"What the hell do you want?" I said and reached in back for my gun.

"Ah shit, man, don't pull the gun," he said, and almost laughed. From his jacket, he pulled a grenade that was lost in his large hand. Without saying anything, he pressed the grenade handle down and pulled out the pin. "Here," he handed the pin to me.

"What am I supposed to do with this?" My gun was still in its holster.

"Give it back to me when we're outside." His expression didn't change. He wasn't angry or excited. "Look it," he went on after a minute of silence, "my job is to get you outside."

"If I don't want to go?"

"Everyone has a choice."

"And mine are?"

"This is a fragmentation grenade." He held it up for me to see. "I have another one," he tapped his other pocket. "You come with me, nothing happens in here. You don't, I toss it into the bar. If I do that, the men waiting outside come in and if they have to do that, there'll be a firefight. Norm and Dick are armed and I expect Dick has half the jarheads from Camp Pendleton with him. They'll fight and a lot of innocent people will die."

"What about you and me?" Our eyes stayed locked on each other. Another friend of Norm's.

"By the time you've pulled your gun and fired a shot, I've tossed the grenade and pulled my gun." His tone remained flat, uncommitted.

"I get the first shot."

"It won't kill me," he said and almost smiled. "My first shot will kill you."

"I thought Cluny wanted me alive?"

"Time's running out for him. Dead or alive, he doesn't care. He's paying me three times my normal rate, that's why I'm here."

"And that's worth dying for?"

"That's the price I put on my life. Hell, you know what we Indians say, don't you?"

"It's a good day to die?"

"Yeah," he smiled. "What about the Irish?"

I didn't answer him. "What do I call you, Chief?"

"Chief will do. I'm not bluffing," he said quietly, returning to his objective.

"All these innocent people, you don't care about them?"

"Naw. But you do," he said triumphantly. "Let me explain something. The government trained me not to care. They dropped me in a God forsaken void called Viet Nam and ordered me to destroy the enemy . . . and the enemy was anything that moved. It's what I do . . . I'm better paid now, but it's what I do."

"What if I just turn and walk out?"

"I won't let you."

"Someone's bound to come in."

"They die with us."

"You're doing this for money?"

"What else is there?"

"Morality."

"Ain't no such thing, Mick. Take some advice. Tell Cluny what he wants to know. You're gonna tell him, one way or another. No reason to die here. I don't know if you work for Norm or not . . . I've never heard of you. Cluny won't kill you, Mick. He's a coward and he'll only kill when there's nothing to come back on him because of it. He knows Norm will find him if he kills you. But there are a lot of other things he can do to get you to talk . . . and by the rules, if you walk away . . ." He didn't finish. "Want to follow me?" he said to break the silence.

"You'll lead the way?"

"Sure, you won't shoot me in the back."

"How do you know?"

"First you should know that time's running out." He glanced at his wristwatch. "If I don't bring you out soon, they'll come in. You won't shoot me because you've got scruples. Norm doesn't have 'em, that's why I think he's covering for you, but there ain't no reason for me to tell anyone that. You coming?" he said and walked past me. "We'll walk through the bar and out the back exit," he said without turning to see what I was doing. "Okay?"

"What choice do I have?"

"Not a good day to die?" He held the door open for me, everything about him cold and empty.

"That's way in my future."

"Be careful, the future has a habit of sneaking up on you," he said and closed the door. "Don't pull the gun on them when we get outside," he said calmly.

I pushed ahead of him, elbowed my way through the bar and into the back of the restaurant. My mind wandered, where were Rob and Jeffrey? How long before they'd wonder about me. If they'd found me, what would I have done? I had no doubt that Chief would toss the grenade at the slightest provocation. There were so many people standing I couldn't see our table. He walked past me with a blank expression on his face and stopped two tables away. He looked at me, our eyes caught, and then he gazed around the crowded room. His callous expression didn't change as he waited for me.

"Leaving?" Alfonso said as he came from the kitchen.

"Fresh air," I smiled weakly and pushed toward the rear exit parking lot, scared shitless.

May 6, 1995
10 p.m.

chapter *TWENTY TWO*

Men mingled in the shadows of the lighted parking lot, talking, smoking, and taking a breath of fresh air after drinking in the congested restaurant. A star filled sky went unnoticed above them, while energized tumult wafted from the building. Chief tapped my shoulder and walked past me. I hesitated. I could've run back into *Alfonso's*. Did the rear door lock? Of course, it did, but could I have locked it? What difference would it have made? Cluny's men would've got in, locked or unlocked and they were probably out front too. The walled in parking lot offered me no choice. Who were those men that milled about? Were they going back inside? Would they have taken a message for me or were they working for Cluny?

Nervousness kept my mind wandering, looking for escape when I knew there was no escape. I went unnoticed as I walked through the dimness.

"Give me the gun, Mick," Chief said calmly as I approached.

We were almost at the street. I looked over my shoulder, saw all the shadowy figures moving about and sadness welled up in me. Was I a coward because I turned the gun over without attempting to use it? Was it cowardly letting it get that far?

Chief held his large hand out and showed me the hand grenade.

"I'm not afraid of that." I half shouted the lie.

"I know," he grinned coolly. "Put the pin back in."

I'd forgotten all about the pin and had to search my pockets for it. When I found the pin, I gazed at it and wondered about all the misery it embodied. On the third try, I slipped the pin in place. Chief made no mention of my shaking hands.

"It would be better if you gave me the gun," he said again, after returning the grenade to his jacket. "Your chances are no better here, than they were in there," he said, his large hand held out, as I faltered.

"Where's your gun?" I asked, still thinking about cowardice.

"In my pocket," he said patting his leather jacket.

"Small caliber," I told him, knowing I would give over my own gun.

"Cop killer bullets, Mick. Effective." His eyes cold and flat, a small half grin on his face,

"At least tell me I'm surrounded," I said as I carefully pulled the automatic from my back.

"You were surrounded before Norm showed up," he said and took my gun.

"What now?"

He nodded toward a white Jeep that was beginning to back out of a parking spot. "You'll go with them. Remember, tell him what he wants to know."

"I don't know where Seámus is," I said and hoped what I did know was too old to be useful.

"I can't help you there," he said grimly. "I'll get the gun back to Dick," he laughed cruelly and drifted to the street, leaving me with the two Latinos who got out of the Jeep.

Both men were neatly dressed in casual attire and each had a large black pistol grip sticking out over his belt. Their stares were noncommittal.

The driver pointed toward the side of the Jeep, spreading his hands to let me know they were going to frisk me. I leaned against the Jeep, as I'd done in many foreign countries, and was frisked. When they were convinced I was unarmed, the door was held open for me. I looked around the busy parking lot and seemed to have gone unnoticed by those that milled about.

Tinted windows and no interior light muted the back of the Jeep. As I began to pull myself inside, a hand, hidden in the shadows, reached out and savagely jerked me in, smashed me solidly between the eyes and as I raised my arms for protection I was punched in the stomach. My lungs emptied as I doubled over onto the floor and as I tried to breathe, a loose sack was yanked over my head.

"Do not remove the hood," someone said in guttural Spanish.

I couldn't breathe and at the same time I was trying not to vomit, the taste of stale beer and spicy tacos inched up into my throat. In a panic, my hands went for the hood and I was kicked in the shoulder, halting my panic with more pain. I began to take shallow breaths, the cotton hood sucked into my mouth as I did. I spit it out and forced myself not to vomit. My head hurt and stars exploded in front of my opened eyes. Dazed, I slowly tried to control my breathing.

I felt the Jeep move out of the parking lot and onto the street, jolting me as I lay on the floor. No one spoke. I probably should've paid more attention to turns and stops, but all my efforts went into not vomiting as the driver sped along. There were sharp turns in the road; quirky sudden stops and potholes hit without care, all of which turned my nauseous stomach and made my already aching head throb worse.

Finally, we slowed and jounced along, and I guessed we were driving on large cobblestones. Splashes of light fell into the Jeep as we continued over the stone road and I thought of streetlights. As I focused more attention to those odd details, my nausea faded. The Jeep slowed almost to a stop and the horn beeped, sending pain through my sensitive head.

I heard a squeaking noise and then the Jeep turned and the squeaking noise was behind us. It had to be a gate opening and closing. For a brief moment, I was proud of my deduction, and then realized it also meant we were where I was being taken. The Jeep stopped.

For an instant, there was silence and I could hear crickets and a rustling of bushes. The door opened, whoever sat above me moved and then helped me without saying anything. As I backed out of the Jeep, a light turned on and the area around me brightened. I could see dimly through the hood and realized there were prints on the cotton material. They had used a pillowcase to distort my vision. The air was cool, a breeze drifted over me and I heard waves wash against the shore.

As frightened as I was, I assumed we were somewhere along the Pacific coast and not too far from Tijuana. There were crowded housing colonies, beginning at the Bullring by the Sea, which stretched the Pacific coast of Baja, to Ensenada, 65 miles away. Many of the colonies were home to Americans who preferred the beachfront prices of Baja to those of Southern California. Other beach areas held large isolated homes within small-gated communities.

"*Muevete,*" I was ordered and a large hand rested on my shoulder and forced me ahead.

I allowed myself to be led along a cobble stone walk. Whispers were lost in the rustling breeze. Where was I? My best guess, then, was somewhere past *Playa Rosarito* and we must have driven the old road, since I knew we hadn't stopped to pay any tolls.

My guide turned me left and the breeze lessened. The light dimmed here too and my vision, what little I had, was gone. We stopped for a moment, I heard a door open to my right, and then I was turned in that direction and forcefully pushed from behind. I tripped over something, caught myself, and heard a door close. Faint light seeped through my pillow case hood and I stood in silence. The light came from above. I waited for someone to say something or move me along. Silence.

I turned, thought I might see someone, but there was no one visible in the shadows. I winced in pain as I raised my arm to remove the hood. I yanked it off and dropped it to the floor. I touched my tender nose and was relieved to find no crusted blood. The swelling would go down and my throbbing head would get back to normal soon enough.

There were no windows in the cinder block room and the only light hung high above. As I walked around, I saw large eyebolts fastened to the block walls, spaced at about five feet, four to each wall. One wall had a small solid door that was locked with a dead bolt. Off in one corner was a waterspout and attached to it a long green garden hose. One wooden chair sat off center of the room and close to it was a large mesh covered floor drain.

Fear wrenched at my aching stomach. After the *Sandanistas* defeated Samoza, journalists were given tours of the National Guard prisons. As bad as the prisons were, the most horrifying tour came when we visited the military buildings within the capital. In the basements, these building held cells, smaller than the room I was in, but similar enough to make my body twinge. Blood stained the walls of those small cells, evidence of the torture that had taken place in them. Here there was a water hose and drain. Samoza's soldiers used buckets of water to wash out their torture chambers.

I quickly reminded myself of what Chief had said about Cluny fearing Norm and because of that I would not be killed. It did little to soothe my anxiety. As I tried to control my breathing, I walked in circles around the square room. When I tried to stay away from the chair, remembering Norm's demonstration at *Alfonso's*, I found myself getting too close to the walls, walls I didn't want to look at. I looked up as I walked, trying to think what I really knew that could hurt Seámus. By then, I assumed, Dick and Norm were looking for me. What good was it going to be? I didn't know. I refused to believe that either Norm or Dick knew of that location, but the thought stayed and add to my anguish. What had happened to Benny?

Before I got too dizzy, I stopped. My eyes had adjusted to the dimness and I walked to the door. It was hard wood, with a good-sized spy hole in it that opened from the outside and was well hinged. I felt along the wall, slowly moving away from the door and toward the closest eyebolts. Below the first two I came to the wall was rough, scratched by something. My hands passively circled the cracks and dents and I knew they were not part of the decor.

My head pounded, as if an explosive pain from the wall rushed up my arm and erupted in my skull. Of course, I knew better, the pain came from the blow I received in the Jeep. As badly as I wanted to sit, I stayed away from the wooden chair.

I circled the room, no longer examining the walls, and avoided the chair. There were mind games I played, trying to figure out how long before I told what I knew and by what method they would get me to talk.

It would be a game to Cluny, I realized, and the longer he prolonged it, the happier he'd be. It was, very possibly, a deadly game for me; one I had no chance of winning. The idea of telling everything I knew, as soon as Cluny walked through the door, spiraled through my mind.

Bright light lit up the room, blinding me. I covered my eyes and winced as I raised my arms, while my head hammered from the brightness. When I looked down at the cement floor, the reflective light forced my eyes to close. The door opened, but my eyes hadn't adjusted to the brightness so I couldn't see who entered. Primal fear told me I knew.

May 6, 1995
    11:45 p.m.

chapter TWENTY THREE

Intense light blinded me, hurt my head as I tried to look into it, but even so, I turned to where I thought the door was. I sensed movement near me and turned slightly, in time to see a foggy ghost image. Breath left me as I bent over in pain from a fierce blow to my stomach and I remember wondering, what hit me? I didn't go down and guess I was supposed to, because the phantom then slapped his open palms against my ears with such force that I went down hard, a ringing sound vibrated through my aching head while I lay in a fetal position. I heard mumbling, or thought I did, but the pain in my head suppressed sounds. Something heavy, a foot forced my head down onto the hard, cold-concrete floor and I prepared myself for a kick, covering my head with my arms, as best I could. Someone kicked me in the back, between my shoulders, forcing my held down head to scrape along the floor.

There were more muffled sounds and then I was picked up and abandoned heedlessly onto the chair. The shock I felt when I realized where I had been dropped jarred me into consciousness.

Parts of my face, that had scraped the floor, burned and as I touched my cheek, I felt the stickiness of fresh blood curdled into my beard. My eyes adjusted to the brightness and I saw three men in front of me. One was Cluny, still in his wrinkled and stained clothing from that afternoon.

"So good of you to join me," Cluny laughed wantonly, when he caught me focused on him.   The men next to him didn't change expression; they stood there silently, my ghost images taking shape. No one was armed.

"If I 'ad the time," he said contently, after a moment, "this would be a long interview." His eyes twinkled in the bright light, his puny mouth smiled as he walked toward me.

I prepared myself for him to come from behind, remembering Norm's example, but he stopped a few steps in front of me.

"One day, Murphy," he smiled monstrously. "One day we will meet on more acceptable terms. I promise." He turned and walked back between the men.

"I 'ave no time for your lies . . . it is a shame, of course, because I am interested in 'ow long it would take to break you . . . another time, as I 'ave promised."

"I'm not lying," I mumbled. "I don't know where Seámus is, so there's nothing to lie about." I forced a smile and felt my insides twist with anxiety as he smiled back.

"All the more shame," he said, a smirk pasted on his fleshy face. "The good doctor will give you a shot and you will tell the truth. If you 'ave nothing to tell me about the priest, maybe you will 'ave something to divulge about our friend, Norm and his Brazilian nigger."

The large door scraped opened and a tall, thin man carrying a small satchel emerged from the shadowy outside. His crumpled clothing hung on him as if they covered a skeleton, while his large bushy eyebrows kept his otherwise hairless, loose flesh from sliding from his skull. Black circles ringed his eyes and his nostrils looked raw, his lank mouth closed, while his upper lip quivered. The rasp of the closing door seemed to hasten his approach.

"There is some activity outside," he said quietly in Spanish as he put the satchel down. He looked at Cluny.

"Do not be concerned," Cluny barked in Spanish. "*El*," he uttered as he leered at me.

If his bones had creaked as he bent to open the bag, I wouldn't have been surprised, but they didn't. From the bag, he took a small bottle and a syringe. He filled the syringe from the bottle of clear liquid and squirted a small stream into the air. When he was satisfied the syringe worked he turned to Cluny, who mumbled something to my two ghosts. They walked swiftly to the chair and held me down by my throbbing shoulders, even though I'd not attempted to stand.

"I don't know where Seámus is," I said, again, vainly and was startled when the door flew open. The shadowy night was gone and bright light shown outside.

"They are here," a fat man yelled in Spanish from the opening. He held an M-16 in his hand.

"Hold them," Cluny growled the command and the fat man left, closing the door behind him. "Now," he said to the doctor.

They are here, I hoped, meant Benny and the Marines had finally arrived. I didn't know what kind of security surrounded the property, but I guessed it to be good, very good. With the door closed, all exterior sounds were locked out. Feeling some relief, I attempted to resist the two men holding me down.

"Keep him still," the doctor whined.

"What good is this going to do?" I was held firmly in the chair.

"Shut up," Cluny wailed. "Now," he yelled at the doctor.

He smelled badly and when I stared at him, I saw shaking, dirty hands holding the syringe. He stabbed the needle through my shirt and into my upper arm. I yelled and then the needle was pulled out, empty of its liquid. I expected to feel something strange, but didn't. The two thugs who held me, walked away and when Cluny nodded toward the door, they escorted the doctor out.

With the door held open, I could hear the soft pop of small arms fire and then the rapid pop, pop, pop, pop, of automatic fire. The outside was lit up and the frail doctor stood by the opened door and turned to Cluny, his eyes void of emotion.

"Come doctor." The fat man appeared and led the doctor away.

"Soon," Cluny said patiently, as if he'd read my mind.

"Soon, what?" I said, no longer caring about the chair. I pressed the soles of my tennis shoes against the hard floor and felt the pressure, relieved I still had feeling in my legs. What would happen? I wondered and stood slowly.

"Where is the terrorist?" Cluny said calmly.

"I don't know," I said proud of myself and stood behind the chair, facing him. "I didn't know when you asked me on Thursday and I don't know now."

"Is 'e in the United States?" He ignored my statement. "'Ow did you get 'im there?"

My face felt flushed and my eyes were sore and hot, they felt like they would explode. I held onto the back of the chair with one hand and painfully raised the other and rubbed my eyes. It didn't help.

"The medication works on the brain," Cluny said slowly. "An overdose will cause blood vessels to burst," he scoffed without moving, "and it appears the victim died from a brain hemorrhage, which is convenient. That is why I did not give you the shot." He continued to sneer, his ugly mouth held in forced grin. "Extended use, over a short period of time, has the same results. At this time, that is not a concern of yours.

"You came 'ere to 'elp the terrorist."

"I didn't know Seámus was here."

"You arranged to meet 'im at *'otel Caesar*."

"He found me there."

"By arrangement?"

"No."

"You took 'im back to your 'otel."

"Yes."

"Why?"

"He looked ill. I wanted to help him."

"Did you?"

"Yes."

" 'Ow?"

"He cleaned up in my hotel room. I fed him, gave him clean clothes and money."

I listened as if the words came from someone else. When he asked a question, his voice was steady, not threatening or demanding. I bit down on my lips, but answered in spite of myself. I held onto the chair, afraid to fall. I didn't want to give Cluny the satisfaction of seeing me look up at him. I wasn't sure how much longer I'd get away with it when the door opened and one of his Indian guards stood there. He was armed as he'd been at *Alfonso's* on Thursday.

He spoke rapidly, but it sounded like gibberish, not a form of Spanish, as it had sounded Thursday when he spoke and Norm had talked with him. My eyes were beginning to water and my arm was numb. Faintly, I heard the retort of small arms fire from outside. One of the thugs left the room, the other one and the Indian stayed.

"Is the priest in Mexico?" Cluny said, his voice edgy.

The Indian stood in the doorway, blocking most of the bright light. I turned from him and looked at Cluny.

"I'm not sure."

"Where is the priest going?"

"Home."

"Where is home?"

"The United States."

The Indian said something in gibberish and when I looked toward the door, he had turned away from us. Cluny answered him, his gibberish spoken in anger.

"Where in the United States?" he said.

"Rockport Beach." I fought myself and tried not to respond. My head began to pound and my eyes watered.

"Where is Rockport Beach?" he said, his words filled with stress. He moved slowly, speaking to the Indian.

"California," I mumbled, biting my lip.

"You live in California."

"Yes."

"In Rockport Beach?"

"Yes," I said.

"You son of a whore," he shouted triumphantly in Spanish and kicked the chair out from my grasp. "I knew you set this up. No one believed me," he cackled.

I went to the floor as soon as the chair slid away. I looked up and Cluny looked down, satisfaction glowed on his stodgy face.

"No." I cried. "No."

"Bloody 'ell." He kicked my shoulder, sending more pain through me. "Where is the priest?" he yelled as he walked away. He stopped at the door and turned to me. "Where?"

"I don't know," I growled.

"I will get you . . . and I will get 'im," he said quietly and took his gun and holster from the Indian. "In the end I will get you both," he said, his back to me. He walked out the door, closed it with a bang and then the room went black. I heard the bolt lock shut in place.

There wasn't a part of me that didn't hurt. I tried to stand, but couldn't, I hadn't any strength left. With considerable effort, I turned onto my stomach and inched my way forward until I came to one of the walls. Cautiously, but with pain, I turned and was able to sit, my back against the wall.

I closed my eyes to the darkness and rubbed them, not knowing if the tears that followed were from the pain in my shoulder or from the medication the dreary doctor had shot into me. Somewhere within the fog I was slowly slipping into, I remembered murmuring a pray of thanks.

A loud banging at the door snapped my eyes open. All I saw was solid darkness. I heard sounds from outside, but was unable to understand them and then more pounding.

I remember wondering if the pounding was in my head and I needed to know when the burning would stop. I had no answers. I covered my ears, was surprised at the pain, and then remembered the foggy palms smashing against them. When I pulled my hands away, the pain in my head and shoulders sent shudders through me. Without warning, the heavy door exploded inward, sending smoky light into the room. I began to choke on the cordite smell and tried to stand, but couldn't.

Images appeared at the door, first one, then another. A beam of light shot into the room and when it found me it stopped. The person holding the light walked toward me. I stared, knowing it had to be one of the Marines.

"Mick," the excited voice called.

I recognized it as Alfonso's, but knew that couldn't be right. As he drew closer I saw him, he held a machine pistol and was dressed in black.

"Alfonso?" I mumbled. My eyes hurt and the smoke choked me, but I knew I saw Alfonso. Something was wrong. He wasn't involved. Where were Norm, Dick, or Sonia?

He helped me up and said, "Walk along with me. Everything is all right."

"Alfonso?" I said again.

"You are safe, Mick. Come on," he said in rapid Spanish and helped me out of the room.

That's all I remember. When I finally came around, I was told what had happened.

May 7, 1995
  1:30 a.m.

chapter TWENTY FOUR

The easiest way to explain it is that it was like watching a movie or a police action from behind the yellow crime scene tape. I viewed from the sidelines as Alfonso carried someone from the block building, observed as he led that person through a group I knew to be Marines, as they returned small arms fire to protect the two escapees. Another way to explain it is to call it an out-of-body experience. That is what it seemed like. When the escape was explained to me, I knew it to be true because I had watched it happen.

. . . .

I knew I was in a downtown produce warehouse, as I became aware of what was happening around me, because I'd observed two Marines move me from the van and into the building.

"Rip Van Winkle," Norm said from his seat as I moved.

"More like Sleeping Beauty," Dick said from across the room.

Men all dressed in dark clothing, moved about, dodging between large wooden crates and hills of fresh produce. I spotted Jeffrey and Rob, not Benny, and didn't know if any of the others I didn't recognize were either Jesses or James. I stood slowly, no help was offered from Norm or Dick. My body ached, my eyes raged and my mouth was dry.

Rifles, mostly M-16s, but a few others I recognized as Galil's, their 50- round magazines black and intimidating, rested against crates, while the group of men rushed about. On top of a table, as I stood, I saw four Street Sweeper shotguns, their portentous round drums held a vast amount of shells and could shoot twelve in about as many seconds.

"Where's Alfonso?" I slowly walked to where Norm and Dick waited.

"He'll be back," Norm smiled. "Sit," he said and held a chair out. "You'll feel better in a little while."

"Says you." I looked around at all the activity. "How'd you find me?"

"Alfonso saw you leave," Dick said. "Benny picked you up as soon as you walked outside.   "Here." Dick handed me the automatic I'd given Chief. "He returned it," he smirked.

"And?" I took the gun and returned it to the holster I had all but forgotten about.

"Jesse followed you in one car and James backed him up in another and they kept in radio contact with Benny," Dick said. "When we knew you were gone, I contacted back up at my place and we waited."

I looked from Dick to Norm and then back to Dick. "Sonia?"

"With Seámus. What did you tell Cluny?"

I looked at Norm.

"I know everything, now," he told me coldly.

"How'd you do it?" I turned back to Dick.

He looked at his watch. "They're in Ensenada. From there a fisherman will take them out to a sea plane," he grinned arrogantly.

"They should be three miles off Rockport Beach and meeting Sully before five. They're a lot safer than you are, right now."

"Sully will pick them up in a boat?" I stammered.

"I don't think he can drive the police cruiser out there."

"Dino will help him," Norm said.

"Now tell me what Cluny knows," Dick said.

"I couldn't help myself," I said sadly. "He knows Seámus is going to Rockport Beach."

"That's it?" Dick said, doubt in his tone.

"I think so. A guy that looked like death shot me up with something. Christ. Was he scary looking. Cluny began to ask questions and I couldn't believe I answered him . . . but I did. He didn't have much time to ask and then your people arrived. What did he give me?"

"An Israeli potion," Norm said. "It's supposed to kill you . . . eventually," he said. "The Israelis stopped using it in their interrogations because it was too lethal. Too many of their prisoners were dying. Now it's finding its way into Central and South America,"

"He told me the part about it killing the prisoner. Said we'd meet again. I guess it was his warning, a threat."

"And probably meant every word. He got away."

"Wasn't he supposed to?"

"Yeah," Norm said. "But he's still here and we've gotta get you across the border."

"I have friends here," I said as firmly as I could.

"They think you've gone back because of a story. Juaquin, Chuy, and a couple of Rául's *federales* are watching them."

"Mick," Dick insisted sharply, "did you tell Cluny about me? My place?"

"He didn't ask about you, just Seámus and where he was."

"And you said . . . "

"I didn't know. It was the truth. I couldn't help answering him, but he didn't ask the right questions. I guess in time. . ." I mumbled and left it at that.

"Sully, he okay with all this?" I said after a minute.

"Juan and Sully are heading back to meet Seámus and Sonia," Norm said. "I called Dino as back up, just incase. I wish you would've trusted me."

"I couldn't give Seámus up . . . and you would've."

"It was all chance?" he said. "You didn't plan this?"

"I hadn't thought of Seámus in a long time," I said.

"No dice nada, gringo." Alfonso scoffed as he entered the room. He hugged me as I stood. "You look better."

"I feel better," I said and rubbed my eyes. "Thank you."

"Been awhile," he said with a leer at Dick.

"Is there anything cold to drink?" I said, my dry mouth began to bother me more than my burning eyes.

Alfonso opened a crate and pulled out a warm bottle of Mexican mineral water. He opened it and handed it to me. "The best we have to offer."

"Thank you," I said and took a long swallow. "What happened?" I said as Alfonso sat. "What's going on here?"

"They knew we'd come," Alfonso began.

"Eventually," Norm said.

"It was all for show," Alfonso grinned. "We blew the gate, they shot up the road, we fired back, and they retreated to the beach. Cluny locked you in and left by boat," he said, feigning disappointment.

"We've got twenty-five men here, now," Dick said. "We're preparing to leave."

"To where?"

From his back pocket, Dick pulled a folded map of Tijuana and San Diego and spread it across the table. "Our first thought was to cross at the *Otay Mesa* border station. It's closed, closes at 10 p.m.," he said to me as he pointed to its location on the map. "The area is unpopulated . . . but there's too much open ground when we get on the other side."

"On the U.S. side?" I said, puzzled at his concern for the American area.

"Something you should be made aware of," Dick mumbled and looked at Norm.

"Information we've received has the Border Patrol and the Immigration people pulled back. We're not sure what it means, but there haven't been any night patrols along the *San Ysidro* area . . . no jeeps through the *arroyo* or choppers, with their spotlights, in the sky. Been that way for two days now."

"The American government's in on this?" I said loudly.

"Who's the government, Mick?" Norm said. "You mean the president? No, he ain't aware of this. Congress? No, probably not, not all of them," he smirked. "This shit here," he opened a drawer and pulled out a large brown envelope and tossed it to me, "will do little more than bring embarrassment to some people. Nothing they can't handle, but it would be better for them if it were avoided. They make a call . . . maybe to Langley, maybe not. A couple of more calls are made, favors called in . . . and the border patrol and everyone else involved is pulled back. It's no big thing, believe me," he said with indifference.

I opened the envelope as he spoke. It contained the documents Seámus had promised me. "Where'd you get these?" I said and thought for a moment everyone there was somehow involved in helping Cluny. "How?" I shouted.

"Thursday night," Alfonso stated quietly, "you remember Thursday night?" he grinned. "After everyone came back to Luis' restaurant, I left to lock up my place. I found them easily, Mick."

"I didn't have much time," I said. "How come you're involved in this?"

"Even Mexico has its secret agents," he taunted with a grin. "I've retired, but I haven't died."

"You should be in the restaurant business," I said to Norm with a snicker.

"Too dangerous," he joked back.

"Explain something to me," I said and was met by silence.

"If you've chased Cluny away and by tomorrow noon the Mexican government demands he leave, what's all this about?"

"This is my city, Mick," Alfonso said, finally breaking the silence. "Come," he beckoned.

The three of us followed him through the maze of crates and hills of produce to the front of the warehouse and then up a narrow stairway to a small office. Alfonso opened the door and led us into the dark room.

"Look out there," he said and then opened louvered blinds.

Streetlights haloed dimly in my view, a few windows reflected light and an eerie darkness palled the neighborhood.

"I don't see anything," I said.

"Out there," Alfonso said, as he pointed out and up.

In the far off hills, where I knew the shantytowns were, a fiery glow danced in the darkness, as if the sun was setting behind them. As I stared harder, I could make out flashing red lights as they darted about.

"What is it?" I kept looking.

"Cluny's making one last effort to locate the priest," Alfonso said hostilely. "Rául's people can't keep up with them . . . and he isn't sure how many are really trying.

"I have never seen Tijuana this unsafe," he said bitterly. "Everything is closed, the streets are dangerous . . . they have even broke into churches. They locate refugees from Central America and terrorize them and when that doesn't work, Cluny's people burn . . . God only knows how many have died tonight."

"How can he get away with this?"

"He isn't doing this." Alfonso roared. "He's at police headquarters preparing his paper work so he can leave tomorrow. But he's responsible. Do you doubt that?" he said as he closed the louvered blinds.

"No," I said as we left the dark room and went back down stairs. "What can we do?"

"We can't stop him," Dick mumbled as we stood over the table that held the map of San Diego and Tijuana. "Impossible."

"We have to make Cluny think Seámus has made it across the border," Norm said. "We have to cross where he'll have men who'll try to stop us."

"That's why all this," Dick grinned. "We'll cross in force and make a hell of a fight of it."

"Okay," I said, hoping my nervousness was hidden. "Where and when?"

"When? Right away. Where?" Alfonso mumbled.

"Has anyone heard from Benny?" Dick yelled out to the active men. No one answered. "We're switching to cars with Mexican plates, old cars and hope we can get through the streets without causing any trouble. That's what they're doing." He motioned towards the men entering and leaving the warehouse.

"Benny's back," Jeffrey called out from the doorway.

Benny swaggered in; his dark baseball cap pulled down tight and was followed closely by a Latin soldier. His eyes were excited and his grin sincere.

"Nice to see you," he said to me. "I keep my promises."

"No one appreciates that more than I do," I said and told myself not to worry about the exhilaration I saw on his face.

"We found a place," he said quickly and pulled a rolled up map from beneath his jacket. He spread it over the larger map. "Past the cemetery, on the route that goes to the Ensenada toll road, there's a couple of old dirt streets . . . narrow and filled with holes . . ." he pointed at a wiggly line on the map. "It's high ground that looks down on the fence and the river." He pointed out the fence that separates Mexico and the United States and the Tijuana River as it flows into San Diego. "There are no street lights and none of Cluny's goons are in the area. It's almost an invitation," he cackled like a witch.

"Can you see across into *San Ysidro?*" Norm said.

"With night goggles," Benny smiled. "Street lights over there ain't workin' either. The river's low and it's darker than my ex-wife's heart."

"Any movement?"

"Me and Wayne and Juan here, we saw some bushes move," he laughed contently. "They're down there, but no way to count 'em. Wayne's there with a radio," he pointed to his own, "Just incase."

"Do you think he'd leave the high ground open?" Dick said.

"What's at our back if we take the high ground?" Norm said.

"The cemetery has walls and gates. Walls can be climbed and gates can be opened. There's a main drag movin' north ... "

"Calle Internacional," Dick said.

"Kind of quiet on that road," Benny's grin seemed to brighten. "After that it's two dirt roads, dilapidated two story apartments, some open yards, a couple of yelping dogs and then you come upon the fence."

"Any activity on the streets or apartments?"

"No lights. Real quite, like they've been deserted." Excitement filled each word; he was ready and looking forward to battle.

"Could be he pulled most everyone for the search and destroy duty," Dick said dubiously.

"He could also have a small cadre hidden in those apartments. We know," Norm looked toward Benny, "that he has people below, in the darkness. The darkness, the high ground, the deserted neighborhood, all suggests it's a good place to cross."

"Maybe he's counting on the inexperience of Seámus and the people he would use to get across," I said.

"Inexperience hasn't kept Seámus from getting this far," Dick said.

"Cluny knows we're here," Alfonso said quietly, "and helping. You have to factor that in."

"Agreed," Norm said. "*Otay Mesa* or here?" He pointed at where Benny had marked the map. "Jesus," Norm moaned as he studied the map. "Could he have mined the hill?"

"He's capable of anything," Dick said seriously.

"We get a couple of fifty-gallon drums and roll 'em down first," Benny said. "Half full of water."

"Can we?" Norm looked at Dick.

"They're used as trash bins all over the streets, it shouldn't be a problem," Dick said.

"What about the noise they'll make?" I said.

"If there are mines there, it'll wake them up," Norm said.

"Cluny's spotters will let them know we're coming before we're out of the cars," Dick said.   "What's our total man power?"

"Counting Alfonso's people . . ."

"And me," I said.

"Of course. Twenty six of us, ten from Alfonso."

"Let's do them." Norm's animosity began to show. "Twenty six of us cut through the fence and head down the hill. Only six hold back, when Cluny's force shows itself our six in frontal position and Alfonso's men from the rear confronts them. He's gotta be thin with all the shit goin' down out there," Norm growled as his arm rose and pointed to where the shanty fires burned.

"Okay with me," Alfonso said. "I am not interested in turning anyone over to Rául."

We all looked at him, understanding what he meant. There would be no prisoners.

"We will be Santa Anna and Cluny will be Davey Crockett," he taunted the three of us, all Americans.

"*Por que no?*" Dick said, speaking for all of us.

"Let's get everyone in here," Norm said, "and make this work. Who has the arms list?"

"I have the inventory," Rob called out and came toward us. "Everything we have is here." He handed Norm a clipboard.

"Hell." Norm yelled as he went through it. "After we kick Cluny's ass, let's take over Costa Rica. Where'd this stuff come from?"

"I only did the inventory, sir," Rob responded. "But my guess is most of it came from Viet Nam surplus."

"Dick." Norm called out humorously. "Are my tax dollars being spent on this?"

"When's the last time you paid taxes?" Dick said as he walked out to get his Marines together.

"Pick a weapon, Mick, any weapon," he smiled at me.

I opened the crate of Mexican mineral water and took a warm bottle out, opened it and drank. My stomach was in knots and if it hadn't been empty, I would've thrown up. I was nervous, very nervous and began to perspire. I felt small rivulets of perspiration run down my side. Was I the only one? Everyone was busy, doing something. I wanted to be busy. I had to find something to do or I was going to explode with fright.

"You're the expert," I told Norm. "What's best for me?"

He looked at the inventory list and then stared at me. "Something light but lethal," he mumbled to himself and read on.

May 7, 1995
  2 a.m.

chapter TWENTY FIVE

Fear. Bone chilling fear overwhelmed me as I sat there and watched young soldiers fatefully prepare to execute their profession. As they primed, Norm, Dick, Alfonso and Benny went over the map one more time.

"How many vehicles?" Norm said.

"Eight cars," Benny said.

"Four men in two cars, three in the rest," Dick said.

"Alfonso?"

"Five, two in each," he said without too much thought. "That's a total of thirteen," he teased blandly. "Hope no one's superstitious."

"We're okay if we don't run over any black cats." I tried to banter away my fear and received dull stares for my effort.

"We only have to put four in one," Norm said after turning away from me, "Wayne's in place."

"Right," Benny said.

"We approach from these three streets," Alfonso suggested and pointed out the three routes. "We meet here, at the cemetery."

"I'll take this street," Dick said, "It's the most direct route. Two of your cars, Alfonso, and two of ours."

"Radios in every car and change channels," Alfonso said. "Let's use channel thirteen" he grinned, "and hope we don't find Mick's black cats." For that twist on my quip, he received small laughs.

"I'll take this road," Norm pointed at the map, "and come in from the back of the cemetery. Alfonso, you come from the South, the Ensenada road."

"We meet behind the cemetery. We can't take the cars to the border fence," Alfonso mumbled, thinking. "Who will stay behind to lead your six men?"

"I will," Benny volunteered.

Alfonso looked to Dick who nodded his approval. "We'll stay in radio contact. As soon as you see someone approach, radio and we'll move. If we're wrong and Cluny isn't planning a rear assault, we'll pick you up."

"If there's no rear assault we should back up the others. I know they're down there waiting," Benny said matter-of-factly.

"This has to be a set up." Dick said coldly. "Cluny doesn't over look things. He may have pulled forces for the search and destroy, but he's hidden some reserve . . . and something we shouldn't forget ...he'll have these small cadres hidden in several places, *Otay Mesa* for one, where we're crossing, probably . . . and when the fight starts they'll be called for . . . as will anyone still in town."

"Maybe we should attempt a few crossings," Benny said. "Keep him wondering."

"No," Dick said quickly. "He's gotta think we're attempting to get the priest across. If he doubts it, he'll continue in the shanty towns."

"I agree," Alfonso said in support. "This is the only way."

They continued to plan and ignored me. I was too edgy to stand there with nothing to do, no reason to be in on their session. I went for another bottle of water and noticed that all the weapons and soldiers were gone. I walked to the door that led out back and was surprised by Jeffrey and Rob. They smiled at me and I nodded back.

"Everyone ready?" I said, not knowing what else to say. I looked out on to the dark parking lot, saw shadowy images move, and heard doors open and close. "No interior lights," I said and tried to make it sound like approval and not a question. The eerie dark calm awaited the four men standing around the table inside.

"We're ready," Rob said, and after a brief silence added, "When you come for the bullfight again, I'd like to tag along."

"Me too," Jeffrey said. "If you don't mind."

"My pleasure," I said, not knowing if there would be a next time for me, since Rául conceivably held me responsible for the marauders launched upon his city. Would he ever believe the truth, could he?

They seemed tranquil compared to my nervousness. Though I'd been in predicaments in the past where I had to defend myself, and know I've killed in those circumstances, there was never the wait, the preparation, as in Tijuana. I may not be a brave man, but I don't think of myself as one who would run when faced with risk. However I thought of myself, now that I'd seen these men, Norm and Dick, Alfonso, Jeffrey, Rob and especially Benny, I knew I could never handle situations like that on a regular basis. How did Norm do it? How did he leave comfort in Los Angeles for confrontations all around the world? I wondered, as I stared into the darkness and watched shadows weave about, if he ever thought he might not return?

When I heard steps behind me, I turned and saw the four of them as they smiled and talked softly.

"You ready, Mick?" Norm said.

"Ready as I'll ever be."

"Good," he smiled. "You two come with us," he said to Rob and Jeffrey.

They nodded but looked toward Dick as they did. He nodded in response and we headed into the darkness.

"You nervous?" Norm whispered and put his arm over my shoulder.

"Scared is more like it," I whispered back.

237

"If you weren't I'd be worried," he said and lightly slapped the back of my neck as he pulled his arm away. "Be as good as you were against the Amerasians in Rockport Beach and everything's gonna be okay."

"Do as I'm told, in other words?" We stopped by a car.

"In those exact words. Got a surprise for you when we get across," he laughed softly. "A big surprise. Our ace in the hole against these fuckers. Listen up," he spoke to Jeffrey and Rob. "We're going through town to the back of the old cemetery. Follow the white Chevy," he pointed at a car off to one side. "The streets may be deserted, but we need to keep our eyes open, anything is possible, take nothing for granted," he said.

It was too dark for me to see who left first, but slowly cars moved through the murky mirage and out into the poorly lighted street. Jeffrey got behind the wheel, Rob took shotgun, and Norm and I got in back. At no time, as doors opened and closed, did dome lights go on.

"Weapons?" I said as we began to move.

"In the trunk," Norm told me. "There's four in our convoy. We're the third car and have to go through town and then an upper middle class neighborhood. Once we're past the tourist sector, we should be okay. But the streets ain't safe, so be prepared and do what you're told," he said in a low voice, but we all knew he was addressing me.

The streets were dark, our headlights the only illumination. It was an eerie ride, moon shadows of buildings gobbled up in our headlights, people darted into doorways as we approached, unsure of who we were, as we were unsure of who they were. Off in the distance, in the direction we were headed, there was still the flicking red tint of the burning shantytowns and as we moved slowly through the darkness the stench of smoke, from the burning hills, became prevalent.

"Look at this," Norm said to no one in particular, his voice steady.

We all looked out side windows and then behind us, only seeing the one car following and the two slowly moving ahead of us. Darkness blanketed everything as we cut our way through the emptiness.

"What?" I said, unable to see what Norm did.

"No lights," he said flatly.

"There haven't been lights most of the way," I said.

"On the streets," he corrected me, "but behind shaded windows there were lights. Now nothing and this is an upscale neighborhood."

"What does it mean?" I looked out at the desolate buildings and knew he was right. We might as well have been in the graveyard we were headed to.

He laughed to himself. "He's shut power down. We're doing everything the way he expects."

"And you find that amusing?"

"Yeah. He's gotta be pulling out hair trying to figure why we're falling into his trap. Once we cross into the States, he'll have us covered on both flanks, with nowhere to run. We're smarter than that and he knows it."

"You've lost me." I said, my anxiety not helped by his amusement. "Why are we walking into a trap?"

"We know it's a trap, so it's not a trap. The point is, he's made a mistake and he's gotta be going bananas trying to figure out where," Norm laughed quietly. "He may even begin to pull men out of the shantytowns, thinking he needs them for a rear offensive. The fact is he's lost this one. Nothing he can do can change that."

"I'm still lost," I mumbled, but was glad to think Cluny might pull back from the shantytowns. Were they all crazy? "Why isn't the trap a trap?"

"My ace in the hole, Mick," he laughed. "The one thing he can't plan for, 'cause he couldn't imagine it."

"And that is?"

"A surprise," he continued to chuckle, "for a lot of people."

We cut through the darkness slowly, constantly prepared for an attack that never materialized. Our headlights offered the only illumination for blocks and it caused window shades to be ever so slightly pulled aside, as those in the upper middle-class neighborhood peeked out to see our nondescript vehicles creep by.   We moved from an area of pleasant homes through a section of up scale apartments, or maybe they were condos, and then the road became narrower and the apartments became older, with stores on the first floors, and as we slowly followed the road up hill, the buildings changed to old businesses and taco stands and with a sharp turn we were at the back wall of the antiquated cemetery.

Jeffrey steered the car next to the high stone wall, pulled close to the car we'd followed and shut off the headlights. We got out and stretched our legs. Dick was already there, his caravan parked further behind us. As he approached, we all quietly pulled our handguns. A nervous laughter came from all as we put the weapons away. Headlights cut through the darkness and we slid behind our four cars and waited, guns drawn. Alfonso's caravan pulled up across the street.

Trunks opened and weapons appeared. Norm handed me a dark jump suit and as I slipped it on, most everyone else suited up. I removed my holster and gun and then re-attached it to the thick belt built into the jump suit. I used the secondary large pockets to put in extra magazines as they were handed to me.

"You know how to use this?" Norm asked. He held out a hand grenade.

"Pull the ring and toss it?" I said nervously. "Count to 10?"

"You won't make it to 10. Pull and toss," he said. "It's a fragmentation grenade, so after you toss it go down and lay flat. Understood?"

"Yeah," I belched and took six grenades as he handed them to me. "Are we crossing the border or declaring war?" I said anxiously and found pockets for the grenades.

"M-16, Mick," he went on without answering me and forced the black weapon into my faltering hands. "It's on semi," he mumbled. "I don't want you letting a whole magazine go at once. Understand?"

"I've fired an M-16 before," I said. "A couple of times with you."

"I remember," he badgered while handing me four heavy ammo magazines. "You stay with these guys." He pulled Jeffrey and Rob to me. "Any questions?"

"Do we have a plan?" I said after waiting for the others to speak up. My pockets were full.

"We will when we get to the fence," he said. "Keep low and stay alive," he said lightly and walked to Dick.

I watched silently as Norm, Dick, and Alfonso passed the mic of a walkie-talkie between them. After a minute they used hand signals to gather us all round one car.

"Alfonso," Dick said, "you know what to do."

"Am doing it now," he smiled in the darkness and walked away with his nine men following.

"Wayne has checked in." Norm said, his voice low but focused. "There's been some activity since we left the warehouse, so we know the trail down isn't mined. It should give us a moment or two before they know we're coming, but it doesn't really matter. Using night vision goggles, he's seen them moving about, repositioning for us. Benny," Norm turned his gaze to Benny, "that's a good sign there are men in the front facing apartments, though Wayne hasn't detected them. Keep your back to us, no matter what. According to Alfonso's last surveillance, the fence is sealed all the way into Tijuana. A rear action has to come from here."

"Got it," Benny snapped back.

"Dick, you gonna be okay?"

"Twenty minutes," he said.

"Good. Five minutes we move out," Norm said and turned to me. "You okay?"

"Where's Dick going?" Dick not coming was something I hadn't even considered.

"Back to his place," Norm said quickly. "You want to know why?" he grumbled.

"Yeah."

"He's our command post," he said and left it at that.

"And?" I persisted.

"From his place he can send us more help, if we need it. Were we're going, Mick, could be as close to hell as you ever wanna be. It's his job to see we only visit and then get out."

"What about your ace in the hole?" I said, knowing I sounded worried.

"It's all in Dick's hands."

"And what if something happens to him? What if he doesn't make it?"

"He's a pro, he's armed to the teeth, and it's only a ten-minute walk, so he's given himself maneuvering time. You ready?" he said as he slid the bolt on his M-16 and took it off safety.

"You didn't answer me," I chided him.

"If he doesn't make it, we could be stuck in hell," he said, "and Father Seámus won't be of any help to you. Stay close to those Marines, Mel wouldn't forgive me for losing you."

"I wouldn't either," I said staidly and smiled to myself as I thought of Mel for the first time since her name had been brought up outside of *Caesar's*, which seemed like years ago, instead of only hours ago. I followed a few men behind Norm, with Rob and Jeffrey, as we moved along, one line against the cemetery wall and another across the street. I felt like a pack mule with everything I carried and tried to focus on the weight and not my anxiety. The air, that close to the ocean, was cool, but I was sweating.

May 7, 1995
3:35 a.m.

chapter TWENTY SIX

Wayne waited for us in the shadows on the cemetery side of the four-lane road we needed to cross. We loitered quietly in the darkness while he and Norm talked. Everything that was going to come down had been discussed earlier, at the produce warehouse, and my ignorance only added to heighten my anxiety. The stillness was disturbed once by the sound of a car as it passed on its way to the Ensenada toll road.

Behind us, we could see the flickering glow of the shantytown fires and even though the cool ocean breezes pushed the smoke away from the border, the rankness of burnt wood and tar paper and clothing, toys, the worldly possessions of people who had nothing to do with our problem, and grass and trees, and other things I didn't want to think about, wafted down. I forced my attention to Norm and Wayne and tried not to think of the savagery and anguish around me. Using hand gestures Norm summoned five Marines. One carried a large duffel bag. They talked quietly and then Wayne and the Marines moved into the night and were gone.

"What's going on?" I said when Norm stopped by me.

"Shit," he mumbled, "I forgot how you have to know everything." He looked into the dimness where Wayne had wandered. "We're giving 'em ten minutes to get to another section of fence," he said, talking as much to Jeffrey and Rob as to me. "There's a drain pipe that takes flood waters from the hills," he pointed to the glowing embers, "and dumps into the bay on the American side. He'll cut the fence and cross there, that'll allow 'em to follow the ocean and come from behind whoever's out there waiting on us." He looked at his watch. "In eight minutes we leave, pass through the fence, and wait for 'em to check in."

"How do you know Cluny won't have men there?"

Norm frowned and shook his head in disappointment. "When we get to the fence, Cluny'll know and he'll place all his attention here. Whatever token man, or two, he leaves behind, Wayne'll neutralize.

"By the way," he said, in a satirical tone, "Dick made it to his club. You feel better?"

"Yeah," I said, harshly.

He left us standing there, Jeffrey and Rob said nothing. Maybe they were comfortable with following orders blindly. I wasn't and I was spooked.

Norm and Benny talked briefly and then five Marines joined them, and were given a large duffel bag. We followed as Norm led us swiftly across the four-lane road and onto the dark dirt path that took us to the border. It seemed like a fast eight minutes to me. Better fast, I thought, than slow.

The battered path was pot holed so we slowed as we single filed to one side, hidden in the dimness of the tattered two story apartment buildings. Far in the distance, a dog barked. As we passed another dirt road, that fronted more apartments, we saw, across the vast blackness, the twinkling lights of *San Ysidro,* California. The path turned to our right and followed along the haggard border fence. The backyards of the worn buildings looked out at the fence and the millions of twinkling lights a mile away, a galaxy away for the people who stood in those yards.

One of the Marines led Norm to the cut in the fence. The rest of us pulled close, knowing we were no longer protected in the shadows, if we ever were. We stood, our backs to buildings some felt held men who wanted to kill us, while we stared at the dark abyss between us and the lights of *San Ysidro*, where we knew men waited, for the sole purpose of killing us. Two Marines pulled the fence open and used tie wraps to hold it extended.

Norm looked past the fence and down to the ground. A cement wall held the barrier within feet of the Mexican dirt path, but there was a drop to reach American soil.

"How far?" Norm said.

"Six feet," someone said.

"I'll go." Benny volunteered and pushed forward. He handed his rifle to Norm and lowered himself down. "Six feet," he called up, his voice muffled.

"Flat?"

"Sloping and rocky."

Norm lowered Benny's rifle. "Benny's men watch our backs," Norm said and took a duffel bag from one Marine and handed it down. "Let's move," he said and one by one, we descended into the darkness. The men who watched our backs finally dropped down, leaving the hole in the fence opened.

"We're over the wall," Norm said quietly into the mic of his radio.

"We are in position." Alfonso's voice crackled back.

"Everything's in motion." Dick statically responded.

"So far so good," Norm said to himself, but we all heard it, as we were supposed to. He took the duffel bag from the ground and opened it.

"Two for you," he said and handed Benny strange looking helmets.

Benny took both and handed them to others.

"What are they?" I mumbled.

"Night vision helmets from the Marine Air Corps," Rob said, his voice hushed.

We pushed toward the cement wall, protecting our backs and looked out toward the blackness between brightly lit *San Ysidro* and us. Norm handed out more helmets. He motioned me forward.

"Before curiosity kills you," he said blandly, "the helmets are for night vision."

"Marine Air Corps issue," I said nonchalantly.

"You want to explain this?" he said.

"No," I said, knowing I was at his mercy.

"Okay," he mumbled. "Six men are gonna spread out and move down the slope . . . they'll be followed by four others, those four have grenade launchers, M-79's . . . you three follow behind them and keep our asses safe . . . is that understood?" His voice was hard and focused on the three of us. I hadn't noticed Rob and Jeffrey approach until Norm mentioned us.

"Yeah." My words were lost in the night.

"Benny and his five men will spread out . . . about a quarter of the way down . . . their backs to us, making sure no one comes through the fence without us knowing. Four night vision helmets go with the men on point . . . two to the next group and Benny has two." He recited the plan and as he did, more men pulled away from the wall so they could hear.

"They're dug in down there . . . we can be sure of that. If we don't spot them first, all we can hope for are some dirt mounds, maybe some large rocks. The 79s have to be our in coming. Wayne's men will be one of our surprises . . . our firepower should match theirs."

"Are you sure?" I said nervously.

"The Uzi's and all the high tech shit we've seen, belong to the few who surround Cluny. What we have out there," he pointed toward *San Ysidro*, "are some of Rául's off duty cops," he laughed at that, "and maybe some local cowboys and a few of the men who came with him. Most of his able body men are there," he nodded toward the glowing hills.

We all stretched our necks to look at the burning shantytowns one last time.

"He knows we're here, so we have to assume he's leaving his compound and bringing his best people with him. They're coming, so we better be gone when they arrive."

"The fishing's fine," Wayne's static voice said, interrupting Norm's speech.

"Bring the catch home," Norm said into the radio mike. "We gotta go. Mick, the 40mm high explosive round has a kill radius of more than 100 meters," he said, almost in my ear. "Those four 79s are gonna get us out of here. Stay behind 'em. "

"I've got it," I uttered and thought they were his secret, his ace.

"By breakfast, you'll be trying to explain Mel to Sonia, or vice versa," he laughed and punched my shoulder. "Keep your head down and listen to these guys," he nodded toward Rob and Jeffrey.

"Where will you be?"

"I'm one of the first six," he said confidently. "Hell, bullets can't hurt me."

The first group of Marines spread out. Four of the soldiers placed the helmets on and adjusted them. They walked as if they'd done this before and I had to remind myself that everyone, but I, was trained at this. I lost sight of Norm as they drifted into the night.

Then the seconds ticked by slowly, as we waited for the remaining men to move out. Their helmets in place, they joked quietly as they watched the six men hidden from the rest of us. Each man had a bandoleer around his waist or across his chest that held the 40mm rounds for the M-79. What appeared to be a short-barreled single shot shotgun rested next to their M-16s. One nervous Marine breached the shotgun repeatedly, pulling the large 40mm shell out and then returning it. I didn't check my wristwatch, so I don't know how long they waited, but it seemed forever and then without saying a word they spread apart and moved into the night.

"How long do we wait?" I said, knowing my nervousness was not concealed.

One of the Marines remaining with Benny said, "I'll tell you when." He stared into the blackness, using the night-vision helmet.

We could see maybe ten to fifteen feet and then the blackness turned to a wall that couldn't be seen through. Heavy layers of clouds played hide and seek with a small moon and starry sky. If you looked too long toward *San Ysidro*, the lights impaired your night vision.

"Go," the Marine said.

"Slow," Jeffrey whispered.

We moved slowly, looking down for objects that might cause us to stumble or make noise. The cant was about forty-five degrees and after a few minutes, it took an effort to hold back, as my body weight wanted me to plunge forward.

The black night wall backed away from us as we inched forward. My night vision adjusted to where I could see a little further, but I was not able to make out the men somewhere in front of us. The inclusive quiet was eerie in itself. To keep from panicking and shooting off at something that wasn't there in the dark, at least I hoped wasn't there, I listened intently, while my eyes evaluated shadowy images. I feared turning around and hoped that no sound would come from there, because I knew where I'd just walked from would be gone from sight.

Silence has sounds, and as I moved forward, I heard the yelps of dogs, a small airplane flew ahead, but I refused to look up into the *San Ysidro* lights for it. Rats, large rats I imagined scurried away from us, their feet scratching them to safety. I held my M-16 forward, at an angle, ready to pull up and fire. The safety was off and the automatic mode was switched to semi, left as Norm had put it.

Screeching tires, the sound you dread to hear when you're stopped on the LA freeway or anywhere at a red light came barreling down from behind us. We stopped, but the sounds continued. We turned, as if we were hooked together. The sounds penetrated the night, but the darkness kept their cause covered.

"Must be Cluny," Rob mumbled. "Anything?" he said to Jeffrey.

"Nothing." Jeffrey pressed one hand against his ear and that's when I knew he had a radio. "Nothing," he whispered again.

We could hear movement far behind us. The fence was torn open and the thud of things, men, equipment, dropping, sent sound waves past us. They wouldn't be surprising Benny.

"How long will he wait?" I whispered into Rob's ear.

"Not long," he whispered back. "Trying to get back over the wall will be their down fall," he continued, his whisper filled with excitement.

While the silence grew again, we turned and even more slowly worked our way down the slope. We had taken less than a dozen steps when a shaft of light pierced the darkness from behind us. We turned toward the source of the light and went to the ground. As quickly as the light had appeared, it stopped and then it slowly swept the area.

What I guessed to have been a large spotlight sent the beam of yellowish illumination toward us from high up at the border fence. A single shot rang out and the spotlight died. We heard the breaking of glass, as if someone had smashed a heavy mirror, as we lay still, once again in the dark. Voices wailed and orders were barked, all in darkness.

Jeffrey whispered into the mike of his radio and then listened to the reply. "Let's go," he said, loud enough for us to hear.

We stood and moved forward. The rumble of activity continued from behind and I wondered why Benny hadn't responded. A feathered light began to glow above us. We turned and high up at the border wall, we saw cars as they pulled forward with their lights on. The lights were aimed too high to be of much use, but our night vision was affected. We moved forward.

Time had taken on another dimension by then, so I can't be sure how long it was before the firefight began. The quick bursts of automatic fire ricocheted through the night from behind us, as we vigilantly moved forward.

I turned, again, Jeffrey and Rob stopped, and I watched muzzle flashes as rivers of bullets flowed down toward Benny's location from the border wall. Short bursts were sent toward the border fence and I could hear more glass breaking and hidden within the retorts of automatic fire, was the clamor of voices. One by one, the headlights were shot out, returning the darkness.

"Christ." I cried in disbelief, watching the multiple muzzle flashes as weapons fired.

"It's okay," Jeffrey said. "They know what they're doin'."

"They're givin' away their positions," Rob laughed quietly, "while tryin' to cover the guys they dropped over."

"We walk away?" I said.

"That's our orders," Rob said flatly.

Before we could move an explosion tore a hole in the night, as a car flamed and then another, at the top of the border wall.

"Alfonso?" I said. The quiet of earlier was gone.

"Those 40mm rounds do their job," Rob said.

"Let's move," Jeffrey ordered.

The tumult continued, as we moved tediously forward, trying to ignore the clamor that eroded the quiet. I had to accept that between Alfonso and Benny, they would keep whatever forces Cluny had amassed at the border from charging us from behind. Without believing that, I probably would have frozen and I didn't want that embarrassment. I kept putting a hand into my pocket, feeling for the hand grenade.

"Down." Jeffrey yelled.

As I went to the ground, I looked quickly behind me, only to see the firefight continuing and no one sneaking up.

From the darkness in front came a thump, thump and then explosions shattered the night. The eruptions were quickly followed by automatic fire, all seeming to be outward. Then muzzle flashes came from the darkness, toward our position, only to be answered with more in-coming explosions.

"M-79s?" I said, lying on the ground.

"Hell, yes." Rob yelled back. He stared behind then forward and at us. "Shit."

"What?" I yelled, nervously.

"We ain't gonna get in it," he shrieked back.

"What are they saying?" I called to Jeffrey.

"Cluny's men have pulled back," he hollered over the battle noise.

"He's leavin' those on this side?" Rob said.

"Guess so," Jeffrey yelled. "Regroupin'?"

"Any word from up there," I said, looking toward the continuing eruptions.

"No," he shouted.

The far off lights of *San Ysidro* were lost in the smoke and glare of the battle in front of us. I didn't know it then, though I should have suspected it, but the reason we were laying there, not moving in any direction, not joining the action was I was being protected. Those were Rob and Jeffrey's orders and they were obeying, much to their disappointment. A yellow flare lit up a section of sky and as it slowly descended, I could see the men in front. Briefly, the automatic retort abated.

After the abrupt pause, heavy automatic fire poured toward the hazy night from where I assumed Norm was, followed by more thump sounds that were followed by small eruptions. Suddenly red smoke rose from in front of Norm's position and another flare was shot into the sky.

"Let's move," Jeffrey said amidst the chaos.

We stood and, in the dimming yellowish light, moved toward the red smoke. Jeffrey turned once, while we walked and then spoke into his radio mic.

Sporadic automatic fire came from the shadows and the men spread out in front of us returned it swiftly. Jeffrey turned again, as we came upon the four men ahead of us.

"What is it?" I yelled, not looking back, but trying to keep up my forward pace without tripping over the uneven ground.

"Benny's comin'," he shouted back.

When we reached the four Marines with the M-79s, we lay spread out behind them. They were quiet, their night vision helmets rested on the ground next to their M-16s, while they patiently aimed their shotgun-like grenade launchers toward the numerous muzzle flashes and awaited orders. Ahead, by a few yards, we heard the small retort of automatic fire, but most of it was lost in the haze from the flares and the red smoke.

I turned on the ground, my back to the smoke and watched for Benny to come, expecting him to be running. Up at the border fence I saw burning vehicles and I could make out figures as they rushed around. The fence was either lost to my sight because of the smoke and distance, or it was gone entirely. The yellowish flare light was dimming again, but I saw men coming at us. It made me nervous, even though I guessed it was Benny.

"Men coming in." I yelled and raised my rifle.

Jeffrey and Rob turned. As the figures got closer, they stood and went toward them, signaling me to stay down. Moments later they returned and helped carry one of two wounded Marines. Benny and another soldier carried the other wounded man. That accounted for four. I looked into the shadowy darkness, but that was all.

"That's it?" I asked.

Benny nodded.

One of the soldiers with the M-79s came over and talked briefly to Benny. While they talked, they carefully placed the wounded men down.

The only reason I could tell they were alive and not dead, were their raw moans. Blood soaked through their jump suits. I surprised myself by making that assumption in the dim light and realized, over the past few years, I'd been witness to too many situations where people were covered in blood. The light ocean breeze eddied the fetor of cordite and sulfurous smoke into the night.

Benny, Rob, and another Marine with their M-16s, and one of the soldiers with the M-79s, moved toward the border in a low run.

"What?" Is all I could say to Jeffrey, as he sat by the wounded men.

"We don't leave bodies," he said and then talked so softly to the wounded men, I couldn't hear.

Fires burned along the border wall, but the gunfire had ceased for the moment. I wondered if there would be men laying in wait, knowing they'd return for the dead? I wanted to ask Jeffrey, but couldn't bring myself to broach the subject. Instead, I walked to where he sat and crouched next to him.

"Can I do anything?"

"We're okay," he said without looking at me.

I stared at the wounded men, but couldn't tell where the wounds were because of all the blood. "Will Benny be okay?"

"Sure," he said, confidently. "They know what they're doin'."

Muzzle flashes flickered at the border, followed by an eruption and more flashes. I was too far away to hear the thump sound the shotgun-like weapon made. Then the muzzle flashes ceased. My stomach sank with the negative thought that the four of them had been stopped.

I looked at Jeffrey, who pointed toward the border. In the murkiness, I saw four men as they ran toward us, two carried bodies over their shoulders, while the others fired indiscriminately toward the wall.

When they arrived, they kept moving, Benny and the other Marine carried a body each. Rob stopped by us.

The fourth Marine passed by, his M-79 slung over his shoulder, an M-16 in his hands.

"Christ." I exhaled.

"I think they're gonna come down the wall again. Give it another try," he said breathlessly, more to Jeffrey than to me.

Jeffrey spoke into his mic. As he talked another flare shot into the cloudy sky, illuminating the barren area in front of us. No one fired from anywhere. A smoke grenade flamed red plumes from the ground far in front of Norm. We were gathering, moving closer together, when shots were heard from behind. Two soldiers hurried to the wounded men and picked them up. Rob grabbed me by the arm and we moved forward, as three Marines prepared for whatever came from the border.

A single muzzle flash came from behind the red smoke, someone cried out close by and most everyone in front of where I stood fired into the smoke. I heard a thump and then the explosion of the 40mm grenade.

As the flare dimmed, two Cobra attack helicopters came from the twinkling horizon, their blades loudly sliced through the night and smoke. As they approached the border wall, their nose guns fired bursts of bullets that ate up the ground in small, dusty chunks, gouging away the cement whenever the wall was hit. The mixture of the thunderous chopper blades and the rapid discharge of the nose guns filled the night with unfathomable violence. It was too shadowy to see what real damage the Cobras did, but their swiftness spoke for itself. The three Marines left to secure our rear joined us.

"When I say I've got an ace up my sleeve," Norm yelled at me as he approached. He looked toward the two Cobras, pointed at them, and laughed. "Cluny's shittin' his pants, wherever he is."

"Where's Wayne?" I yelled back at him, not laughing at the Cobras, but watched them maneuver and attack.

"In a car, somewhere over there," he pointed toward *San Ysidro*. "It was easier than I thought," he shouted.

"Yeah," I hollered back, cacophony still filled the night. I didn't want to ask him if the wounded boys thought that, or the two dead soldiers.

A Sea Knight helicopter, its sizable front and rear blades reverberated through the night, approached from *San Ysidro*. It filled the sky as it neared. Norm talked into his radio and used hand signals that must have meant for us to move forward, because Rob and Jeffrey pushed me along. The Cobras circled the border and continued firing their nose guns, the sound of the rapid retorts vibrating though the night. I couldn't tell from my quick glances at the shadowy border, if anyone was firing at the Cobras. I didn't think anyone would be that foolish, but I've thought wrong before.

The Sea Knight landed its side door opened and Norm and Benny rushed the dead and wounded men aboard as quickly as they could. Those of us remaining didn't need to be told to rush we did it naturally. The wind from the two whipping blades blew dust, smoke, and debris around, miring up the landing zone.

The men manning the Sea Knight were in civilian clothing. The man at the door had earphones over his head and a small mic extended to his mouth. He handed a similar set to Norm, who put it on and talked. The pandemonium inside the restricted compartment was overpowering. Norm nodded and the civilian closed the door as the helicopter rose sharply, forcing everyone to try for balance.

Two bodies were off to one corner and three wounded men sat crumpled in another. The third wounded soldier must have been hit when the shot came from behind the red smoke. A man in civilian clothing sat next to a small doctor's bag and worked over one of the wounded. One Marine, dirty from battle, seemed to be helping. He ignored the blood from the wounded as it dripped onto the floor. There was an odor filling the compartment that I can't explain in words. Maybe it was death? Or the after-effects of fear? I'd never smelled it before and it would be all right with me, if I never smelled it again.

Some of the Marines began to whistle, others clapped and hollered. I stole a glance out one of the small windows and saw the lights of *San Ysidro*, or maybe San Diego. It didn't matter most of us were home safe.

The helicopter landed in a dirt lot along a small two-lane road. Norm helped me out and we both ran from the whirling dirt. From next to a streetlight we watched the Sea Knight rise and move off.

"Take off the jump suit," he said, as he removed his.

I did and we both tossed them down as a van pulled up and stopped. Wayne opened the side door and smiled.

"What's that?" I said, when I noticed the heavy vest Norm wore.

"Flack jacket," he said and picked up both our jump suits. "Didn't you use anything I gave you?"

"No," I said and knew my jump suit was still loaded down with the ammo magazines and grenades he'd given me. "How come you have a flack jacket?"

"We only had six," he said, "and the point men needed them."

I couldn't argue with that. We got in the van.

"Now what?" I said as the van sped away, an unknown driver at the wheel.

"Rockport Beach," Norm sighed, removed the ponderous flack jacket and stretched. He looked at his wristwatch. "We might beat them there."

"Seámus?" I said. My body ached.

"Damn right."

I felt in my pocket for the crumpled documents that Seámus had wanted me to get across the border. I took them out, tried to straighten them, and thought how costly the wrinkled pieces of paper had been. The few black and white negatives were in pretty good shape, considering everything.

"What about all this?" I said. I was still wound up.

"What about it?"

"There was just a battle on the American side of the border, for Christ's sake. Not to mention what Alfonso did on the Mexican side."

"Mick. Calm down. You're talking about the coordinated Mexican and American DEA effort that took place as the smugglers were attempting to enter the United States. Due to the cooperation of both countries, a large drug-smuggle ring has been smashed," he recited and smiled. "See Mick, everyone can pull in favors. The truth's too embarrassing to both governments, but with a little imagination and cooperation, it's all worked out. Great, ain't it?"

"Yeah," I tried to smile, "great." I didn't ask him if it was great for the two dead soldiers or the three wounded kids flying in the helicopter, or for Sonia's murdered family or for that old man killed Thursday night in front of *Alfonso's*. At that time I wasn't even thinking of all those that were killed trying to kill us and I didn't have any idea of how Alfonso came out of all this.

I stared at the papers again, I felt their wrinkled edges, but it was too dark to read them. I hoped silently that Norm was wrong, that everything wasn't great, but that there would be people who cared enough to work with these documents and make things better for some, by revealing the truth of American involvement with death squads. One-step at a time, I thought as I sat in the van as it sped me to my rendezvous with Seámus and Sonia.

"Damn. It's good to be alive. Ain't it?" Norm said, his eyes closed.

May 11, 1995
    5:30 p.m.

chapter TWENTY SEVEN

Wakes from incoming boats softly rocked us, as Sully and I sat in the aft section of the *Fenian Bastard*, a forty-foot sloop I was, at that time, living aboard. My burned out condominium was almost rebuilt and I had it up for sale. It was Wednesday, four days since I'd crossed the border, and the so-called cooperative Mexican-American drug bust had gone down. The story appeared in the news as Norm had quoted it. Sully and I nursed a pint of Guinness and a double shot of Jameson, over ice, and watched as the day sailors motored in.

"We got there a half hour early," Sully said for the umpteenth time. "Juan even agreed to stay past sun rise. You know what could've happened to us if the Coast Guard came by . . ." He let the sentence die and sipped from the Jameson's.

"Sully," I moaned, "we've been over it, and I believe you." I'd been telling him the same thing since Sunday afternoon.

"Nothing new from Dick?"

"No," I said and drank some Guinness.

It was late afternoon and the large May sun slowly prepared to dip into the cold ocean. A cool breeze came with the setting sun, but we stayed aft wearing our daytime shorts and tee shirts.

"I've check again this morning," he said slowly, his usual flushed face burned from the afternoons in the sun, keeping me company, "and the Coast Guard has found nothing new. Just the gas slick in that general area on Sunday. I talked to a couple of guys I know at harbor patrol and they come back with the same info."

"We know how easily the truth can be orchestrated, don't we?" I said.

"Yeah," he mumbled and sipped more Jameson's. "Dick can't locate the plane in Ensenada, right?"

"Right," I said with a mouthful of Guinness.

"Alfonso?"

"Hasn't got back to me."

"Norm?"

"He should be here soon," I said and went below for another Guinness. "You want another beer?"

"Ice," was all he said.

I came back with a small tub of ice. Sully put a couple of cubes in his glass and poured more Jameson's. I held my glass out and he added to it.

"I wish there was something I could say or do," he said, sipping the whiskey.

"Don't beat yourself up, Sully. You did everything you were supposed to." I sipped the Jameson's and wished it made me feel better.

"Ahoy, captain, permission to come aboard," Norm called out as he climbed from the dock. He went below and came back with an empty glass, which he filled with ice and Irish whiskey. "You gotta get another kind of beer," he grumbled as he leaned against the rail. "Mick," he began after a long swallow of whiskey, "you have to accept fate. You did everything you could. Hell, we all did."

"I just want to know . . . I need to know that what I know is the truth." I stared at him. "You have the ability of manipulating facts."

"Jesus Christ," he yelled. "I put my ass on the line for you in Tijuana and so did Dick. Neither of us is manipulating anything. The damn pilot made two mayday calls, damn close to where he was supposed to land. I had a request put in to the Coast Guard, thank you," he mumbled and went on, "and the gas slick was analyzed and came up Mexican aviation fuel. The water is too deep for divers."

"I checked that, Mick," Sully cut in. "The location is out past the drop. There's a sand waterfall, where the ocean floor drops, that divers go to see all the time. Where we waited was past that by a good mile."

"Yeah. How'd you do it?" I said, letting my curiosity get the better of me.

"Do what?" Norm said and sipped the whiskey, a silly grin pasted on his face.

"The weapons, the choppers, the press release," I quoted from a mental list I'd made since Sunday.

"Dick supplied the weapons and choppers. He has a stockpile of Vietnam era surplus," he said clearly and I knew he knew I'd ask eventually. "They're for sale to those who can afford 'em. His contacts at Pendleton got him the choppers, but I pulled a few strings and had them under the Agency umbrella, just in case."

"One other thing?" I gulped from my glass of Guinness.

"Get it over with," he said, cynically.

"Is there any chance that you were right about Dick? Do you think he double crossed me and turned Seámus and Sonia over to the Guatemalans?" I asked anxiously, my insides jolted with the horrid thought. "You said, maybe he was my jailer, not my protector."

"I remember," he said. "If you think about it, you'll see you were right and I was wrong. If he was gonna double cross you, we wouldn't have had as much of a problem at the border.

"There might've been a token effort to stop us, but that would've been it. He wouldn't put those many of his Marines in danger. That and the reward offered for Seámus didn't amount to much. Not to Dick, anyway." His expression was serious; he'd given the idea some thought too.

We sat there, drank, and watched as small pleasure crafts went by, their wake rocking us, and didn't talk. Norm was dressed in jeans, a sweatshirt, and old sneakers. Sully looked cold, I was cold.

"Where's Wayne?" I said to hear myself say something.

"Running an errand," Norm frowned and poured himself more Irish whiskey. "The condo done?"

"Just about."

"You put it up already?"

"Yeah. With the low market I'll lose money." Sea gulls flew overhead and cried aloud for me.

"So keep it."

"He won't," Sully smiled slyly and winked at me. "Mel sold hers and moved down the road. Right?"

"She did," I said.

"Maybe there's a place in her building?" Norm said.

"I wouldn't know," I said back and gave them each a look of disgust.

Norm laughed at me. "Damn, Mick, how can a guy with your education be so dumb?"

Sully joined the laughter and as I was about to say something the phone below deck rang. I did my best sneer and went to answer it.

"Hello." I snapped.

"Nice to talk to you too," Dick answered back.

"Sorry, Dick. I'm just in the middle of nothing with Norm and Sully," I said in lieu of a long explanation.

"Yeah, well that's understandable, then. I told you I'd call," he said.

"You did."

"Alfonso went to Ensenada himself and looked around, that's why he hasn't got back to you. He talked with people we both know. The plane hasn't returned and no one's seen or heard from Chico."

"Chico?" I said, never having heard the name mentioned before.

"The pilot," Dick said. "He was the best, Mick. He could fly anything, anywhere. I don't understand what happened," he said tediously. "If I didn't have faith in him, I wouldn't have used him. You know that, right?"

"Yeah," I said. "Norm said to accept fate. I guess it was Chico's fate to go down off Rockport Beach. "

"Yeah," he half-heartily agreed. "Fate, kismet, it gets us all in the end, don't it? Look, Mick, between Alfonso and me, we'll keep word out we're interested in Chico's whereabouts. If he shows up anywhere in Mexico, we'll hear and if we do, you do. That's a promise. But Mick, I trust him and if he ain't around, something happened."

"Thanks," I mumbled, there seemed little else to say that wouldn't have sounded argumentative. "Have you talked with Rául?" I hated asking, but I had to.

"Yeah. We both did and he believes your story, but I think you should kind of, ah, miss this bullfight season. Give him time."

"That bad?" I knew, from reading the papers about the fires that hundreds were homeless and many had died.

"Time, Mick. Give him time."

"Sure, I understand. I'll see you around the holidays . . . maybe," I proposed and waited for his reply.

"Sounds about right. I'll keep in touch and if I hear anything, you'll be the first one I call. *Adios,*" he said and hung up before I could say anything.

"Dick," I said as I came on deck and sat down. I added ice and Jameson's to my watered down drink. "Nothing," I griped and they remained silent. "Rául is okay with my story, but Dick thinks I should miss the Bullfights for awhile."

"There are other things to do, other people to see," Norm said.

"It just isn't right." I shouted at the ocean, angry at the world. "I can't find anyone in Washington interested in the information." I looked at Norm, expecting an I-told-you-so stare, but it wasn't there. "It's nothing new, they say. Sure, the pictures are new, but they don't relate, there's no proof. Can you believe that? What the hell do they want? Pictures of smoking guns and the priest's bodies?" Sully and Norm drank quietly and let me continue to rave. "I made copies and sent them overnight to a couple of Senators and a few Congressmen I know and nothing. They aren't even interested in how I obtained the documents."

"Mick, you gotta remember that that's secondary. No matter what the response here, Seámus was in danger. Real danger, as we all discovered. Even if you believed the papers were useless, what you tried to do was necessary. Seámus' safety came first, the documents second. You had the documents, you didn't need to go through what you did," Norm said, the first time he spoke like a friend, supportive.

"It just doesn't seem right," I said and drank.

"You do what's right," Sully said from his chair, "because it's the right thing to do. As Norm said, the results are secondary. You hope it turns out okay, but if it doesn't, like now, you don't change what you did.

"Somebody explain to me what I just said," Sully blushed and drank. "You know what I mean, Mick."

"Yeah, I do." I stood and walked to the stern and looked over into the grimy water. "Damn you, Norm. People care. They do," I howled to the ocean, "they have to."

"You wouldn't be you, if you weren't trying to save the world. Hell with the world." Norm toasted and drank.

"If it ain't the world, it's some other cause. The whale, or dolphin, or manatee," Sully added in agreement and drank.

I turned to their smiling faces and knew they were trying to take the edge off my guilt. I toasted them, "To friends." I drained my Guinness. "Beer?" I asked the two of them and received no response.

From below, I felt the boat rock as someone got on. I opened my beer and went above. Wayne stood by the stern, he was dressed for the approaching cold in jeans, boots, held in his hand to keep from ruining the deck and a sweater. Mel sat in my chair. She was as beautiful as ever, her hair longer than I remember, but it had been awhile. I smiled foolishly, while staring into her deep brown, puppy dog eyes.

"May a lady have a drink?" she said quietly.

"Not much of a bar on this boat," I said trying to hold a thin smile. "No wine. Beer or Irish whiskey."

"Guinness stout ain't beer," Norm griped.

"A pint of Guinness would be fine," she grinned.

I smiled and went below for her beer. I poured it over the small sink and my hands shook with excitement. We hadn't spoken in months and now she was there. Wayne's errand, I thought as the glass filled with black stout and a frothy head. For what purpose, I wondered as I climbed the steps to the deck.

"It's nice to see you," I mumbled and gave her the glass.

"Thank you," she said and sipped the beer. The foam slightly covered her upper lip for a moment, before she licked it off. "I've meant to come by and see the boat. Sean owns her?"

"Yes. He's been letting me stay since last Christmas, I think I'll buy her."

"I've gotta run," Sully said and finished his drinks. "I'll be by tomorrow."

"Sure. And thanks Sully."

"I only wish it did some good," he told me as he stepped onto the dock and walked away.

The sun had begun to surrender to the horizon, its shades of reds and yellows rippling along the surface. I walked to the stern and stared. Mel stood next to me before I realized she'd gotten up.

"I'm sorry about Seámus," she said softly.

She was dressed in faded jeans, an old white fisherman's sweater, and battered sneakers. She'd never looked prettier. Her perfume was soft, a mixture of baby powder and flowers.

"Thank you," was all I could mumble.

"I liked him. I liked the stories you both told about each other. They were funny. I never got use to his being a priest," she said with a smile. "You're a lot alike."

"Amen to that," Norm said from the hatch.

"Go away," she yelled, but the smile stayed.

"Aye, aye, captain," he saluted and went below with Wayne.

"You can't live here forever," she said and sipped beer and tore at my heart as she licked the froth from her lips.

"No I can't," I said.

"You'll take a loss on your condo. You should keep it."

"No offers, yet," I laughed. "Maybe."

"Do you have any plans?"

"I think so." She was so close and smelled so damn good.

"Would it be too much to ask what they are?"

"See the sun set?"

"Yes. It's beautiful," she said and I could hear a little annoyance in her voice. She thought I was putting her off.

"I think I'll go where the sun sets are one hundred times more beautiful," I said and for the first time in days had an idea of what I should do.

"It must be beautiful there." She looked at me now, not the sunset.

"Key West," I told her and felt some excitement in my voice. "It's very beautiful there, if you like the tropics."

"It's almost hurricane season, isn't it?" Her voice was soft, almost caressing.

"Usually begins in July. But that's okay. At least you have a warning and can do something. Not like earthquakes," I said, and knew how she feared them.

"Or do nothing," she added with a soft laugh, remembering how little we both did to prepare for earthquakes.

"I'm going there and write about last weekend. It doesn't matter no one will believe it. I owe them that," I said.

"Hot and humid, isn't it?" she asked slyly, avoiding the more serious subject.

"It's an island, Mel, not Orlando," I assured her. "There won't be much packing."

"My new string bikini, some shorts, and tees," she said blithely, sipped some Guinness and tore at my heart.

"A string bikini?" I murmured and tried not to think of her in it.

"Yes and it's very sexy," she purred. "Can I come?"

I pulled her close and hugged her as tight as I could. "Could I stop you?" I whispered.

She pushed back and looked me straight in the eyes. "Yes," she said, resolutely. "You can stop me by saying no. Or you can say yes and we're gone whenever you're ready. I've missed you too much, but this is as far as the chase goes." Her eyes were large and excited.

"I can be packed for the morning flight," I told her.

"I'll help you pack, if you'll help me."

"What a deal." I laughed and kissed her.

"You two fighting or making up?" Norm said as he came on deck, followed by Wayne.

"We need to leave our cars at your gym," I said.

"Sure. For how long?"

"For a while."

"Just about what I thought," he laughed. "Where are you going?"

"Key West," Mel yelled cheerfully.

"You kiddin' me?" Norm bellowed lightheartedly.

"No," I told him and held onto Mel. "I'm going to write about last weekend. I'm doing it for me, I'll keep your name out of it," I said before he could warn me about keeping him out of it.

"Hell." he cried with excitement. "I'm flyin' to Key West this weekend."

"No." I shrieked. "Don't fool around."

"I'm not. I'm checking out a Cuban boxer that lives there. I may want to sign him if he's as good as I hear."

"How long are you staying?" I held onto Mel.

"However long it takes to get him to sign. Hey, we can get together in the evenings," he said with a smirk.

"Bye Norm, bye Wayne," I said and watched them leave the *Fenian Basta*rd, laughing, as they walked to their car.

"Is he really going there?" Mel said holding my hand.

"Probably," I moaned. "We'll avoid him."

"He's your friend," she said. "We can't avoid him forever."

"For a week or two."

"Maybe three," she smiled and kissed me.

END

15919445R00143

Made in the USA
Charleston, SC
27 November 2012